Evald Flisar

THE SORCERER'S APPRENTICE

Translated from the Slovene by the author and David Limon

Texture Press
Norman, Oklahoma
2012

EVALD FLISAR (1945, Slovenia). Novelist, short story writer, playwright, essayist, editor. Studied comparative literature in Ljubljana, English literature in London, psychology in Australia. Globe-trotter (travelled in more than 80 countries), underground train driver in Sydney, Australia, editor of (among other things) an encyclopaedia of science and invention in London, author of short stories and radio plays for the BBC, president of the Slovene Writers' Association (1995 – 2002), since 1998 editor of the oldest Slovenian literary journal Sodobnost (Contemporary Review). Author of eleven novels (six short-listed for *kresnik*, the Slovenian "Booker"), two collections of short stories, three travelogues (regarded as the best of Slovenian travel writing), two books for children and teenagers (shortlisted for Best Children's Book Award) and thirteen stage plays (six nominated for Best Play of the Year Award, twice won the award). Winner of the Prešeren Foundation Prize, the highest state award for prose and drama. Various works, especially short stories and plays, translated into 32 languages, among them Bengali, Hindi, Malay, Nepali, Indonesian, Turkish, Greek, Japanese, Chinese, Arabic, Polish, Czech, Albanian, Lithuanian, Icelandic, Russian, Italian, Spanish etc. Stage plays regularly performed all over the world, most recently in Austria, Egypt, India, Indonesia, Japan, Taiwan, Nepal, Bosnia & Herzegovina, Bulgaria and Belarus. Attended more than 50 literary readings and festivals on all continents. Lived abroad for 20 years (three years in Australia, 17 years in London). Since 1990, resident in Ljubljana, Slovenia.

*t*P
Texture Press

Evald Flisar

THE SORCERER'S APPRENTICE

Translated from the Slovene by the author and David Limon

Texture Press
Norman, Oklahoma
2012

David Limon has received a grant from the Slovenian Book Agency.

Originally published in Slovenia (European Union) as *Čarovnikov vajenec* by Pomurska založba in 1986. Subsequent editions published by various other publishers in 1988, 1990, 1995, 2000, 2003, 2008, 2010.

Published in the United States by
Texture Press, 1108 Westbrooke Terrace, Norman, OK 73072.

Editor
Susan Smith Nash, PhD

Sub-editor
Arlene Ang

Cover design by
Arlene Ang

Published with the financial assistance of Trubar Foundation, Ljubljana, Slovenia.

The names, characters, and events portrayed in these pages are the product of the author's imagination. Any resemblance to actual persons, living or dead, or to real events is entirely coincidental.

This is a limited edition.
World rights (also for the US) are available from the European Literary Agency.
Please contact Sandra B. Naylor: sandra@europeanliteraryagency.co.uk

ISBN:978-0615694740

Printed in the United States of America.

The fool
who persists
in his
folly
will
become
wise.

William Blake

Contents

1.

Have I come too late?

At the end of the canyon the old man drew my attention to one of the snow bridges that abound in Kashmir. Every winter, snow fills the deep ravines and riverbeds to the brim and freezes over, while underneath water digs a tunnel and flows through it invisible, inaudible except to a trained ear. On top, one can cross the bridge without the fear of crashing through its frozen layer. But in late spring, as the snows start to melt, the water tunnel grows steadily larger and the snow span above it thinner. Finally, a gap appears in the middle. Before it widens, one can leap across it, but towards the end of July this becomes hazardous. At the end of September, before the onset of winter, only a fool would venture on to one of those structures.

"Each of us carries his winter with him," pronounced my companion. "And his snow bridge. And his gap."

These were startling words for the old mule driver who had offered to take me to Amarnath Cave for less than half the usual fee. But he was right. All of a sudden I saw my journey as a symbolic attempt to leap across such a gap in my soul, and my recent life as a series of such attempts, of jumps undertaken to reach the other side; of vertiginous falls; of attempts to find a crossing point where the gap was not so wide.

I had always been aware of having a second self. As children we used to be very close, but gradually distrust grew between us. The world took the side of my intellectual "I", while my instinctive part, repeatedly shamed, withdrew. It settled in a dimension to which my intellectual "I" refused to grant equal rights, for to him it appeared inexplicable, non-scientific, however much it continued to be confirmed by experience.

As the old man and I continued our ride towards Amarnath Cave, I suddenly felt that on the other side of the canyon I could see, astride a Himalayan pony just like mine, and riding in the same direction, my rejected self whose absence had made my life so unbearable. But I had waited too long; the bridges that could have brought us together had melted. Now there was a gap between us that my distrustful intellect couldn't clear without risking a catastrophic fall into mental illness.

Farther up we came upon a group of pilgrims who were returning from a visit to the caves; a small number of men and women who rested, drenched by the afternoon sun, on the rocks by the wayside. The old man threw them a few Kashmiri words that drew surprised comments and laughter. As we rode on I could hear them exchanging scornful remarks.

"It is too late," said the old man. "Lingam in the cave is no more. You should have come a month earlier."

I knew I would not see the stalagmite of ice which mysteriously appears inside Amarnath Cave each summer and waxes and wanes with the phases of the Moon, reaching its highest point some time in August. But that didn't bother me. My pilgrimage had a different reason. I had been told that inside the cave I would find a remarkable holy man who might amuse himself by letting me stay by his side and help me across the gap in the snow bridge in my soul.

After crossing the Mahagunas Pass we reached a plain at an altitude of ten thousand feet. It was inevitable that years of inactive life would sooner or later exact their toll, but until that moment I had felt nothing more than a slight touch of vertigo and an occasional stabbing pain in my lungs. But as we descended towards the wind-swept shadowy plain, the grey rocks and granulated mountain slopes suddenly swayed and sank into darkness.

The first thing I saw when I opened my eyes was the mule driver, a mixture of apprehension and irritation on his face. I felt something gluey on my left cheek; licking my lips, I tasted blood. I must have fainted and rolled off the back of my pony, striking a rock as I fell. I could feel another patch of slippery moisture on the right side of my skull. I dragged myself to the nearby stream and lowered my head into the icy water rushing over the rocks. I watched it grow dark with the blood.

"Shall we go back?" asked the old man.

"No," I said.

"You have altitude sickness."

He was right. Vertigo, buzzing in the ears, shortness of breath, pain behind the eyes, rapid pulse, nausea, thirst – all were indications that I had climbed too far too fast. But never before had I been so close to the most important goal of my life! To turn back now would mean giving up at the very beginning. And for that it was too late. After a brief rest I struggled back into the saddle and we continued on our way.

Before long we had to dismount. The narrow path was becoming very steep, winding dangerously through precipitous cliffs. Mist began to appear in front of my eyes.

"Rest." I gasped. "A short rest."

And I slid to the ground, with my ears throbbing, on the edge of consciousness. I could see something luminous in the distance; it took me a while to realise it was the setting sun. The cold was taking on the quality of steel.

"We can't rest here," I heard the old man's voice somewhere above me, "the horses will lose their footing and tumble into the ravine." He was half-dragging, half-kicking them up the mountain.

I was lying on a rocky ledge, shivering, exposed to the hungry shadows of the approaching night. The old man returned and helped me to my feet. I let him grip my arm and drag me up the path, with a short rest behind each corner.

"It's not far now," he kept saying, his voice in the wind sounding miles away. "A few more steps, just a few more, make an effort, look at me, I'm twice your age."

This wasn't the first time he used my weakness to rise above the insignificance he must have felt as a mule driver. But this time I responded with kindness rather than impatience, not only because he was, after all, over seventy, but also because I myself was suddenly robbed of significance – by the dimensions of the landscape which had opened before us in all its naked cruelty. It was so simple in composition, so unreal that my gasping physical presence was *on it* rather than *in it*: just as the finger touches a photograph without being able to penetrate the picture across which it slides.

This was truly God's world, distant in spite of its nearness, inaccessible in spite of its presence. In its remoteness the old man and I looked like exhausted midges climbing across the canvass of a huge natural picture in the gallery of creation.

Finally we reached our ponies, which were shivering in the freezing wind, and resumed our journey. Soon a long valley opened before us, so narrow that probably even the sun could not penetrate it for more than two hours a day. It was covered from end to end in dirty brown snow. As we entered it, leaving the wind on the slopes behind us, deep silence enveloped us. All we could hear was the muffled sound of a hoof striking stone here and there.

Through this cold shadowy valley we finally reached an opening from where we could see, rising before us, the broad face of Amarnath Mountain, casting a threatening shadow, much steeper than I had expected, strewn with white rocks. High up the slope I could see the dark mouth of the holy cave.

"There," the old man said, pointing at it as if claiming credit for a wonder of nature.

I dismounted for the final ascent to the cave. It took me a while to reach the entrance. As I passed into the damp and dripping interior I could see nothing at first; my only sensation was of being touched by cold, stuffy air as if licked by a huge dog. Gradually, the interior of the cave became visible. It was hardly more than a hundred feet high. I descended a steep ramp to an iron railing behind which I noticed a small mound of what looked like decomposed flowers: perhaps the garlands which devotees had offered to Shiva's lingam during the August pilgrimage. The wet ground was strewn with litter. I held my breath, listening.

The silence finally persuaded me that I was alone in the cave.

As I emerged into the dying light of the day, I was choking. Where was the holy man I had come to find? He was not in the cave. He was not at the entrance. He was not at the foot of the mountain. How could he possibly live in that empty wilderness?

I had imagined, God knows why, that there would be a village or a monastery nearby. Assured in London, and again in Delhi, and again in Srinagar by ten reliable people that I would find the man I was looking for in Amarnath Cave, I did not expect disappointment. Ten people, I thought, cannot be wrong.

I sank to my knees, leaning against the nearest rock. Tears welled up in my eyes, tears of an offended child. And the voice, which I felt had been summoning me to this cave, whose was it? Merely an aural hallucination, a subconscious excuse for the journey which otherwise would have seemed stupid?

Alone in the Himalayan wilderness, I suddenly felt that it *was* stupid; everything from the start: my naive wish for a psycho-physical transformation; my decision to find, despite my doubts in the usefulness of such things, a teacher, a guru; and, above all, my conviction that my investigations had been thorough enough. Equally stupid was my readiness to believe the old mule driver who was the last to confirm that I would find Yogananda in the remote mountain cave.

At the foot of the mountain he had already unpacked the ponies, pitched a small tent, rolled out two sleeping bags, lit a kerosene burner and boiled water for tea.

"Did you see Shiva's lingam?" he asked with a touch of malice. "You should've come in August, now it's too late."

"You know perfectly well I didn't come to see Shiva's lingam," I snapped. "I came to find Yogananda, the holy man. You swore he would be here."

"How could a man live in that cave?" He affected surprise. "What would he eat? Yes, during the summer pilgrimage there are sadhus here, hundreds of them, all kinds of yogis and holy men. But they all leave. There is nothing to keep them here."

"Why didn't you tell me that before we set off?"

"You didn't want facts," he said simply. "You wanted a dream. And you employed me to guide you, not to put you in touch with reality."

I found his words stranger than ever, completely at odds not only with his appearance but also with his occupation.

Even so, I felt I had been taken for a ride for no reason other than the old man's desire to see me bursting with hope and then deflated. I did not fail to notice the glimmer of satisfaction in his cunning eyes and the smirk on his face as he busied himself with the gas burner.

"You're a liar and a cheat," I said, stepping towards him. "And I hate being treated like a fool."

I struck him in the face.

"I won't pay you," I said, "and that's final."

"I didn't bring you here to get paid," he replied, gently rubbing his painful jaw, but not really upset. "I brought you here to get to know what sort of man you are."

"Well, you know now."

"Indeed," he said. "So don't worry about payment. And if you want to find Yogananda at this time of year, your best bet would be Leh, in Ladakh."

"What makes you think I believe you?"

"What you believe has nothing to do with me," he said. "Would you like some tea?"

I was about to hit him again, but something in his eyes told me that this time he would strike back.

"I would," I said. "Thank you."

2.

“You look for me, and I find you!”

As soon as I arrived in Leh I found a modest room and collapsed on a rickety bed. My head was buzzing, my mind was awash with strange faces of the Baltis, Tibetans, Ladakhis, Indian state officials and Muslim traders with whom I had shared a two-day bus ride, and with the greenery of the Kashmir valleys which seemed to belong in another world – a much pleasanter one than promised to be “little Tibet”, as Ladakh is known.

On the bus, a bearded Kashmiri merchant had warned me not to overdo things. I should spend the first two days resting under three blankets. In Ladakh, he said, strangers encounter strange things. In the open sun, where the temperature often reaches thirty degrees above zero, they remove their coats. Then they pass under a cliff and are struck as if by an axe, for they have crossed the line of permanent shade where it is always at least twenty degrees below zero. The air is so thin that they become breathless after a brief dash across the road. This doesn’t apply to the natives, of course, whose heart muscles are permanently enlarged.

“But that’s because of hundreds of years of adaptation,” the merchant said. “Please don’t think you can catch up with them in a few days!”

I expected the high plains to be covered by snowdrifts, but even in winter most of the snow remains on the slopes of the mountains piercing the sky on all sides. The winds are violent, sometimes warm, most often cold. They are caused by sudden drops in temperature, which fluctuates wildly. There are few trees; in most places all one finds are stunted bushes.

Before nightfall I rose and went to the window. I gazed at the Indus River and at the sprawling city of Leh before me. I saw a sixteenth-century royal palace, empty and full of dangerous cracks. I saw a city of brown and grey houses with terraced roofs and rectangular windows, shabby, Asiatic, seemingly without secrets. Where in this place would I find Yogananda? What on earth would he be doing in this crowd of Tibetan faces, in the heart of traditional Lamaism, he, an Indian Brahmin? No doubt the old mule driver had sold me another lie.

Next morning I checked my provisions. I had cans of beans, dried sausages, soup packets, potato chips, vitamin supplements. I had tea bags, thank God, because Ladakhi yak butter tea was nauseating, to say the least. I had a bottle of paracetamol capsules, although I wasn't sure what sort of pain I was trying to guard against. And, of course, three different types of antibiotics, just in case. I had decided to live modestly and get used as soon as possible to the local fare, although friends had warned me that in the mountain villages I could expect little more than *tsampa*, a barley porridge, and, if I was lucky, an occasional piece of cheese.

Out in the street, the high-altitude sun gathered me into a stunning embrace. I was glad to reach the winding alleys of the old city, which the sun could not penetrate. Passing a profusion of little shops, I decided that a stab in the dark was the best option I had. So I entered a shop selling padded winter jackets and asked the trader if he knew an Indian holy man by the name of Yogananda.

He grabbed me by the elbow and rushed me to the door. I thought I was about to be thrown out. But the trader dragged me across the road to a shop opposite, in front of which sat a plump young Ladakhi with a round cap on his head. A conversation ensued, during which the plump young man listened attentively, but kept shaking his head. Then a middle-aged lama with glasses came past, carrying two travelling bags. He paused for a chat, which went on for almost ten minutes. I was forgotten.

When the lama finally took his leave I, too, turned to go, but the trader reached out and held me back.

"The lama knows Yogananda," he said. "Maybe you'll find him at the lamasery of Thikse. Or Lamayuru. Or some other. When he comes to Ladakh he always stays in one of the lamaseries."

I raced to the government information office to find out how many lamaseries there were in Ladakh. A sleepy official explained that there was one in almost every village. In some there were hardly more than three or four monks, but the largest held hundreds. Reluctantly, he made a list of the most important ones. Outside, in front of the entrance, I spread out the map of Ladakh and Zanskar and soon realised that even to visit a few of the largest monasteries would take more than three weeks!

I closed my eyes; I had to lean against the nearest wall. My head was spinning. It was a mixture of rage, helplessness and self-pity. Rage, above all. If the wily old mule driver had suddenly appeared before me, I would have knocked him to the ground and spat in his face. After some minutes, I opened my eyes again and realised with shock that in my rage I had actually visualised him so well that he seemed to be standing before me, almost real, watching me with a mixture of curiosity and surprise – even amusement.

"Where have you been so long?" he asked. "You look for me and I find you. Is that a good beginning?"

His voice was certainly not an illusion, and neither was he. The old mule driver was standing right in front of me. But he looked very different. He was dressed in a faded yellow gown, the usual garb of an itinerant holy man, with a necklace of beads round his neck. In his right hand he was holding a thick bamboo stick. Because he was no longer wearing a turban I could see he was bald on top of his head, with plenty of greying hair falling down to his shoulders. He seemed to be taller, and his bearing more dignified. His eyes were different, too: less conniving, more astute, more spiritual.

It came to me in a flash. "Are you...?

He nodded before I could finish my question.

"But why did you...?"

"Because I was hoping you might hit me again." He smiled very gently. "Won't you?"

"I'm sorry," I said.

"Why?" He laughed. "Hitting old men is a matter of principle for you, is it not?"

I said I felt ashamed for losing my temper so disrespectfully. And I would, of course, pay him for taking me to Amarnath Cave, as agreed, and with interest.

"Don't worry," he said. "Forgiving fools is my favourite pastime."

An hour later we were on our way to the lamasery of Thikse. Old Yogananda was far from talkative. Occasionally he paused in his stride, turned and looked me up and down with a cynical grin. His wiry body exuded strength that was astonishing for a man of seventy, although strength may not be the right word; it was more a question of lightness and physical harmony. Why had I failed to notice that in the mule driver?

He walked very fast. Before long I fell behind, increasingly short of breath, unable to understand why he preferred steep mountain paths to the more leisurely road along the river. Witch each step, my backpack grew heavier. But the old man would not wait. He soon vanished behind the steep rocks overhanging the path.

Go to hell, I thought as I paused to regain my breath. Far below I could see the city of Leh, half-bathed in sunlight, half-sunk in deep shadow, with me in a far deeper shadow under a vaulted rock, and with my hopes, which had blossomed an hour earlier, in the deepest shadow of all. The old man was so scornful and taciturn that I felt he did not like me at all. Obviously he was not prepared to adapt his tempo to my lumbering progress.

Lifting my backpack, I staggered on.

Behind the first corner I was greeted by an unusual sight. In the middle of the rocky path, Yogananda was standing on his head, perfectly vertical, immobile. Only the bottom ends of his gown, which had collected round his waist, were trembling in the wind. The top of his head was resting on a flat stone. His feet were held slightly apart.

I waited. After five minutes he slowly bent his knees, arched his back, touched the ground with his feet without lifting the head off the stone, then manoeuvred himself onto his knees and finally, without any visible effort, extended himself into a standing position.

"Now it's your turn," he said.

I explained that my doctor had warned me, on account of a weakened vertebra in my neck, never to stand on my head. He laughed so loudly that the chilling sound flew down the mountainside and vanished somewhere above the valley. This was the first time I heard the laughter with which he would later greet each of what he called my intellecto-idiocies. I almost shivered when I heard it; it was rude, gross and derisive.

"So you have brought your doctor with you," he said. "Well, don't worry. You *are* standing on your head. You must've been doing so for the best part of your life."

He picked up his bamboo stick and walked on.

The path began to descend, so I found it easier to keep up with him. He even slowed down, as if wanting to tease me. Once or twice, in a moment of inattention, I almost bumped into him. Then, without any warning, he sat down on a rock beside the path.

"Carry on," he said. "Don't wait for me."

I said I would prefer to stay with him.

"Why?"

Expecting the question, I had prepared a number of what I thought were meaningful answers. Unfortunately at that particular moment I could not remember a single one. All I could say was that I wanted to change, to become different.

"You *are* different," he said. "If you wanted to become what you are, you would have better reasons for staying with me."

"But that's it," I said. "I want to find myself in my essence. I want to transform myself into what I used to be. I want to heal the gap inside me, become whole again."

His smacked his lips contemptuously. "What *is* your essence? Are you human? If you understand what is, then you are. Truth is what is. Do you know truth?"

I said I was still searching for it. I had come in the hope of finding it with his help.

"Truth is with me?" he asked, surprised. "In my pocket? In my stomach? Between my toes?" He seemed quite amused.

"It's not something tangible," I said. "It's a form of insight. The sort of knowledge that brings peace of mind." I added that truth was something that transcended temporal notions, something that simply was, present in the past *and* future.

"My dear friend, these are just beautiful words, the most worthless kind of poetry." He laughed. "So I tell you: don't seek, because you will miss. Don't seek, simply find."

He grinned, waiting for me to continue. By now it was more than obvious that he was not teasing me. But all his statements were so paradoxical that they failed to penetrate the defences of my rational mind. I said that I understood what he meant, in a way, but at the same time, perhaps, I did not.

"And why not?" he asked, almost jumping at me. "Because you understand. That's why you don't understand. Can I put it simpler than that? Peace of mind is achieved by a method that is neither spiritual nor intellectual, but physiological. You do something, and something follows. The mind grows peaceful along the way."

"That's why I'm here," I said.

He narrowed his eyes and wrinkled his forehead. "You lack innocence. Ideas and philosophies sprout from you like a multitude of weeds. You planted every seed the wind brought you, rejecting nothing. Now you're overgrown by a thick forest of nonsense. Are you prepared to burn it? If not, no method will be of any use. It'll just be another weed."

I said I was prepared to sacrifice many things, including what he called my garden of weeds, which is, in fact, a collection of my experiences, my knowledge of the world. But yes, I was prepared to let go even of that. Perhaps not by erasing it entirely, but by paying it less attention...

He interrupted me with a chilling laugh.

"Why don't you go to the bazaar in Leh? You'll make good money there. But at this bazaar, my little friend, there is no bargaining. And prices are steep! Playing this game, you have to put everything on the table. And there is no guarantee that you will not lose it! Even so, you will never lose more than weeds."

Gradually we were enveloped by moonlight, by a hollow night in the Himalayan heights. In the stillness, I became aware of my breathing, of the movement of lungs, of how much I owe to air.

I was zipped up in my sleeping bag. My guru was happy with a blanket across his knees. In the moonlight his eyes burned like those of a wild tiger. I told him how some eight years earlier, during my first visit to the Himalayas, I had tried to familiarise myself with Tibetan secrets and learn the art of *tummo*, heating the body with an inner fire. And how I failed because I lacked determination and was too superficial, merely a seeker of sensations.

"Are you different now?"

Yes, I said. I am different because my search is no longer an intellectual game. I am different because I am no longer interested in the panoramic breadth of the visible world, but want to descend to its core. For a long time my distress resembled the distant rumblings of a storm which never came close. Now I am in the eye of that storm. Now my distress is so real that I find it painful even to talk about it.

I am like a furrow waiting for the seed of something, anything, that will save me. I am like a man with a terminal illness, willing to try and accept anything that might help me.

"Even a kick in the arse?" His voice reached me through semi-darkness. "If it comes with a guarantee to free you of the burden of your unwisdom?"

He said that in reality my distress was nothing more than the burden of my intellecto-idiocies, which had started to suffocate me. What would I do if he assured me that a kick in the arse would bring me relief?

Yes, I said, I would accept even a kick in the arse, or whatever he meant by that.

"When I say kick in the arse, I mean the kind that knocks you flat on your face." He laughed. "I can't handle this overblown language of yours in which everything you say means something else. If I use words instead of actions, I do it because you're not ready for actions. If you were not blinded by words I would have kicked you in the arse hours ago. Then, perhaps, you would have understood."

So simple, I thought. But is it so simple?

I began to speak, to explain, not so much to him as to myself, as if trying – again – to achieve some sort of overview of my situation. I said I was an outcast, a fugitive from the world of scientific materialism in which I am unable to live in a way that would make me feel at home. Knowledge I do not lack, but this is not knowledge of insight and understanding, this is merely a plethora of facts and opinions, a richness of habits and mental reflexes. My Western world of scientific objectivity disallows questions that can have only subjective answers.

I am a fugitive from the world, I continued, in which the "objective" scientists do their utmost to convince me that my values are nothing more than reactions to the threats posed by the environment. That my entire value system is nothing more than a result of my longing for happiness, and so an attempt to prove what is pure illusion, and so the source of my *un*happiness. In my world I am laughed at if I mention enlightenment and salvation; I am told that the idea of salvation is no more than immaturity, lack of courage to come to terms with the fact that I am a biochemical machine without added dimensions.

I long for knowledge that embraces the world not only in its appearance, but also in all its hidden aspects. I long to be able to penetrate everything that is not visible, to reach deeper than what the world appears to be, and to remain permanently in touch with that hidden dimension.

I am a fugitive from the world in which a man by the name of Descartes said, "Cogito ergo sum," thus narrowing the frame of valid experiences to what can be counted and measured –

"And now," interrupted Yogananda, "you want me to save you? So you can save your people? So they can save the world?"

I said I was neither naive nor a fool. All I wanted was for someone to show me the way. Because, I said, the first step was the most important.

"The first step you've taken," he said. "You believe you can reach understanding by methods that your rational world does not recognise. Why else would you come to an old man who lives like a beggar and stands on his head twice a day?"

3.

The blow

I could not sleep, it was too cold. The moon was setting behind the shadowy bulk of the mountains. Yogananda was quiet and blissful. Master of the moment. Not so I. The usual chaos of memories, worries and ruminations boiled and bubbled, independently of my will, inside me. Thoughts shaped themselves into questions and other thoughts into answers, without any order or depth; I was merely a witness to a series of disjointed neural explosions.

Who was he that was watching? That thoughtless "I" which was experiencing, witnessing the untameable dance in his brain? In whose brain?

"What are you *really* after?" Yogananda, who was not asleep after all, suddenly asked.

"Wholeness," I said without hesitation. "The feeling of oneness with myself and my experience of the world."

"Childhood?"

"Perhaps. Not so much because in childhood most possibilities were still open, but because of that undaunted belief that the world is a place of miracles and that life is an endless sea of enthusiasm."

I told him that as a child I used to experience the world, and life, and myself in both, without standing outside and judging my actions. Then something happened, and I am still not sure what.

"You lost the world," he said, "and you were lost to the world."

Maybe, I said. All I can say with certainty is that for the last twenty years I have been plagued by a feeling of loss. With each of the passing years, this feeling grew stronger. Whatever I did, whether plunging, as a young man, into the sensual, material world or exploring the shadowy regions of the inexpressible, I could always feel, at least vaguely, that all my efforts, and even my pranks, were dedicated to some kind of journey. For a long time I had no idea what it was that I felt I had to find. Only gradually it dawned on me that my restlessness was not a desire for something new, but an urge to reconnect with something known and long lost.

"Suppose," he said, "that your soul is already saved and there is nothing you have to do about it."

I thought about this for a long time.

Then I said, "Anybody whose soul is saved would surely know about it, would he not?"

There was no reply. Old Yogananda had fallen asleep.

"Good morning," I said seven hours later, as I climbed out of my sleeping bag. I felt stiff all over. I started to jump up and down, slapping my thighs with my hands. Yogananda watched me with great curiosity. He asked me why I was doing this.

I told him it was my morning exercise, meant to loosen the joints, improve circulation, warm up the cells.

"Have you ever seen a tiger or a dog jumping up and down, slapping himself?"

No, I said. An animal wakes up, stretches and is fully alert. A tiger uncoils from the deepest sleep like a spring and extends himself without effort into fight or flight. A tiger neither thinks nor calculates. A tiger does not sit eight hours a day at a writing desk. He knows neither love nor hatred, or past, or future. I, on the other hand, am aware not only of myself but also of myself being aware of myself. Wedged between me and my environment is my construction of reality. How can I compare myself to a tiger?

"You can't," said Yogananda. "The tiger lives in his centre, while you live on the outskirts of yourself."

Like most of his statements this one, too, caused a sudden halt in my train of thought. For a brief moment I was suspended in terrifying emptiness. He was looking at me and was obviously amused by my startled expression.

"The tiger knows how to breathe," he said. "You don't."

"I do," I said.

I closed my eyes and slowly took a deep breath, following its passage all the way to the lungs. Then, just as slowly, I breathed out.

As I did, something horrible struck me across my back. I opened my eyes and could just see the old man raising his bamboo stick to deliver another blow. I threw myself out of its reach.

"What?" He grinned, almost viciously. "Did you suddenly feel you were close to the door?"

"What door?" I cried, suppressing tears.

"The door through which you could enter this moment. The only moment in which you exist."

We continued our way down the winding path towards the misty valley. I staggered after him in complete confusion.

Why did he do that?

"I wanted to wake you," he said.

There are moments when this is possible, he explained. When the pupil is relaxed and convinced that the teacher is satisfied with his progress, a sudden blow with a stick, especially if it comes when the pupil expects approval, can make him see the door and push him through it into the light of self-realisation. In my case the attempt failed. I may have caught a glimpse of the door, but my intellectual armour is so heavy and cumbersome that any inkling of it was dissipated before I knew what was happening.

And now it was too late. Now the stick would not work any more. At each blow my first reaction would be the thought: "Oh yes, the old man is trying to knock me into being awake." And thought is a wall with no door, no exit.

Then he spoke of the interval between the ingoing breath and the outgoing breath. There is one, he said, but I failed to notice it. That is how the Buddha became the Buddha. By paying attention to his breathing he one day unexpectedly caught the fleeting moment of non-breath, and through it he entered the present, where he remained.

This, of course, goes against everything that my intellect is capable of accepting as possible. I believe that important goals can be reached only gradually, by painful accumulation. How could the Buddha reach enlightenment suddenly, in a flash of realisation? I believe, and so does my world, that only results of effort have any value, and the greater the effort so much greater the value. That is why, for me, the way to enlightenment is a thorny path of renunciations, hard work, study, philosophy. I cannot accept that truth is within me this very moment, and only this moment.

"Or can you?" he asked me.

"Maybe not," I conceded. "Is this a big problem?"

Only as long as I consider the situation rationally, he said. To the rational mind everything is a problem. And every solution to a problem creates another problem. Reality itself is not problematic. What is problematic is my concept of it. Everything goes through my head. My head is like a state border, and my intellect is the customs service that confiscates most of the precious imports, everything that is new and foreign, everything that is different and could be subversive. The intellect's role is to safeguard the system. It is very conservative, a democrat on the outside but in fact a cunning dictator who never sleeps.

That is why I dare not believe that a blow with a bamboo stick could knock me straight into a state of enlightenment. For my intellect that would mean capitulation. So many years of study, reading, collecting and checking facts, ideas, opinions! All these accumulated treasures must be very precious to me. They cannot be blown away just like that.

"And it's true," he said. "They cannot. Not easily. Only the right method will do it. But the attempt should not be undertaken lightly. The shock of suddenly finding yourself in the heart of emptiness might kill you."

But I should not be afraid, he said with a laugh. My intellect is too cunning to let a sudden method get the better of it. We tried that, and it failed. My customs service is too conscientious.

"So?" I asked. "If the sudden method will not work any more, what is left?"

What is left is the gradual path, he said. But I must remember that this is not a path in terms of developing special skills and so on. By studying Buddhist texts I can become an excellent scholar, but not the Buddha. If I want to become the Buddha, I must wait for it to happen.

"How long?"

"Anything from five seconds to three thousand years," he said.

4.

A moment of doubt

In the valley we came upon a wide oasis of fields and meadows, interspersed with groups of poplar-like trees which the locals call *chenar*. A scattered herd of yaks was grazing on the bank of the nearby river. The sun began to burn like a furnace. I instantly rummaged inside my backpack and pulled out a tube of sun cream. The weather-beaten face of old Yogananda twisted into inaudible laughter.

"Use this," he said. He bent down, scooped up a handful of damp brown soil. Before I got the chance to move away, he grabbed me with his left hand by the scruff of the neck and with his right one spread the dirt all over my face.

He laughed. "So, now you look like a native!"

I swallowed my anger and even managed a bland smile, as if trying to say that mud was indeed a better protection than sun cream. But when we reached the shallow river I announced that the muddy sun lotion wasn't quite to my liking and I would wash it off. I bent down, pushed my hands into the fast-flowing water – and let out a yell that must have frightened the hell out of my companion.

But he merely laughed. "Cold, is it?" My head was burning from the sun, but the icy water felt as if I had touched a live wire. I gasped and quickly scrubbed the foul-smelling mud off my face.

What must life be like here in winter, I wondered.

"Dear boy." Yogananda laughed. "Everything freezes over, the only way to reach water is to break the ice, but you can do that only on larger rivers; the small ones freeze right to the bottom. Sharp winds whistle across the plain and there is so much snow that you can't reach your nearest neighbour. The villagers cut narrow passageways into the frozen snow, and these walkways, often haunted by wolves, remain the only means of communication among the farms and villages throughout the long winter."

We walked on towards a cluster of rectangular whitewashed houses that hung to a rocky hillside. We reached a *chorten* that marked the entrance to the monastery grounds. Buddhist Himalaya is full of *chortens*. Reminiscent of ancient Indian tombs, they are symbolic structures expressing the Buddhist conception of reality. The square base represents the earth, the round mound represents water, the pointed red pagoda is a symbol of fire, and the umbrella at the top represents wind. The four constituent elements of man and the world.

Behind the chorten the path diverged and continued on both sides of a rocky mound which was covered in flat prayer stones. All were engraved with the words *Om Mani Padme Hum*, hail to the jewel in the lotus, the Tibetan equivalent of The Lord's Prayer. There are few places where you cannot find it; it is chiselled into wayside rocks, mountain sides, walls of houses and temples, the monks keep repeating it during prayers and it is said to be an effective mantra for meditation.

The monks received us with broad smiles and polite bows. Unsure of my role, I kept smiling and nodding. I noticed that the monks were looking at me with discreet curiosity. The walls of the large prayer hall were covered in luxurious Tibetan *tangkas*, depicting scenes from Buddhist mythology. Leaning against the left wall were stacks of yellowed Buddhist texts, most of them printed three hundred years ago in Tibet. Lively flames of the fire burning in a large fireplace at the end of the hall threw shivering shadows on the ceiling and surrounding walls. Some of the twenty odd monks around us were very young, still only boys, while others were older, some nearly bent over with age.

After the greeting ceremonies Yogananda took hold of my elbow and ushered me into the middle of the hall. Loquaciously and theatrically he started to introduce me. He spoke Tibetan, so I tried to gauge the meaning of his words from the expressions on the monks' faces; an impossible task. Against my will I had become the centre of attention, and yet I didn't know what was being said about me. How should I react? Modestly? With humility? Proudly? Indifferently? Or should I assume an expression of seriousness? Severe? Placid? All-knowing?

The choice was limitless, so I merely stood there staring at my feet and waiting for the painful moments to pass. For the first time in my life I became aware that embarrassment is a form helplessness, and for the first time I felt it as a physical pain.

When the old man concluded his introduction I asked him what he had told them.

"Why do you want to know?" He looked at me in surprise.

"I feel awkward because I don't know what they think about me," I said.

Without a word he turned his back to me and started to talk to an old lama who was standing nearby. Less than a minute later loud laughter exploded behind me.

"Let's go," Yogananda said. Half-mechanically and half in a dream-like state I followed him out of the prayer hall. A young monk, Lama Lobsang, insisted on carrying my backpack.

We passed through rooms with frescoes and statues, through halls with frightening ritual masks, swords and ancient guns, then through rooms filled with drums, trumpets and books. Finally we reached a long terrace from which there led narrow doors into monks' cells. Lama Lobsang opened the door of the eighth one in the row.

"Take a rest," Yogananda said.

The shuffling sounds of their sandals drew away along the terrace.

I stepped to the small window. Sharp breeze was forcing its way inside and into my face; there was no pane. I saw the sunlit valley we had crossed, the shadowy blue-grey slopes of the nearby mountains and, far behind them, the snowy peaks of the Himalayan range.

Suddenly I heard a sound. Yogananda was standing behind me.

"Tell me," he said. "When I was introducing you to the monks you wanted to know what I was telling them, so you could figure out what they thought about you, so you could then, on the basis of that, figure out what you are. Don't you know what you are?"

I bent my head. "It's true that occasionally I behave too mechanically –"

"A net of illusions," he said, almost shouting. "A play of shadows and light. I want to know what you are. Why you want to stay with me. I'm a strange old man who is tramping around without a purpose, without any aims. That's my life, ideal for me. But you have started to tramp around with me. Why? If you don't know that, then it's pointless for us to continue."

Abruptly, he turned and left the cell.

The sound of a gong could be heard from a building lower down. It was probably calling the monks to a meal. Or to prayer. I thought: isn't this too far from the world I know, from the place I call home?

The sudden awareness of the cultural gap shocked me. What am I doing among these mountain folk who don't wash and whose staple diet is barley porridge? And who use tattered flags and spinning wheels to pray for them?

Where does it come from, this urge to change, to spread out, to widen and deepen myself? Isn't that sort of thing out of fashion? Suppose this urge doesn't lead to liberation but to a form of madness, not closer but further away from the world? And what is the nature of this urge? Is it religious? Philosophical? Do I want to become a mystic?

Mystic, scientist, philosopher, poet, composer – they all draw energy from the urge to create meaning in the meaningless world. The mystic differs from the others in that he seeks salvation: he wants to awake from the night into the light of day.

Is that what I should tell Yogananda? That I would like to awaken? The word Buddha comes from the Sanskrit root "budh", which means to know, to awaken to what is. When I truly awake, I become the Buddha. But only in the sense that I begin to think and live like the Buddha.

The Buddhist thinking doesn't change processes into things and events into objects. Buddhism, no matter how much some dislike the idea, is an unassailable composition of philosophy and psychology, a demanding method of getting to know oneself and one's role and value in the world. And thus simultaneously the art of connecting with true reality. Doesn't that mean that spiritual awakening is really nothing more than optimal mental health?

I had come to Yogananda as a victim of my European cultural moulding – a child of Aristotle, Plato, Descartes, Hegel, Nietzsche, Heidegger, Sartre, Derrida and other purveyors of ideas about existence and the meaning of life. I had come to transcend this heritage and escape its suffocating grasp; to create a distance that would become the measure of my freedom.

Then it is clear what I want from Yogananda! Therapy! I had come as a patient: divided, neurotic, mistrustful, impatient, full of "useless poetry", stuffed with metaphysical shit, a slave of habits and instilled reflexes, nailed to the cross of conflicting illusions. Had I not?

I rushed from the cell to tell Yogananda that I finally knew what I want from him. Let him do with me what he wants. Let him cut me into as many pieces as he likes, and let him rejoin the pieces the way he thinks fit.

At the end of the terrace I encountered Lama Lobsang who asked me if I was looking for my friend.

I nodded.

"Unfortunately he is no longer here. He left for the valley of Zanskar."

And he waved his hand towards the blue-grey mountains whose tops were hidden in a swathe of white clouds.

5.

A journey to Zanskar

All right, said the insulted little boy within me. Go to hell. Stand on your head, wander through these mountains from dawn to dusk, but humiliate someone else. If you really fancy yourself so much that you're incapable even of little patience, I don't give a dime for your wisdom. Only a charlatan would disappear without saying goodbye.

When the bus reached Kargil, where passengers from Leh to Srinagar have to spend the night, I was already glad I was leaving. I began to look forward to the advantages of civilised life: tasty food, good wine, regular showers, books, intelligent conversation, Mozart. And sex.

But the following morning a strange force made me rise before dawn and walk past the resting bus towards a small cluster of tents by the road. Camping there was a small mountaineering team from Lille in northern France; one of them told me the night before that they were on their way to Zanskar. After some initial reluctance they finally said there was room for one more person in one of their jeeps. But only as far as Ringdom, they warned me; there the road deteriorated and they would have to continue on the backs of ponies.

I ran back to the bus to fetch my backpack.

Half an hour later four battered jeeps were rattling and squealing along the narrow road leading southeast. It wasn't long before we reached the Suru River valley. It was lonely and without vegetation; not a twig could be seen poking from among the rocks on the steep slopes rising up to the glaciers at the top. Very few villages in the valley were blessed with modest greenery. The road snaked its way along the river and two rows of white mountain peaks accompanied us for hours on end like a guard of honour.

I tried not to think of my change of plans. But eventually I had to find a reason for my decision, so I said to myself: Well, why shouldn't I travel a little, see these outlandish places now that I'm here? After all, didn't the Indian government open them to foreigners only a few years earlier? The fact that Yogananda, too, had gone to Zanskar, is mere coincidence; that doesn't mean that I'm looking for him. And where would I find him in a valley that's three hundred kilometres long?

"We Westerners are so stupid," Jules, a member of the French team, was saying. "What we see in these Buddhist *gompas* are monasteries. But in fact they're schools in which the young monks are pupils, taught ancient wisdom by the old ones."

"We smirk," he carried on, "when we see prayer flags and prayer wheels and mandalas. We can't understand that they are symbols. Just like the French flag. For someone who can't understand the value of symbols even the French flag would be no more than a piece of cloth."

"And that is the problem." He showed no signs of letting up. "We can't grasp the reality that lies behind the Buddhist symbols. If we see a Ladakhi spinning his prayer wheel all day long we call it superstition. But if someone could prove to us that this daily ritual is capable of curing neurotic illness we would exclaim that it's psychology!"

Towards the evening we stopped in the valley of Ringdom and the French brewed some coffee. The setting sun was giving the glaciers above us a golden hue. Cold shadows were spreading along the valley. Jules spread out a map and looked east.

"There." He pointed towards two snowy mountain caps glowing high above us, almost floating in the sky. "Nun and Kun, the highest mountains in the Zanskar range. Between them lies a pass leading to the valley of white copper."

After a brief conversation, they decided to set up tents and spend the night by the river instead of continuing on. It turned out to be a wise decision. By the time everything was ready, Nun and Kun had already disappeared in deep evening shadows while the bottom of the valley became enveloped in translucent darkness. A multitude of twinkling stars appeared in the sky above us. We were so exhausted from the long journey that the camp soon sank into silence. Only a whisper here and there, subdued laughter, an occasional cough. Then snoring. And not far away, the whispering flow of the river.

And the night. Which brought remorse. And anger. And disappointment with the apprentice who, only a day earlier, had deluded himself that he could say goodbye to these mountains with barely a shrug. Who *knew* that he was deluding himself and yet had no courage to admit that to his innermost self. "Fuck you!" I kept berating myself in the warmth of my sleeping bag. "Fuck you!"

But who was the person berating himself? I pushed my head into the open and looked at the sky.

And suddenly it hit home as if all the mountains had crashed on top of me. Isn't it clear who I am looking for? The master in myself. So many quarrelsome "I"s, so many little Flisars are having a ball inside me. The one who blows his top for hardly a reason at all, and the one who swears never to forgive a slight, however small, and the paralysed melancholic who decides never to leave his little shell, and the thoughtless optimist who steps on thin ice and begins to dance; and the one who falls in love with an idea and tries to mould the world in its shape; as well as the one who is able to surrender to the moment and feel happy.

Who is the master of all these "I"s?

Who is the one who keeps them in check, makes them calm down when they go overboard, pulls them back when they venture too far? There is no order without a master and where there is no master anarchy rules.

On the threshold of the land of white copper I remain a land without a ruler; a land in which power is passed from one usurper to another. What my "I"s need is a master.

In the morning, as we crawled out of our tents, we noticed they were covered with a thin layer of ice. The French mountaineers threw themselves into vigorous morning exercises. Politely, I did a few push-ups with them, but as soon as my lungs began to wheeze I wandered off towards a solitary *stupa* standing not far away. I still hadn't got used to the high altitude; low pressure was making me dizzy and tired. Looking east, I could see the peaks of Nun and Kun already gleaming in the rays of the morning sun. Still in darkness between them was Pensi-la, the only pass leading to the valley of Zanskar, lying 4500 metres above sea level. Jules told me that Zanskar was one of the most mysterious lands in the world, an old Buddhist kingdom in which power was by agreement shared by two kings, a valley of villages, monasteries and temples carved into steep rocky mountain sides, a valley of deep canyons and fast-flowing rivers, arched over by rickety hanging bridges; a valley of ancient rituals, a fairy-tale world in which even the richest imagination was unable to compete with reality.

Suddenly the sun sent its rays across the mountain ridge and dispelled the shadowy gloom of the valley as if by magic. The reddish mound of the Ringdom lamasery, perched on a rounded hill at the foot of the mountains, became clearly visible. I could see a long caravan of heavily loaded yaks and ponies slowly moving towards it, accompanied by a group of drivers in long dark-red coats.

Light on the northern side of the Himalayan range is unusually sharp. Because the air is so dry and clear, the mountains a hundred miles away seem much nearer than they are. You get the feeling that the world had moved closer, crowded in on you, and that you only have to reach out to touch the snow on top of the mountains.

Distorted perceptions made me feel knitted into the texture of nature, part of the dance of matter and energy. That I cannot die, because I have always existed and will continue to do so, although not forever in the same shape and form. For a while, at least, I succeeded in leaving the anarchic company of my "I's" to connect with the world of which I was an inseparable part.

Now! I thought. Now Yogananda *could* get hold of me. Now he wouldn't grasp only at empty air!

I said goodbye to the French and set off towards the Ringdom lamasery. To my surprise, I caught up with the caravan quickly. Not one of the men understood English, but they received me graciously with broad smiles. They relieved me of my backpack and tied it to the back of the sturdiest of the ponies.

"Zanskar, Zanskar," the toothless leader of the caravan kept repeating and pointing towards Nun and Kun.

"Zanskar, Zanskar," was my refrain as I tried to explain that that was also my destination.

The journey was very long. My clearest memories are of the moments when the monotony was broken by unexpected events. How one of the ponies stuck its teeth into my left buttock, making the sunburnt Tibetan faces break into sympathetic smiles. How my behind got so sore from the rough saddle that I had to dismount and continue on foot. How the pony that bit me a little later added insult to injury by honouring me with a well-aimed kick that missed my knee by less than an inch. How a man by the name of Songsten twisted his ankle on a rocky path and had to be lifted into a saddle where, in spite of pain, he continued to smile.

And how on the slopes close to the pass we spotted fox-like furry animals that sat on their tails close to the entrances of their lairs, watching us with almost amazed curiosity. And how suddenly they began to rush around as if demented, whistling "feeuuu, feeuuu, feeuuuu," and then disappeared. The men said the animals were called "feeuuuu", but to me they looked like marmots.

Around midday we stopped. The men made a fire with dry flakes of horse manure, boiled a pot of water, threw in some tea leaves and finally added four handfuls of barley flour. "*Tsampa*," they said. I didn't like *tsampa*, the staple meal in this part of the world, so I opened a can of corned beef. Polite as I was, and believing they would refuse, I offered the can to one of the men. "Try some," I said. All the faces lit up as if I had offered them gold. They emptied the can with their spoons in less than a minute. Then, with genuine gratitude, they offered me half of their *tsampa*!

I remember falling into fitful sleep in the afternoon sun – blue and yellow flowers on the nearby slopes, the undulating sea of snowy peaks, deaf loneliness of the rocky mountain path along which the caravan continued on its way, wild sheep and goats whose twisted horns could be seen flitting among the rocks.

I remember the moment we reached the top of the pass and stopped by a large mound of rocks adorned with a multitude of yellow, white and blue prayer flags. I remember how the merchant emissaries of the king of Zangla added their own flag to the others, no doubt in gratitude because the treacherous path hadn't cost them any of their precious animals.

But apparently one flag wasn't enough, for towards the evening, as the caravan began to wind its way along a particularly narrow path carved out of the rocky slope, one of the ponies made a wrong step, loosened a large stone on the edge of the precipice, which tumbled loudly into the depths below. The sound frightened the pony which made a sideways jump and knocked even more stones over the precipice before it finally lost its footing and rolled, pack and all, into a deep ravine.

At the foot of the pass we found a grassy patch and set up tents for the night. Two of the five drivers walked back to retrieve the sacks that had been strapped to the unfortunate pony's back. The other three unpacked the animals and used the sacks and saddles and wooden boxes to build a wall that might, so they hoped, protect us against the low wind.

I remember that the following morning we crossed a thundering mountain stream flowing from a glacier high above us and continued across desolate slopes towards the plain below. We were already in the western province of the kingdom of Zanskar, the land of the white copper.

Soon we reached the first villages. They were not much different from the ones in Ladakh: clusters of rectangular flat-roofed houses with tiny windows, set in rare oases of greenery, some at the foot of high slopes, others built into the sides of perpendicular rocks. Once more we spent the night in the open.

The next morning we found the sky literally stuffed with rain clouds. The air became warmer and noticeably damper. I could read relief and freshness on the faces of the merchant emissaries of the king of Zangla; on the northern side of the Himalaya rain is a sign of God's mercy.

But suppose it is going to snow?

The thought didn't fill me with pleasure. The snow separates Zanskar from the rest of the world for eight months. I noted down the names of the villages through which we passed: Arsho, Abrang, Kusul, Baharse, Remala, Pe, Trokta, Ating, Drokang, Ramtasha. I remember a herd of yaks which, together with their shepherd, followed us with doleful stares, and packs of emaciated dogs that barked and growled at us near the villages, and the chortens and temples near the road, and lamaseries on the slopes of the mountains.

Most villages were surrounded by yellowing fields of recently mowed barley. As far as I could see there wasn't a single tree. These villages, at four and a half thousand metres above sea level, are the highest in the world. It was late afternoon before we reached one that was not without trees. Along narrow ditches that guided water from the glaciers above to the terraced fields at the foot of the slopes, rows of poplars and willows grew.

It started to rain. The caravan continued on its way. Towards the evening, when the rain thickened and started to slap our faces, the leader of the caravan led us towards a small village half-hidden in gathering darkness. Ponies were given shelter behind the walls of the local lamasery. Good-hearted villagers offered roofs over our heads.

A tall man in a thick wool coat led me towards a rather large house on the outskirts of the village. Lighting his way with a flickering torch, he guided me to a small backroom and showed me a dusty mattress in the corner. Without hesitation I started to unroll my sleeping bag.

"Thank you," I muttered, "thank you so much." I fell asleep in less than a minute.

When I opened my eyes it was already late morning; sun was shining through the narrow window. I turned to climb out of my sleeping bag. As I did, I became aware that there was someone else in the room. A man leaning against the opposite wall.

"How is that now?" I heard a deep fatherly voice. "Again you look for me, and again I find you."

Instantly, my eyes filled with tears.

Oh, you holy grey-bearded face! You who understand! My teacher! If only you knew how desperately I have missed you!

6.

My dangerous friend

The next morning we set off across the central plain of the kingdom of Zanskar. Some rain had fallen during the night, so the ground was soft, fresh and green. We headed for the slope on the northern side of the plain and eventually climbed a narrow path that wound its way round the ridges of the slope. After an hour of walking, as we turned a corner, I suddenly felt as though we had been pushed through a time tunnel into a distant past. Far away, four mountain villages perched on a gently rounded slope, growing out of rocky foundations as if a natural part of the ground. From a glacier high above them three narrow streams flowed gently among the villages into the river at the foot of the mountain.

"There." Yogananda pointed towards a distant house, standing on its own and glowing white in the morning sun. "There we will stop for a day. Maybe two. Maybe three?"

In the afternoon we caught sight of the famous lamasery of Karsha. It was like a vision from another world. Almost a hundred white buildings, clamped together in a grape-like fashion, were bathed in the setting sun like huge rectangular mushrooms with a multitude of tiny square windows. Yogananda told me the lamasery belonged to the Tibetan Buddhist sect of Reformed Yellow Hats, the leader of which was the fourteenth Dalai Lama. Lamaseries are places of learning and education. The monks have to survive the way they can. Some are supported by their parents while others work in the lamaseries as cooks, cleaners, workers in the fields. If a lamasery is rich enough, it gives poorer monks annual grants. Younger monks have to pass exams. They can earn a degree. Any monk can stay in the lamasery for life, but some return to their families, get married and continue to lead normal lies. The monks perform funeral rites, bless houses and fields, and exorcise demons. They are doctors, healers, herbalists, even psychiatrists.

"No different than in your world," Yogananda said. "Only simpler."

"It seems to me," I replied, "that it's rather more complicated."

"Many things seem to you," he said. "It seems to me this, it seems to me that, I keep hearing from you. A good way of keeping a safe distance between yourself and events, between yourself and the world. As long as it only seems to you, you can place responsibility for wrong decisions on the vagueness of your feelings. Convenient, but cowardly. Only when you're able to say: no, it doesn't just seem to me, I know, only then have you stepped from behind your shelter and into the open battlefield. Where anything may happen. Where you can lose your head. But you're a hero who is fighting his battles in his imagination. And even there you mostly end up defeated."

It's not *quite* like that, I objected. When I say that something merely seems to me, I am just being honest. I am aware of the inconstancy of the quarrelsome individuals inside me. If I could force them under a central rule, my feelings would become my knowledge, my certainty. And then the feeling of the ruler would turn into the action of the ruled. My problem is the absence of central rule. I miss a master inside me. My mind is like a country of hundreds of provinces. I would like to unite them, bring them all under a central rule.

"Why don't you?" he said. "Make one of these provincial governors king."

I said that either one or the other always usurps the throne. Sometimes he is elected to rule by the others. Occasionally the others force him to rule. The problem appears when the master, elected or not, gives an order. Then, instead of implementing it, the parliament in my mind starts debating, criticising, rejecting it.

These parliamentary debates rage in my mind night and day, without respite. Occasionally one of the delegates suggests something that the others accept unanimously and the result is action. At other times five or ten of them leap to their feet all at once, each demanding the acceptance of his suggestion, and then I have to witness conflicts, quarrels, a neurotic strife in my mind, and the result is paralysis. It happens that one of the delegates disappears without trace or is forced out by the united will of the others.

It also happens that out of the blue new ones appear. Or they start knocking at the door, at first gently and then insistently, until they are allowed to enter and join the crowd already inside. Some start to waste away and finally become so weak that they can't be heard any more. In the meantime some of the others grow louder, more devious, even violent, and turn into dictators. But only for a short time, for the others almost always unite and force them out.

Yogananda looked at me warmly. "Do you realise who these delegates are, and whose interest they have at heart?"

After some thought I said that these quarrelsome entities are my urges, ideas that were planted in my mind when I was a child, wishes that insist on being fulfilled, metaphysical speculations implanted in me by my peers; my hereditary, physiological leanings; habits, memories and experiences that I found pleasant and would like to have repeated; and the self-images I had created and would like to strengthen – all these things are fighting for their rights and privileges inside me. Results of their eternal debates and struggles form the chain of events and non-events that is the history of my presence in the world. And this history is my life.

"Society has given you the illusion that you are what you think you are," he said.

But there is no other reality, I objected. I don't live in an empty space; my identity and my life's meaning grow out of my interaction with others; I cannot brush away the dimension that is the basis of what I am, not without annihilating my self.

It is society that determines the shape of my consciousness. And this consciousness, this *construction* of reality, denies me the possibility of reacting to outside stimuli directly. My consciousness is a safety filter. I may indeed say that I feel and experience the world, but this experience is only partial, made up of fragments let through by the filter. This filter is so good at its work that I am aware of the deeper, truer reality only in the form of indefinable longing. Even when I try to escape my "I", or quietly steal away from it, I cannot do it. My mind knows what I am up to; it has spies everywhere. So there is no way out. My way of thinking is a prisoner of my brain. And without brain there is no me.

"You move in circles," Yogananda said. "The Buddhists call this state of imprisonment *samsara*. You keep returning to where you have already been many times. What you must do is to move from *samsara*, the state of illusions, to the state of nirvana, wakefulness. Then you will realise that you're not what you think you are, but that you are what you think."

Below the lamasery he approached the stream that was running past the houses and removed his shoes. I thought he was going to wash his feet. But instead of stepping into the shallow water her pulled a tin mug from his bag and beckoned me to come closer.

"Fill the mug with water," he said, "and bring it here."

I unloaded my backpack and did what he wanted.

"I'm going to stand on my head," he said. "When I do, I want you to pour the water, drop by drop, on the soles of my feet. Very slowly, one drop a minute."

And before I knew it, there he was, standing on his head right next to me. His legs wobbled a little, but the next moment he was completely still, as if frozen. The skin on his soles was unusually young, soft, and smooth. Carefully, I tilted the mug and let a drop of water fall on his left sole. His foot twitched a little. Then I let a drop fall on the sole of his right foot; it, too, twitched a little.

I waited a minute. When the second drop fell on his left sole, the foot remained still. So did the old man. Not even when water began to run down his ankles and seep into his trousers, gathered in folds around his knees, did he show that he was made of flesh and blood. His breathing was slow and measured, his eyes were closed.

After half an hour I had to move the mug into my left hand; the right one had become almost rigid. I could feel impatience welling up inside me. I could feel its tentacles spreading through my body until I could hardly breathe. I was mindful of this process, all the while hoping that the old man would tire of what seemed completely senseless.

An evil voice inside me began to whisper, "Shorten the minutes. Make the drops larger. Pour some water on the ground."

Which of the delegates in my internal parliament was saying these things? It seemed to me there was an entire party behind him, the Let's Hurry Party which has no time to pause and reflect, and is prepared to expend effort only if the goal is within reach. This is the party that has never heard of persistence; the party that lets down a runner a quarter of the way to the winning post; that weakens the drive of the artist at a point where, with some extra effort, he could have created a masterpiece; that offers you reasons to withdraw once something ceases to be fun. This is a party of halfway heroes and self-indulgent hypocrites.

And suddenly this party started to make pronouncements: "Dripping water on the soles of an old man is crazy. Who does he think he is, daring to treat you like this? Pour some of the water away. He won't notice it. And if he does, he won't say anything. And if he does, tell him that enough is enough."

The voice of the opposition was at first barely audible, but it kept getting louder. Before long, a full-scale debate was running between the two camps inside me. It doesn't matter, objected the Party of Consistency, if the whole thing looks crazy; the old man surely knows what he is doing. He asked for a favour, and once a promise is made it has to be kept. It's as simple as that.

Then the Let's Hurry Party got unexpected allies. A small group of ragged boys appeared from among the houses. They stopped a few yards away, watching us. One of them said something and the other three responded with laughter. That forced me to look at the scene through their eyes, and suddenly I was overcome by embarrassment. The kids continued to pass derisive remarks. Then they started to run around us in circles, pulling at each other and yelling. I began to hope that the noise would weaken Yogananda's concentration.

It didn't; he remained completely still.

The boys eventually disappeared among the houses. I remained by the side of my old companion and in the growing chill of the evening shadows continued to drop water on his soles for another twenty minutes. Having overcome the crisis of confidence, I stopped asking myself if any of this made any sense. The whole thing became easier, until finally it became fun. When the last drop of water slipped out of the mug I was filled with a sense of peace and deep satisfaction. Yogananda (how did he know the mug was empty?) deftly jumped back on his feet and thanked me with a sly grin.

As we walked on I asked him if the drops of water were meant to help him with meditation.

"Me?" He turned around with surprise. "It was you they were meant to help. But if I told you you were undergoing a trial you would have tried too hard, and the result wouldn't tell me the truth about you. Now I know you're a disciple worthy of my attention. That's good enough."

I asked him if I can expect more tests like that.

He laughed. "Imagine that I have a gun and want to shoot you. You don't know where I am, but I'm stalking you, I'm close and a bullet can come whistling at any moment. Do you expect me to shout: here I come, be careful? You must understand that our game is different. If I warn you, you will rely on my warnings, and then you won't be careful, you won't be awake. The bullet can come at any moment. At any moment, without the slightest warning, you can find yourself being tested. And if you don't pass the test, it's goodbye."

We walked on. After a while he turned and said, "I'm not your nurse. I'm your friend. But a dangerous friend."

7.

I am stupid because I am clever?

Our shadows, long at first but gradually shortening, walked before us. Yogananda's steps were light and easy. I tried to fall in with his rhythm, but his legs were longer. And without a heavy backpack, he was moving softly and in a leisurely fashion. As soon as I managed to synchronise my steps with his, I began to lose the rhythm. If I tried very hard, I could hold it for ten, fifteen steps, after that it was broken and I had to start from scratch.

The old man eventually became aware of strange shuffling behind his back. He turned and looked at my feet. "Something wrong with your shoes?"

Embarrassed, I shook my head.

"Come." He grinned and stepped aside. "You go first."

I moved on and soon the sound of his steps behind me got lost in the sound of mine; we walked like a four-legged animal. Our walk became like a song that soon drew into its rhythm our breathing as well. It wasn't long before the entire world was vibrating in our easy rhythm.

The voice of old Yogananda came to me as if from a distance. "Everything is moving in the rhythm of your steps. Isn't it great to live in a world that is infinitely compliant?"

I began to dance. A strange force got hold of my feet and started to twist them this way and that. Behind me my dangerous friend also began to dance, jumping in unison with me and laughing as loudly as

I was, and our laughter was resonating across the plane from which the sun was just taking its leave. The sky, too, was laughing with us, and the slopes, and the snowy peaks of the mountains.

"There you are," said Yogananda.

The path began to wind its way up a slope which was so steep that every ten minutes we had to stop to get back our breath. The valley below us was opening up and simultaneously disappearing in the growing darkness. Night wasn't far away. Eventually we reached an isolated house set in an oasis of terraced fields. The house was square, flat-roofed and rather dilapidated, with shutters closed, half-dug, so it seemed, into the slope. Cool air was descending from the glacier high above it.

We climbed along a steep winding path onto a rocky ledge above the house. From there we lowered ourselves down a rickety wooden ladder onto the earthen roof of the house. Yogananda asked me to unload my backpack and tent, sit down, and wait. In the middle of the flat roof there was a square hole, from which another ladder led down into the interior of the house. Yogananda carefully stepped on the first rung, then on the next one, and the next one, until he disappeared.

This was the first house I had ever seen that had an entrance on the roof. Bundles of firewood were stashed in the corner. I was overcome by the feeling that I was standing on the viewing terrace of the world. Undulating before me was the western Himalayan range. Clusters of mountain villages were scattered on the plain below. Two streams separated the sloping fields that surrounded the house.

Yogananda's head emerged from the square hole and he invited me into the house. It took me some time before I managed to get my backpack and tent through the hole and down the rickety ladder. I found myself in a dark room without any windows. Sitting among cooking pots in front of a blackened fireplace were two toothless old ladies. Standing next to the ladder was a short-cropped middle-aged man who turned to me and said, "Nawang."

Yogananda explained that that was his name, that the two ladies were his aunts, and that he was making ends meet by making wooden tubs for barley beer and trading Himalayan ponies. And by what grew in the fields round the house, which wasn't much. He emphasised that his family was poor, very poor, but in spite of that we could stay with them for as long as we wanted.

He added that he himself had rejected the possession of money a long time ago, but if I wanted to contribute a small part of the European riches I had brought with me, I should do so right at the beginning. In this way the money will be a welcoming present, on leaving it would look like payment for services rendered. Payment would be firmly if politely declined, but to decline a present would not be polite. What Nawang needs most of all is money. Cash. If I gave him three hundred rupees he would dream sweet dreams for the next seven nights and his two aunts would cook us their unappetising barley stew with the enthusiasm well beyond their culinary capacity.

Without the slightest hesitation I rummaged inside my pocket and pulled out three hundred rupees. Having had few opportunities to spend money, the sum seemed less a reward than an offence to our hosts, so I added another hundred. I pressed the banknotes into Nawang's reluctant hand. His two aunts opened toothless mouths and offered me grateful smiles.

Yogananda stood up. Nawang led us to a little room that smelled of stuffy wet soil. He opened the window and pushed out the wooden shutters. A view of the valley and the snow-capped mountains opened up before me.

"This is where we're going to sleep," Yogananda said.

Nawang brought two mattresses and threw them on the floor. A cool wind blew in through the window. It will be cold at night, I thought. But then Nawang opened a trapdoor in the corner of the room, allowing warm air to waft up from the space below. The room had the Himalayan "central heating": there were stables under it.

We remained alone.

"How do you like your four-star accommodation?" Yogananda grinned.

After lunch Nawang brought a tub of homemade barley beer. We sipped it from wooden mugs, even the two old ladies, with one of them reaching out to touch my winter jacket. Nawang was talking, God knows what about; Yogananda listened and nodded, but it didn't occur to him to translate.

I rose and said I would go up to the roof; I needed space and a view of the mountains.

The sun wrapped me in its embrace like a warm blanket. The mountain peaks were sparkling white. My heart was filled with a mixture of contradictory feelings. I wished I could stay on that roof until the end of my days, with my eyes caressing the panorama of the towering mountain range until I was absorbed by it, becoming a mountain, snow, rock, a part of the Himalayas. Only that. Nothing else. Nothing more.

Had I grown tired of being a man?

A little later I was joined by Yogananda. Sitting on the roof, we stared at the sunlit plain below us. A sort of telepathic energy vibrated between us.

"Now you see," he said. "Now you're aware of the dangers."

Yes, I said. The search for oneself, for one's true "I", for an answer to the question of what it is all about can become a habit. It can become an obsession. It can become a routine. The one who is doing the searching can become a robot. He can become an actor, replaying his part, the one and only part, on different stages. He can become his worst imitator. It is good to search, but it is even better to find. It is good to find at least a small part of what *can* be found. Although I have found much many times, I have never found anything permanent. I have written books about my spiritual adventures, and I have stated categorically that I had found "it" and that the search is over.

So how is it possible that I have ended up here, on the roof of a house above the central plain of the kingdom of Zanskar, the land of white copper? I, a restless young man who cannot find refuge in political dogma, who cannot embrace intellectual opportunism, who cannot escape into the comforting illusion of consumerism? And who is afraid, in fact terrified, of hovering in a permanent state of homelessness. What am I dong here?

It seems to me that I'm looking for insight. For a conclusive answer to the question: What is the purpose of my being here, in this world, at this very moment? So I can fulfil that purpose. And if there is no purpose – well, let's wait and see.

However, what I'm most afraid of, I said, is my urge to *justify* this search of mine, even to myself. As if I was doing something reprehensible. As if my search was something unworthy of a grown man. As if my restless mind was a symptom of immaturity or mental disease. A great deal of what I have written is, apart from anything else, a veiled apology for my goals and aims. Why?

"Because you're an idiot," Yogananda cut short my eager confession. "Because you're clever you think you can't be an idiot. Stupidity is just simple stupidity, but cleverness that believes the limits of its reach are the limits of the world as it really is, and the limits of life as it really is, that sort of cleverness is a farce. There is no humility in your cleverness. You're trying to escape the prison of your mind, and you fall in love with the act of escaping, with the role of a seeker of liberation, with your intellectual daring. Here we are, gazing at the beauty of nature, the only thing that can ever be truly yours, and what do you do? You babble. What you don't understand is the fact that there is no difference between the Buddha and an ordinary mortal, between an awakened man and an ignorant one. The only difference is that the Buddha is aware of that, while the ignorant man is not. You're an idiot not in spite of but because of your cleverness."

Well, I said almost aggressively, how can I stop being an idiot?

"By being mindful," my dangerous friend replied. "That is the wisdom you seek. Be mindful of the swirling of your thoughts, so mindful that not one of them will escape you. Then become a traffic regulator. Guide the traffic of your thoughts to the left, to the right. Raise a stop sign, bring it to a standstill. Then the disorder in your mind will cease. It will be followed by peace. And in that peace: a door into the universe."

He said that I could begin right there, on the roof. For a start, I should become aware of the sounds, of even the tiniest sound that reached my ears. I should hold on to these sounds, isolate them, examine them, and try to determine their origin. When they turn into images of their origin, I should fix the images in my mind. Of course they will try to elude me. But I should hold on to them until they become as sharp as if I were really seeing them. When I achieve that, my thought disorder will stop.

And then: silence!

I closed my eyes. I heard Yogananda's steps softly withdrawing. Silence came floating towards me. This wasn't the silence of my eternally turbulent mind; it was the silence in my ears, which at first registered no sound at all. Then they started to come: the sounds I had heard before but paid no attention to them. The soft rustling of the wind in the trees. The murmur of the stream. My breathing. Muttering voices in the rooms below. The bleating of a goat.

In the darkness behind my closed eyes I began to notice vague shapes of the origins of the sounds. But no matter how hard I tried, I could not sharpen them; they remained misty, flighty moments from memory rather than visual images of the tree, the stream, the goat. I began to concentrate on my breathing. I followed my breath on the way in; I followed it on the way out.

Suddenly something moved inside me, something split apart, I could almost hear the tearing noise. Never before had I heard anything like it. I felt that I was leaving my body. I was able to see myself from a distance. I saw a youngish man sitting cross-legged on the flat roof of a mountain house on the northern side of the Himalayas. His feet were stuck in a pair of muddy, heavily-worn mountain boots with flexible rubber soles. He was dressed in loose woollen trousers and a brown woollen pullover. His face was gaunt and smudged with patches of sunburn. His sloping shoulders looked tired, as if he weren't quite up to the task of carrying a heavy backpack up and down the steep slopes.

The sounds entering my ears were also different; as soon as I heard them I could see them so clearly that I could touch them. When the goat bleated I could see the curved shape of its back and the rather stupid gaze of its eyes; I could see how it bent down and nibbled at a tuft of grass. When a dog barked further down the slope, I could see the whitish breath escaping its open mouth, and I saw how it pricked its ears, waved its tail, sniffed at the ground and twisted its body into a comfortable resting position.

Increasingly penetrating the ordinary sounds was a rhythmic tinkling of a tiny bell, accompanied by a barely audible wooden moaning. Both sounds were enveloped in a deep rush of water. The wooden moaning reminded me of the turning of a waterwheel that keeps getting slightly stuck in its bearing.

I realised that these sounds were produced by Nawang's *mani-chokor*, the prayer wheel that was being turned by the force of the rushing water in the nearby stream. All other sounds withdrew. I could still hear them, but they remained in the background. My attention was concentrated on the turning of the water-driven prayer wheel that, with each turn, made a tiny copper bell produce a tinkling sound. And in the darkness behind my eyes I saw the wheel clearly. I saw how water poured on its cross-sections and made it turn with measured thrusts. There were traces of greenish mould on the wood. In the middle of the wheel there was a little drum that contained Nawang's mantra, the prayer, which was repeated with each turn of the wheel.

By repeating his mantra, the Buddhist cleanses his soul, renews the vows to live rightly, disavows selfish and violent behaviour. Every time the wheel turns and the bell tinkles, all those that hear it in their minds repeat *Om Mani Padme Hum*, knowing that *padma* means lotus, which is their heart, and *mani* means jewel, which is the Buddha that lives in their heart.

Rotation is the basic law of the psychophysical world. *Manichokor*, the Tibetan prayer wheel, is the symbol of this law. And the symbol that keeps turning and, with the tinkling of the little bell, draws attention to itself is a hypnotic way of drawing our attention to the rotation of all the bodies and galaxies in the universe. And so to the rotation of our spiritual axle, the eternal faith in love and goodwill.

Suddenly I rose in the air and floated across the plain. I began to echo among the mountains. I felt that this was the sound of the universe. The whole world was vibrating inside me. I had caught the rhythm of cosmic energy and became one with it.

I rose even higher. Lying below me, interspersed with white clouds, was the beauty of the countryside. The clouds were swirling, joining, parting, rushing past each other, getting bloated, deflating, widening, diffusing and offering to my view in turn a glacier, dark canyon, a valley of fields, a splashing waterfall, a lake. The colours of everything were sharper, clearer than ever. The sky above me was solid blue. It gave no impression of being hollow; it was almost tangible, a velvety blue curtain above the scenery of fiery red and yellow cliffs.

I began to experience new time. Not the time of minutes, hours and seconds, but the rhythm of the sun, moon and stars. I could feel how heavenly bodies regulate the pulse of life on Earth. Through the clouds, past snowy peaks, across glacial lakes and shadowy canyons I was floating towards the flat roof on which sat a bearded youngish man and, with his eyes closed, stared into the vastness of the world inside him.

The spirit was returning into the body. But before it slipped back inside, it noticed Yogananda, who was sitting behind the bearded man, intensely staring at the back of his head. An unforgettable moment: my body on the roof, my spirit above the mountains, Yogananda behind me, his eyes on me. It was just a split second; then the spirit and the body were reunited.

I opened my eyes and turned. I wasn't dreaming, Yogananda really was sitting behind me! He gave me a curious smile. He looked strangely tired, almost exhausted. I realised that the wonderful vision from which I had returned wasn't a hallucination; it was a trick of magic, his magic. Sitting behind me, he must have telepathically guided my thoughts and feelings through an experience that was real only insofar that he had created it.

I was almost paralysed by fear and respect. I rose, made a few steps towards him, fell on my knees and pressed my forehead to the floor before him.

"What happened?" I asked.

"Nothing special," he said. "I wanted to show you that you possess unusual powers which you can use. For any good purpose you can use them until you die. For any bad purpose you can use them only once, because when you do you will destroy them. I also wanted to show you that I'm not what you think I am. You're thirsty and you think that I'm water that can quench your thirst. I'm not water, I'm merely a pitcher. The pitcher isn't empty, there is water inside it, and this water is the Buddha. I wanted to show you that only the Buddha can quench your thirst, and I'm the pitcher from which you can drink.

It's up to you how you will drink, and how much. Just be careful you don't spill the water."

An evening breeze was beginning to blow across the plain, bringing with it the sounds of rivers and cascading streams. In the evening chill I began to shiver. I wanted to climb down the ladder to get close the fireplace, but as soon as I got to my feet, the old man pulled me back down.

"Stay," he said.

I explained that I would like to put on some warmer clothes. Once again he pulled me back down. "If you're cold that's just an idea; push it out of your mind and you'll be warm."

I said that cold was certainly not an idea, it was a real feeling experienced by my body.

"Can you see the jewel glistening above those mountains?" he asked.

"That's a star," I said, "not a jewel."

"How do you know?"

By association, I said. My memory tells me that little dots glistening in the sky are stars, or in a few cases planets. They are certainly not jewels; only a child would believe that.

"What is the mental event that enables you to know things by association? To put them in files, like letters and documents?"

I thought: without this ability I would experience the world as chaos. If I couldn't draw borders and separate things I couldn't live. The true organiser of the world I experience is my conceptualising ability. This ability is quite simply wonderful – until it turns into a robot. And this happens sooner rather than later. Instead of experiencing the world directly and freshly, I break it up into little pieces, which I stash away in labelled drawers. It is I, my true "I", who experiences first love. The second love is experienced by the one who has already experienced (and filed away in a drawer) the first one. A robot. A concept of love. This ability makes it possible for me to have a life. But if I don't keep it under control my life will be stale, a series of rehashed stories.

"Well done," Yogananda said. "Let's go to sleep."

8.

The first jolts of an earthquake

Once inside the sleeping bag, I soon began to feel warm. The smell of fresh dung wafting up through the trapdoor made me sleepy. Suddenly, Yogananda said, "We're going to listen to silence and observe darkness."

And so I listened, peering into the blackness around me.

"What do you hear, what do you see?"

I said that silence wasn't complete, for I could hear the murmur of the stream, the moaning sound of the prayer wheel, and the movements of animals in the stable below. Darkness, too, wasn't impenetrable: A moon ray was shining through a gap in the shutters and in its light I could see a small part of the wall and the shape of the gap through which it was shining. I was not listening to silence, but to barely audible sounds within it; I was not observing darkness, but a sliver of light within it.

"Right," he said. "Now push the sounds out. Be mindful only of what the sounds disturb."

I couldn't. If, for a brief moment, I did succeed in pushing the sounds away, I was instantly overcome by the memory of them, or I intensely awaited their return. This neurotic struggle lasted a good ten minutes. Then I gave up. I said that my awareness was like a helpless deer attacked by sound beasts, which tore at it and dragged it in all directions.

"Because you're not truly mindful," he said. "Because all you're capable of are negative mental states."

Anger, pride, vanity, sloth, fear, envy, lust, worry, doubts, self-pity, resentment, boredom, moodiness, despair, nervousness, sentimentality, pessimism, distrust, depression, cynicism: Are any of these unknown to me?

I asked him if these mental states were not, after all, constituent parts of a normal human personality. Surely there are moments in every man's life when depression is natural; one cannot live in a permanent state of bliss.

"Why not? If you know the true nature of bliss, you can. You think bliss is the euphoric feeling that overcomes you when you win the lottery or receive an award for your work. Which part of you delights in that? Your ego. Bliss is like a jewel in mud. It's inside you, but you're unable to feel it. It dwells in positive feelings. Do you know any?"

"How could I not?" I replied. "Love. Compassion. Joy. And perhaps the feeling of peace and quiet, when everything is all right and in its place, and there is no fear and no expectation."

"Well," he said, "if that is bliss, why is it so difficult to achieve?"

Because it's not possible to hold on to such feelings, I said. Because they are always replaced by negative ones.

"They're poisoned by the ego," he said. "When a feeling slips to the level of ego consciousness, it becomes a lie, its own caricature. Love turns into jealousy, lust, possessiveness. Compassion becomes sentimentality, inner peace becomes apathy. And joy becomes blind enthusiasm, self-satisfied ecstasy. This process of slipping from higher to lower states runs continuously."

"How can I prevent that?"

By observing my thoughts, he said. I must observe how they are formed, how they connect into chains, how they emerge from the depths of memory and rise to the surface. I must observe the birth of my fears and desires, I must follow them. I must accompany all phases of all my feelings and thoughts. Sooner or later I will notice that they are dispersing. Increasingly, there will be fewer of them and finally there will be none. When I see that all my problems are localised, I will be able to sort them like letters and put each into an appropriate file. They will stop piling up and threatening to suffocate me. I will open up to everything that *isn't* a problem. And then all my negativism will vanish; instead of mud I will have clear water inside my head.

"You will discover," he said, "that the pause between the moment you become aware of something and the moment you react to it is so brief that only a peaceful mind can register it. That pause is your opportunity. During that pause, however brief, you'll be able to bypass your habits and react in a completely fresh way. Then you will stop saddling your essence with unimportant things and leave them to resolve by themselves. Your mind will once again be young and innocent. It will be unspoiled. And the unspoiled mind registers only what is. What is real, what's happening. And what's happening is the beauty of truth.

"I will grant you a secret word. It has no meaning. It's a pure sound, two syllables. Close your eyes and place the word in the middle of your head. Imagine it as a strip inside your brain, a sticky patch meant to attract and catch flies. Allow your thoughts to buzz around it and get stuck to it. Let every thought that arises gravitate towards it. Try to keep this word in your head both as a sound and a sticky patch. Do that whenever you feel like it, but at least twice a day for ten minutes. Sooner or later you will reach a moment when all your thoughts will be stuck. Then simply extinguish the patch. Like a candle."

He gave me the secret word and I began to catch "flies".

The next morning he taught me six yoga exercises. The first was *savasana*, or death pose. I had to lie on my back, breathing naturally and rhythmically. I tried to imagine my body five times heavier and sinking into the ground. Then, deliberately, I began to relax my muscles. First the head. Then the neck, shoulders, chest. Then arms, hands, fingers and so on until I reached my toes. I tried to imagine I was a piece of cast-out rope, a dry twig, a pile of earth. I stared at the clouds in the sky. I closed my eyes and stared at the clouds in my memory. Going from head to foot and back again, I tried to unravel individual knots of tension.

To my astonishment, I discovered that tension in my body was a permanent state. I could feel how individual muscles were contracting quite automatically. I discovered that I live in a permanent state of readiness: to be hit, to strike back, to flee. I live in a continuous state of defensive attention. Deep inside me I discovered the fear that if I stopped being on guard, the entire structure of my life would collapse.

The aim of the second pose was not relaxation but concentration. That was *padmasana*, also known as the Buddha or lotus pose. The Buddha is usually depicted as sitting on his behind, with legs crossed in front of him, with his hands on his knees, palms facing upwards. Despite its apparent simplicity, *padmasana* is really the most difficult of all yoga poses. But Yogananda assured me it was also the most rewarding.

Sadly, after the first few attempts I concluded that it would bring no rewards to me. My knees were not flexible enough. Nor were the ankles. Not to mention the hips.

Yogananda sat down on the ground and crossed his legs. He gripped his right ankle with both hands and lifted the toes of his right foot on to the thigh of his left leg, with the sole turned upwards and the heel close to the vertical centre of the body and with the big toe's protuberance horizontally in line with the top of the thigh. Then he gripped his left foot and, in a similar way, lifted it onto his right thigh. He placed his wrists on his knees, opened his hands and turned the palms upward, then he formed a circle by joining the tips of his thumb and the middle finger.

His knees were touching the ground. But mine remained stubbornly five inches above it. Regardless of all my efforts I could not get them down, except by pressing on them with my hands, but as soon as the pressure ceased the knees jerked up again.

"Keep pressing them down," Yogananda said. "Play ball with them. That way you'll loosen the joints and stretch the ligaments. Give yourself five or six months. Only when you master this pose, can you devote yourself to concentration. Not a minute before."

The third pose is called *ustrasana*, or camel pose. In vain I tried to execute it correctly. I managed to achieve something that resembled the correct pose, but the old man warned me that this was not only useless; it could be dangerous. Only the correct pose brings rewards that are its aim. I tried again. I pressed my legs together, kneeled, and placed my buttocks on my soles. I leaned back, placing my hands next to the soles. I extended my neck as far as it would go and pushed my head back until the nape of my neck started to hurt. Slowly and deeply I breathed in. Simultaneously, I lifted my posterior off my soles and arched my back. Then I froze and stopped breathing. After a while I returned to the starting pose, leaned forward and breathed out.

The fourth pose was *bhujangasana*, or cobra pose. I lay down on my belly, my forehead pressed against the ground. I bent my elbows and placed my hands under my shoulder. I stretched out my legs. Then, very slowly, I started to rise. Leaning on my hands I lifted my head and torso, at the same time arching my back until my lumbar region reached the point of breaking.

Yoganada said that I presented a miserable version of cobra. From the navel down I should be pressed flat to the ground, from the navel up I should be almost vertical. He showed me. He achieved the right pose in an instant. His astonishing flexibility filled me with a mixture of envy and despair.

Finally he showed me the "royal asana", the headstand. When he realised that I was afraid of injuring the vertebrae in my neck, he explained how I could achieve my aim step by step. I felt incredible pain in my heart when I remembered how many times I stood on my head as a child. Yogananda wasn't young, he was twice my age, around seventy, but judging by our physical and mental conditions, I was the old man, and he was the youngster. How was that possible?

"There you are," he said, looking at me with his moist, sparkling eyes. "You have to learn how to stand on your head. That is the shortest path to what you think you no longer have. The youth. It floods your brain with blood and cleans it. It improves your sight and hearing, it sharpens your senses, it balances your nervous system. It frees your heart of the usual burdens and lengthens your life. Even more! It frees you from the feeling that you are stuck to the ground with your feet. When this feeling is gone, you'll be able to float in the air."

Not only did I not float, I felt that I was rapidly sinking. Chasms of forgotten problems and suppressed pains kept opening up inside me. Night after night, my dreams became increasingly frightening. It seemed to me I was descending into some kind of madness. I believed

I was horrified by the collapse of the familiar forms of the world. But when a strange light began to shine through the gaps in the defence walls, the sort of light I had not seen before, I realised I was afraid of emptiness awaiting me out there in Freedom: the emptiness of Nothing, the loneliness of Vacuity.

"I'm losing myself," I said when the horror became unbearable. "I feel as if I were dying."

"Carry on, carry on," he encouraged me, his face shining with satisfaction. "Kill yourself. Extinguish yourself. I'm waiting for you in the present moment. Join me."

When he saw that I was paralysed by fear he began to comfort me. When I get rid of everything, I'll still have what I'm losing, he said. I will still retain memory. The only difference will be that I won't be a slave of memory. Memory is a repository of facts, and that is all right. What isn't right is that my mind experiences these facts as a burdensome weight which determines my reactions to life's impulses.

The most dangerous "facts" embedded in my memory are emotional states in which I mistakenly see my life. If I don't splash around in this or that emotional tub, I feel as if I weren't alive. Often I cling even to suffering and disappointment – only because I want my life to have a "meaning", a recognisable form. Only because I'm horrified of emptiness.

I said I wasn't afraid only of losing my memory and facing the great hollowness, I was also afraid of losing my future, my conviction that tomorrow won't be empty but full of rich possibilities,

"You speak of possibilities as if they were real," Yogananda said. "They are no more than projections. They are merely forms of memory. You live by throwing hooks into emptiness that you call future, and by climbing the hooked rope to what you call tomorrow. The hooks are no more than projections of your desires."

"So what remains, then?" I asked him. "There are things and people, and also desires and goals that I can't and don't want to renounce."

"Renunciation doesn't mean giving things up; it is the awareness that you can't keep them."

When I become mindful in the right way, he said, I will realize that things aren't important. In reality I am not dependent on health, on income, on books, reputation, love, knowledge, acknowledgments and all that, but on the idea that life without them wouldn't be worthwhile. I am dependent on my convictions. The world as I perceive it is a slave of my thoughts. When I become mindful, this slavery will end and mindfulness will give birth to spontaneity.

That doesn't mean that the fruit of my attention will be bliss, or that I will never again be angry, disappointed, cold, and rejected. Of course I will be. What will differ will be my experience of those feelings. They will no longer claw at me. I will still be angry, but anger won't chain itself to me like a dog. Disappointment will no longer lock me into its dungeon. Things will move into a distance, they will cease to be in my way.

"And then?" I asked him.

"Then you will stop being afraid that you'll loose your livelihood. Or that people will think badly of you. You won't be afraid of death any more and of what may be awaiting you after death. You will lose you fear of everything that may still lie in wait for you in your life. Can you imagine what your life will be like when all those fears let you off the hook? You will become an eagle!"

And what will happen when I abandon this Himalayan solitude and return to my people? Into the heart of the society that renews itself by emphasising the very things I should get rid of while I'm here? My society tells me the meaning of life is not in renouncing but in obtaining as many things as I possibly can. Obtain, own, keep, get attached – these are the unspoken orders of the society to which I will have to return.

"Every society fills you with illusions and then confirms and strengthens them. That is the reason you have to withdraw to a lonesome place where nobody watches you. Only in such a place can you divest yourself of your clothing. In front of whom would you want to defend your illusions about yourself? Himalayan peasants? Monks, yaks, goats? In front of me? I know what you are. Here you can undress to the naked core. And when you return to your people you will remain aware of this core."

He repeated that the psychophysical exercises he prescribed me have only one purpose: to loosen me up and unravel me. But the process is paradoxical; it also contains withdrawals and regressions. Before I move on I may have to take a step or two back. Quite often a step back is already a step forward. A step back is often a return to childhood. But many times it is a steep fall into the horror of darkness, depression, mental illness. And yet mental illness is often a manifestation of the inner reorganisation that is a precondition of mental health. Among the things awaiting me on the path, few can be anticipated. If I am afraid, I can still change my mind.

And what is he going to say if I do?

He looked at me. "I know you'll change your mind only when it's too late."

9.

Unravelling the cobweb

The more I lost the ground under my feet, the more I realised I was a spider which had, in the manner of making a web, spun itself. I needed assurance that the ground under me was endless and that I couldn't stumble over a precipice. Every time I felt that I was beginning to slip, I widened the ground, added an extension, and then an extension to the existing extension, and so on in a vicious circle forever.

Yogananda told me my self-deception began with the ignorance of what is. Nothing is. Or, in other words, Nothing is all there is. Because I didn't know that (or if I did, simply couldn't believe it), I attempted to fill the vacuum with form. Because of my ignorance of the nature of the world I began to shape concepts and create structures. However, because Nothing (absence of me as a fixed entity) is empty space, I could only create forms by freezing my experiences of space. Terrified of Nothing, I kept creating threads to which I could cling; lighthouses that would guide my ships. These projections gave me the feeling that I existed, and the feeling kept confirming itself by creating new projections.

Emerging from this process was my "I", my ego, the absolute ruler of the land that was my experience. This ruler employed three strategic moves: disinterest, greediness and aggressiveness. He established a secret information service that kept him informed of what was happening. He had a complete overview of events and my mental states. The strategy of disinterest, indifference, was passive: it was manifested in my ability to close my eyes before unpleasant facts, before anything that could hurt me, awake me, or slip me up. That was the strategy of false power, of false manliness, of disingenuous power over circumstances.

Greediness was born of my fear of poverty, of lacking things that would give me the feeling I was alive, independent, and successful. It was manifested in a blind assimilation and accumulation of experiences, facts, events and "understandings"; in a burning desire for everything. In times of plenty I was desperate to create reserves for leaner times. Afraid of depersonalization, I accumulated huge mounds of material and spiritual (especially spiritual) food, an illusory basis of my certainty. But these reserves never seemed sufficient. I wanted more. I wanted absolute certainty that I will never be naked and hungry; that I will "understand" and "experience" the world optimally.

The strategy which the ego, my ruler, used to defend its territory was instinctive. But it was so widespread and so complicated that my ego needed headquarters for my defensive forces. It needed an ability to distinguish among things by name. What came into being was intellect. Which became some sort of secret service of cruel fanatics, devoted to the ego/ruler beyond the call of duty, a sort of state within a state, inquisition and spiritual elite at the same time. Its mental battalions were always in a state of readiness; all conspiracies were nipped in the bud.

In spite of this, the kingdom of the ego was not an orderly realm. The defensive system was chaotic, contradictory and wasteful. The ego kept abusing its defensive elites, it forced them to work till exhaustion, to rush this way and that, spy on each other, repeat the tasks already accomplished, report on each other. The territory of my "I" resembled a chaotic battlefield without generals that could influence the events: tremendous noise and disorder, and rushing from one end to the other: from financial problems to sexual fantasies, to God, to the respect of friends, to getting old; everywhere there was a threat of danger.

What danger? That a gap would appear in the constructed kingdom of reality, and through that gap I would be faced with illusory nature of everything that my ego tells me I am? With the truth of emptiness? With the realization that I am Nothing?

Yogananda continued to ask what was happening inside me, what I thought and felt was happening. I realised I couldn't report real events to him, only my feelings, my ideas of those events. Only the Informbiro of my intellect could report to him the state of affairs on my spiritual battlefield. These were not reports of independent witnesses; somewhere along the way they were hijacked by the intellectual censor who adapted them to his own judgement.

"I cannot express the truth," I admitted. "My intellect is an absolute owner of my expressive abilities. Whatever I have to say has to go through its channels, be poured into its mould, come across in its words. I cannot, I simply cannot convey the truth about what is happening inside me."

"Leave the words," he said. "Show it."

I tried to demonstrate the dilemma with a childish joke. "It's as if I had collected all the potholes on the road and loaded them onto a truck. All except one. Every time I drive back to collect it, I fall into it!

He said I was trying to pull myself up by the strings of my shoes. My meditation is self-absorption. I meditate to reconfirm myself, my existence, my ego; everything I want to escape. My attitude to the process launched by my mental exercises is "all or nothing". I am filled with a violent hope that I will succeed, and to this hope I cling like a tick. I am suffused with the fear that I will fail, and this fear clings to me like a tick.

It may happen that in this way I will gain unusual, "higher", more spiritual states of mind. It may happen that I will achieve even a sort of bliss, which my ego (the usurper of my longing for it) will declare to be "nirvana". I will end up with a magnificent shop of plastic flowers. Everybody will notice they are not real. Everybody but me. My ego will not admit that all my efforts have created nothing more than a fake. My way of meditating is merely a process of manufacturing new chains. The chains with which my ego will bind me to itself.

"Then I don't know," I said in despair. "I simply don't know. If all my efforts are a waste of time I should perhaps give up."

"Look at this statement of yours," he said, pouncing on me. "If you are a spider unravelling its web as well as itself, do not at the same time be a spider that is already weaving a new web in which to get stuck. Allow the threads from which you are made to unravel by themselves. Don't spur yourself on all the time like a schoolboy during an exam: it'll work, if only I try hard enough. And stop moaning all the time: oh my God, what now, what now? Be mindful of the process of the dissolution of illusory reality. But also be mindful of the attempts of your ego to subjugate the process to its own aims."

I continued with my exercises. Now I was doubly mindful: not only of my feelings, thoughts and sensations, but also of the manner of my mindfulness.

It wasn't long before I began to realise how appropriate the old man's warnings were. I could see what my ego was doing: it was rushing around, beating its chest and proclaiming: "The old order is collapsing, new times are coming, and all thanks to me!" I could see how my ego was deviously taking charge of the revolution that was meant to depose it, and how it started to present itself as the only one able to insure that it would succeed. I could see its sentries manning all corners, its barricades on all the main streets, spies everywhere. I could see how furiously it was seeking allies, how desperate it was for new ideas, possibilities; how it resurrected rejected thoughts and combined them into new patterns, forever making new plans. I could see it was afraid. And I could see it was fighting for its life in a thousand devious ways.

I realised that my situation was quite untenable. If my ego is really the owner of my thoughts and feelings, the architect of my plans and the leader of my conspiracies, then everything that happens inside me (also the unravelling of the spider's web) is no more than one of the ways of its defence. Every attack on my ego immediately turns into a form of its defence. That means that I am doing things that, by doing them, I would like to give up. That means that what I'm doing is stupid.

Here I sit, performing psychophysical exercises, while the ego is all the time poking fun at me! Am I an idiot?

Yogananda gave me a good-natured smile. "Well said. You twist your limbs, gaze into your inner depths, execute breathing exercises, and repeat strange mantras. Only a fool would do things like that. It should be obvious to everybody that you're a fool. But so far your ego has not allowed you to realise that. But now you've marked your first victory. Modestly and with humility you have agreed that you are a fool. The path ahead is now clear. Now you will cease to ascribe mystical elements to your exercises. Now you will know they're merely a crutch required by an invalid in the first stages of his cure. As soon as he can walk he throws the crutch away. You have realised that your ego steals not only your actions but also your ideas about the meaning of those actions. Renounce these ideas. Then your ego will have nothing to grasp at. Be simple and don't try to become better, more clever, more moral. Accept your shortcomings; they are your starting point. As long as you try to transcend them, they will remain obstacles on your path. When you accept them, they become integral to your path."

As soon as the valley below is flooded with sunlight, I walk to the stream rushing past the house. I take off my clothes, then I soap my body from head to toe, and step into the water. I kneel. The water is freezing cold; I let out an ear-piercing cry. I repeat the process. I hiss, and gasp, and yell. When I gather enough courage I spread my arms and throw myself face first into the water. The speeding stream splashes over my body. You'll catch a cold, reason keeps warning me; you'll catch pneumonia, you'll die!

Shut up, I firmly resist what reason is telling me, deliberately surrendering to the icy water. On the point of fainting I scramble out of the stream, grab the towel and rub my body all over as hard as I can. My yelling and shouting has gained the attention of one of Nawang's aunts. She is standing on the roof and looking at me as if I weren't normal.

Cover your private parts with the towel, reason whispers to me. Smile and tell the old lady, "Good morning, have you slept well?" Show her you are polite, well-brought up, that you respect old people and are grateful for their hospitality.

Go fuck yourself, I tell my reason. "What are you staring at, you hag?" I shout at the shrivelled woman on the roof, in Slovene, since I don't know a word of Tibetan. I remove the towel and swing my pendulous member from left to right. The old lady, startled, moves out of sight.

Many people, while standing on the edge of a precipice, have experienced a sudden urge to throw themselves off the ledge. Not so much out of curiosity about death but because of an impulse to do something they didn't expect from themselves. To cheat reason and, with a sudden move, escape its grip. My behaviour springs from a similar source. I don't want to shock other people, I want to shock myself. I want to derail myself.

I return to the house and demand breakfast. Nawang's aunt turns away and ignores me. Yogananda is sitting in front of the fireplace, noisily eating his portion of tsampa. He, too, ignores me. Nawang rises and without a word leaves the room for his workshop. There is no sign of his other aunt; she must have gone to the village.

From the disorder behind the door I fish out a wooden bowl and ladle out some barley porridge from the cooking pot. I sit down in front of Yogananda and start eating like a pig, challenging him with a defiant stare.

"What's the matter, old man?" I ask him in Slovene. "How am I getting on? In any case, I don't give a shit what you think. I don't depend on you. Do you think I respect you? Actually, I see you as a big joke. Why are you suddenly pretending you're deaf? I don't need you any more! Can you hear me, you asshole? I'm renouncing gratitude, respect and other projections of an imprisoned mind. You're in for a surprise if you think I'm ready to fulfil your expectations. Or mine. I am free; the word responsibility has vanished from my vocabulary."

With a sudden gesture I toss the contents of the bowl on his head. Tsampa is trickling down his forehead and into his eyes and down his hair behind his collar. Without a word, he gets to his feet, walks to the hearth and picks up a dirty dishcloth. He uses it to wipe his face and his hair and his neck. Then he quietly walks into the front room.

As for me, I rush down the slope towards the village. Among the houses I encounter dogs and kids. I knock at the nearest door. As it opens, revealing a brown Tibetan face, I turn around and push out a loud fart.

I walk to the next house. By now I am being followed by a group of unwashed kids who find my behaviour amusing. I knock at the door. A red-faced young man appears on the doorstep. I offer him my hand. "Good morning, Herr Professor, my answer to your question about the meaning of life is brrrrrrt-ziiink-tlezzzubl-dstrekfitzbun-lep-trebdbrdvuntr-batrndrdr-aprevijotrgatrpintr-suckatrlarbenttr-pa-ra-tutrrdtretcetera."

Then I stick out my tongue at him.

The villagers are now watching from all the windows and doorways. I walk into the middle of the little square and bow all around. I lower my trousers and exhibit my behind to everyone within sight. The children scream with amusement, a few dogs suddenly bark, a few people respond with tittering laughter.

I tighten my trouser belt and, with my head held as high as I can, I march out of the village and back up the slope. The children run after me, some of them playfully displaying their butts. For them it's a game, they have found a clown and don't want to lose him.

I pause and start throwing stones at them.

Surprised and a little frightened they rush back to the village.

I continue to climb back towards Nawang's house. I turn around and climb backwards, with my eyes on the valley below, softly green and opaque brown in between. I stumble and fall. I remain on the ground.

I close my eyes.

In my thoughts I ride the clouds across the sky. I fly across the valley of Karsha and watch the monks at their morning ritual. I sail around mountain tops, watch the thrusting peaks, jagged backs, snowdrifts, perpendicular cliffs swept clean by the wind. I alight on the edge of a cliff and peek into the abyss below me. Headlong I throw myself into it. I am falling. I hear how my body whistles through the air. The bottom is fast approaching. We collide, and I am thrown back like a ball, I keep rebounding until I am back on the edge of the cliff, from where I fly back to the sky.

Suddenly I hear laughter. I open my eyes. Two red-cheeked girls are panting up the steep path, no older than sixteen, seventeen, each of them carrying a sack of flour on her head. Because of the weight they stare at the ground in front of their feet.

Say hello to them, reason tells me. Tell them how pretty they are, offer them help, the sacks are heavy and you are a man. Shut your gob, I reply to the dictates of reason. Keep quiet, you old squeaky barrel organ. Your eyes tell you that a woman is approaching and immediately you start issuing automatic orders: be friendly, be helpful, be a knight, be charming, say please, allow me, thank you. And then you expect me to perform the part like a well-oiled marionette.

What do you take me for? And what do you think *you* are?

I undo my trousers, pull them down to my knees, lean on my elbow and begin to masturbate. The girls are now very close. I keep growing, and growing, and growing, excited by the prospect of their confrontation with the sight that will surely take their breath away. The first one becomes aware of me and stops. Hoarsely, and noisily, she draws in her breath. The other one peeks from behind her back; when she sees me she utters a wild sound of disbelief. With their mouths hanging open, they stare at the aggressive tumescence in my hand as if they had just been electrocuted.

Looking them in the eyes, I continue with my thrusting movements. Then I start explaining, in Slovene, *why* I am doing this. "I'm trying to prove I can distance myself from what I normally think I am, and do everything I normally never do, and normally never would, but without losing the ability to remain what I am, what I am normally. I am creating a gap between my self-image and myself."

The first girl awakes from her trance and says something. The other one raps her forehead with the knuckles of her right hand to indicate that I must be mad. Balancing the sacks on their hands, they turn around and hurry back down the slope.

I get to my feet and follow them with my eyes until they disappear behind a mound of rocks. A strong wind is blowing across the valley. I can see heavy clouds in the north. Winter is on its way. I will be snowed in and cut off from the rest of the world for eight months. Wonderful!

I close my eyes and begin to catch flies. I place a magic two-syllable word into the heart of my brain. My mantra. A strip of sticky tape. My thoughts swarm around it and, one by one, get stuck to it. I keep the mantra in my head until it's covered with layers of my thoughts, all stuck and immobile. Then I extinguish it.

I stare into Emptiness.

I become aware of the mental state the Tibetans call *kunji*. That is the basis of my experiences; the screen on which I watch the projection of my ideas about the world and myself. *Kunji* is an echo of my essence, not always the same, sometimes deep and heavy, at other times light and translucent. This is not an emotional state; this is the ground in which feelings and thoughts, as soon as they appear, put down their roots. And this state is not hidden, I am aware of it all the time. But I'm not always aware that I'm aware of it.

When, after a while, I awake from this awareness of pre-awareness, I suddenly realise that I have again (yet again, yet again) constructed a trap which has pulled me into the illusion that I exist!

As I walk up the path back to Nawang's house, the excitement fades and with each step my legs become heavier. Close to the house, I am crawling up the path on all fours. My heart is throbbing inside my throat; soon, I feel, I will blow up and be scattered across the valley. Yogananda is waiting for me on the roof. When I reach him, he greets me with a devious smile as if he had known in what shape I would drag myself back to his feet.

"Help me." I clutch at his hand. "I'm sinking into some kind of psychosis. Please pull me out before it's too late!"

"Why should I care what happens to you," he says. "Sink into hell. If you want to go mad, your desire will be granted. After all, you are free, aren't you? That's what you're trying to prove to yourself. Whatever you do is a fruit of free choice. But in reality, friend: isn't this a denial of the possibility of free choice? A self-loving rebellious gesture? Everyone can be free like that. Even me. Don't you believe me?"

He grabs my shoulders with his hands and forcefully thrusts his knee between my legs. I gasp with pain and bend over. I collapse on the roof and roll around, moaning and swearing and sobbing. Yogananda is standing above me with a spiteful grin on his face.

"Does it hurt?" He feigns surprise. "Your suffering is the measure of my freedom. I've proved to you I'm not a slave of your expectations. Do you want me to prove I'm not a slave of compassion?"

He pulls me up and strikes me in the face. I start to bleed from the nose.

"Long live freedom," he says and strikes me in the stomach with his right fist. His left fist, landing on my right eye, nearly blinds me. Then his right fist slams into my temple with such force that I pass out.

When I re-emerge from Nothing, I find myself lying on the roof, exposed to the wind which had already blown pregnant clouds over the valley; the air is sharp, smelling of snow.

I knew I was letting myself into danger. I knew many people who took up spiritual yoga ended up mentally unbalanced. But all the time I was hoping I could escape this danger. Now I realise I lack the inner strength that would save me. Squeezed empty like an old dishcloth, I lie on the roof.

And cry.

10.

Ripe for the Devil's bath

For the last two days it's been raining. Sometimes it's no more than a drizzle, but every now and then aggressive wind comes swishing round the slope, pushing water through the slats in the shutters, and through the gaps in the walls. The flat roof has softened in many parts and water drips and pours onto our heads, onto the pots in front of the hearth, onto the wood in Nawang's workshop.

Rain is a rarity on the northern side of the Himalayas. Flat roofs – made of twigs, birches and mud – normally offer sufficient protection. Except when it rains. Occasionally a very old roof collapses or the whole house disintegrates and slides down the slope into the valley. Although he is aware of danger, Nawang remains completely calm. The only thing he worries about is the rain ruining the wood he uses to make beer tubs. In a valley with only a few scattered trees, wood is a precious commodity.

Every time rainwater starts penetrating the ceiling we rush into his workshop to move the wood and the finished tubs to a dry spot. We know that sooner or later the dry spots will run out. Finally we get the idea to stack the tubs and the pieces of wood on top of each other and cover them with my sleeping bag.

Nawang breathes a sigh of relief. He brings barley beer. We drink and wait.

The rain helps me to create an impression that, in spite of my outburst, I am still normal. I can hardly wait for the moment when it will start dripping again from the ceiling and we have to move something to a dry spot. The more helpful I can be, the sooner my madness will be forgotten, I hope.

Yogananda is watching me with his shining eyes and encouraging me with a barely perceptible smile. He seems to approve of my wily attempt to turn rain into my ally. He knows we cannot proceed until everything has been forgiven. He also knows (and knows that I know) that that won't be enough. Even when I will be able to look the locals in the eye again without shame, there will still remain the question where to go next. And why.

As the rain abates and turns into a gentle drizzle, he invites me to follow him to the precipitous cliffs that rise from the slope high above the house. The path is narrow, at times almost perpendicular. The valley below is hidden by a thick fog and loose clouds are sailing past Nawang's house. Soon we are alone among cliffs and clouds. We stop on a wide ledge that overhangs, like a natural balcony, a foggy precipice.

"Look." The old man waves his hand. "What do you see? Nothing. We are alone among the clouds, like two angels. Or maybe devils?"

We approach the edge of the ledge, sit down and dangle our legs above the invisible precipice.

"Are you afraid?" He looks at me.

Slowly, I shake my head.

"No?" he asks, surprised. "Then jump. Throw yourself into the fog below us."

Why, I ask.

"To prove that you're not bluffing. That you really have accepted me as your teacher. I warned you that one day I would require proof. This is the day. Demonstrate your submission."

Couldn't I do that with something less dangerous? Surely he doesn't expect me to kill myself in front of his eyes; being submissive doesn't mean being stupid. If he does need proof I will do anything he wants.

"Anything." He gives a snort. "Except what I really want."

I am not saying, I said, that I couldn't throw myself into the abyss without a thought. I could. And many times I was tempted to do just that. But I never did. And never will. I doubt I will ever have a good enough reason. If I did that now, my act would be meaningless.

"You think of life as a piece of drama in which you play the central character. The hero. But this hero is an actor who wants to play all the parts that could strengthen his illusion that he is living a worthwhile life. At the same time he is sitting in the front row, watching the play. His own hero, his own audience. Break this illusion. It's in your head. Break your head and you will break the illusion."

And then what, I ask him. I have come to him in the hope that he would teach me how to live wisely; to die is easy. My loyalty is the respect I feel for him as a teacher. I am doing my best to enact his lessons in practice. Occasionally I do go too far, but surely he must have expected that. It's not easy to find the ideal balance. I'm grateful to him, and that, too, is part of my respect for him. I have come –

"I don't care why you've come," he cuts me short. "Give me proof that you're unconditionally devoted to me. Not with words. With deeds. For you I'm not a man of flesh and blood, for you I'm merely a stranger playing an episodic part in your play. A walk-on. You are using me as a tool."

I admire you, I said. I would love to have all that you have: understanding, inner peace, non-attachment to things and events, the ability to savour life without hopes and disappointments, mental and physical agility –

"You know what I've noticed? That you're trying to impress me. To convince me that the pupil is worthy of his teacher. Otherwise, you think, I might kick you in the ass and send you home."

I'm afraid of you, I say. You are invulnerable and strong beyond any limit and unstoppable like a runaway train bearing down on me. Of course I rebel, of course I get angry, but only because I know that in the end you will run me over.

"You hate me because you can't cheat me. I keep offending you, but you have no courage to offend me back. You're a weakling. What do you expect from me? That I chop you up into little pieces and then reassemble you? How are you going to pay me? I demand payment: complete submission. Give me what you treasure most. Not empty words about gratitude and respect, which is more fear than respect.

Give me your faith in the future. Give up your future. Jump into the abyss."

Surely he must be joking. Surely he is only teasing me. What would he do if I suddenly rolled over the edge?

"Then give me your pride. That you can do without danger. You won't be hurt, you won't get killed. Give me a present, your pride."

That I can do, I reply. I long for humility. Humility is the mother of mental agility. I am giving him my pride, let him do with it what he wants, I have no need of it.

He laughs and gets to his feet. "Let's see if the master of sweet words and empty promises is capable also of deeds." He pulls down his trousers. "Lick my arse," he says. "Clean it with your tongue so it will shine and smell like a mountain flower."

He is staring at me and grinning. "Why are you hesitating? You refuse to give me your life, you won't give me your pride; what, then, are you prepared to give me? Only something you're not going to miss?"

He pulls his trousers back up and moves away.

You're demanding impossible things, I shout after him. What will I prove by licking your arse? Humiliation is not humility. That doesn't mean I'm not prepared to give you my pride. It's a question of basic human dignity. And that I'm not going to give you!

"You know what?" He turns back. "You have started to gnaw at my nerves. My arse seems dirty to you, and yet all the time shit keeps pouring out of your mouth. That doesn't bother you. Highly dignified shit keeps pouring in a dignified way out of your mouth. And very little more. I've had enough of that. Dig yourself out of your mess any way you can."

He steps to the edge of the ledge, spreads out his arms, utters a bone-chilling laughter, and plunges headlong into the abyss.

The fog silently swallows him.

What I feel more than anything is a desire to throw myself after him. Surrounded by clouds I feel rather than see the depths below. They are a composition of all the abysses I carry with me in my memory: of jagged rocks and crumbling cliffs, of gravel bottom full of sharp stones.

And lying on the stones, the crumpled body of Yogananda. Broken neck, blood-spattered face, wide open eyes, staring into the great Beyond. And next to him my body: flattened, twisted, deformed. The fluttering wings of sharp-beaked mountain birds can be heard in the fog; they will tear me to pieces and fly off with them into thousands of directions. Perhaps they'll be beaten by mountain tigers whose slouching shapes can be seen approaching through the mist; they will claw me apart and swallow me, head and all. And digest me, and dispose of me in chunks of excrement round the slopes, from where rain will wash me away and the wind will scatter me all over the valley.

Where will then be my "I"? Where will be my "home"?

What will then be worth everything that I call mine?

I would like to step back from the edge of the abyss, but I have no strength; my will is deserting me, surrendering to a strange longing for the end. I remain suspended on the verge of the decisive move that can't be undone.

And suddenly I realise what I should have known all along. I am afraid of evil. I am afraid of evil in my heart. I have dedicated most of my efforts to the suppression of urges that spring from the dark side of my nature. From the side that refuses to serve the carefully constructed image of a responsible and moral European, and wants to realise its dark side unhindered.

It is the mind that creates the illusion of reality. It invents a distance between itself and the things outside it, and forgets that it had created those things. The mind paints a picture of the world and calls it reality. In the universal process of passing through life there is no difference between living and dying; birth and death are merely stages of the process; stages invented by the mind, for in nature there are no stages, there is merely a continuous flow.

Life and the world are like the cloud into which I am falling: formless. But the mind insists on the form, it needs a frame for its painting of the surroundings, for the image of its own importance. The mind is an untiring bird, constructing the nest in which it could dwell as comfortably as it thinks it deserves; a nest of illusions.

I lose my balance and lean over the edge of the cliff. As I'm about to fall, I'm grabbed round the waist by a pair of strong arms which pull me back. And turn me around. Facing me is the smiling face of old Yogananda, who gently leans me against the side of the rock behind us.

"Tantra," he says. "Tantra will set you free."

I touch him; he is real.

"Look." He points over the edge of the cliff. The rainy fog had dispersed, and I can see the bottom of the "abyss". It is hardly five metres deep. It isn't rocky; it is soft and sandy, made even softer by tufts of grass. And from it a winding path leads back up to the ledge.

"You have jumped into the abyss in your mind," the old man says. "I can see now that only tantra will save you from the danger you are to yourself. The walls that imprison your mind are too thick; you will never be able to shatter them. You must plunge into the heart of evil. If it doesn't destroy you, it will let you pass through it to the light on the other side."

The house below us and the whole valley are suddenly bathed in sunlight. Above the line of departing clouds in the east I can see a jagged range of snowy peaks. We return to the roof, which Nawang had already filled with his rain-soaked possessions.

"Thank him for hospitality," Yogananda says.

I roll up my sleeping bag, fold and tighten my little tent, tie both to my backpack. I say goodbye to Nawang and his two grinning aunts. They are glad to see me go. Yogananda has already disappeared behind a corner on the path leading down to the village.

When I catch up with him, he grins and asks: "Would you like to know where we're going?"

"No," I reply, still angry with him for putting me through such fear on top of the cliff.

"We are going to look for evil. You are ripe for the Devil's bath. But I warn you; don't ask me stupid questions. For each I will smack you straight in the gob. Take pity on my hand and let it rest. Tell me what went through your mind up on the ledge. Did you think I was dead?"

I start immediately and speak for half an hour. Not about events on the ledge; I feel the need to tell him about my new discoveries. In nature, I say, there is no difference between pure and impure, between good and evil. Distinctions are made by the mind which is caught inside the body and needs opposites to be able to function in the material world. The mind weaves the illusion of reality with the threads of duality. It can't create patterns with a white thread alone, so it needs the black one for contrast; only so can both become visible.

I want to continue, but suddenly Yogananda's fist comes flying at me from the side, almost knocking out my teeth. As I lick my lips, my tongue tastes blood.

"You are so excited about our new journey," he says. "So thirsty for new places and new adventures. As long as you cling to your fears and hopes, your attempts to understand the functioning of your mental clockwork merely add additional chains to the ones you would like to break. We're on our way. We're walking in the direction of evil. Many things are waiting for us. But I warn you: don't expect anything. Much will happen, but that's not important. The main thing is to be on the way."

11.

Dreams can spy

After crossing a stone-covered plain we reached the almost perpendicular bank of the river Zanskar. Frothily swirling in its rocky bed, the swift-flowing water rumbled as it carried fragments of rocks along the riverbed. Because of the rain in the southern province it had swelled and gained momentum as it hissed through narrow gorges, trying to find a way to the Indus in the north. Here and there the path took us down to the water's edge, where the rumbling sound turned into deafening thunder, and the icily cold spray soon made us wet through and through.

I was glad when the path rose again and we drew away from the violence of the river. But even there we were soon embraced by a shadowy cold; the sun was hidden behind a mountain. It was almost evening when we finally reached another plain with rare trees among the fields and a lonely village forlornly sitting among them.

"Here we're going to spend the night," Yogananda announced. These were his first words after five hours of walking.

We turned towards the nearest houses. A boisterous group of ragged and dust-covered children came rushing towards us, accompanied by jumping and barking dogs. Tightly clutching our hands and sleeves, they led us towards the biggest house. As is usual in most houses in Zanskar, we had to enter the stable first and then climb up a ladder to the living quarters on the first floor. The owner hospitably invited us to the hearth. We discovered we were not the only guests;

sitting on a low three-legged stool near the hearth was a tall turbaned Indian stuffing himself with *tsampa*. Something about his face didn't appeal to me. In the flickering light of the candles I could see he wasn't too happy with our arrival.

He put the bowl of *tsampa* on the floor, rose to his full height, nearly knocking his head against the low ceiling, joined his hands into a Hindu greeting, bowed to Yogananda and said: "Namaste." Completely ignoring me, he sat down and resumed eating.

Something strange filled my heart in the presence of the tall Indian: the feeling that this was not our last meeting, but merely the first knot with which Fate intended to weave him into the tapestry of my journey. The respect he showed Yogananda (respect traditionally shown to all *sadhus*) didn't seem genuine.

At the same time it occurred to me that I might be exaggerating. I was exhausted and dizzy as if suffering from the first symptoms of sunstroke. After a cup of butter tea I calmed down, especially when I saw that Yogananda and the dark-skinned Indian were engaged in a relaxed conversation in Hindi.

After *tsampa* we drank *chang*, the local beer. Slightly dizzy and with my fears suppressed, I switched my attention to the owner's young wife, who was clattering with pots and pans and moving around in front of the hearth: firm-bodied, with round swaying hips, and with a cluster of precious stones on the tail of her traditional head covering.

After what seemed like a very long time, the thought of sex re-entered my mind. In the warmth of the sweet-smelling wood fire I surrendered to fantasies in which the young woman and I performed yoga exercises that would astonish even Yogananda. Before she left the room, she sent me a cheeky sideways glance as if she knew what I was doing with her (and to her) in my thoughts.

Unfortunately she was the mother of four children and the householder's wife. Zanskaris are not as hospitable as the Eskimos, who, if they like you, offer you their wife as an after-dinner dessert. In addition, the willowy beauty was married not only to the house owner, but also to his younger brother who was away on that particular evening. The children were also (at least partly) his; they called the older brother "big father", and the younger one "little father".

In the middle of the night I climbed out of my sleeping bag and clenched my fingers round the torch. Stepping over Yogananda's supine body, I went in search of what might be called a toilet. In Zanskar such things are usually on the first floor, which is reserved for humans. They consist of a square hole in the corner. You crouch above it and, after relieving yourself, take a little spade and cover the ill smells wafting up through the hole with dry soil piled up in a basket nearby. In some houses you find chopped-up straw for the purpose. The mixture at the bottom of the hole is cleared away twice a week, depending on how many people live in the house. In richer houses this is done by the farmhand, who then scatters the manure on the fields, the only manure available in this part of the world. Whatever plops from the behinds of yaks and other animals, the Zanskaris assiduously collect, flatten, dry in the sun and use as fuel; using wood for fire would quickly denude the valleys.

I was crouching above the toilet hole, thinking about the lama who (according to legend) awoke and reached nirvana at the very moment he heard his "sausage" plonk in the stream over which he had lowered his behind. Everything is holy for those who understand.

Except for me. I felt I was further away from awakening and nirvana than ever before. More than ever I felt that I was more than anything a neurotic mass of twitching nerves, desires and forebodings: a man who had peeked over the edge of reason into the swirling sea of madness without achieving any change that would make a difference.

As I carefully made my way back to the front room where Yogananda and I were allotted a sleeping place, I spotted the silhouette of the tall Indian in front of the hearth where a weak glow of the evening fire still remained. I was struck by the unusual gestures of his hands. I put out the torch and pressed myself against the wall. I could see the Indian sitting on his three-legged stool and cleaning a long-barrelled rifle.

My suspicions returned and swept over me like a wave of cold water. Back in my sleeping bag, I shook Yogananda by the shoulder and whispered to him that the bandit sitting in front of the hearth was going to rob and kill us.

"Only you," he muttered, half-asleep. "He will hit you on the head with the butt of his gun. He is a hunter; all he kills are blue sheep."

In the middle of the night a twelve-headed monster appeared before me. Its body was covered in greenish scales that mirrored my face in hundreds of contorted reflections. Undulating above me was an exuberance of hands with a restless multitude of fingers that were inviting and threatening at the same time.

The lowest head, from which sprouted smaller ones like grinning grapes (while the smallest protruded like warts from its forehead) resembled the head of a black bull with bared teeth. A sharp, pointed tongue twitched like a flame inside its mouth. A red demon, displaying two bloodstained molars, stared at me from among the many horns. Gaping skulls jutted from the top of its head. On the very top of the pyramid of these horrible faces, however, there perched a head with an angelic expression of understanding and peace.

Before me, the monster danced and twisted its shape in teeming reflections of its disgusting colours – and with it, the reflections of my contorted face. It swung its many hands all around, gradually pushing me towards a hanging bridge – made of rotting flexible twigs riddled with holes – that swayed dangerously in the blasts of the wind. Blowing from the bull's mouth was a horrible breath, not unlike the heat from hell.

"I don't want to go the other side!" was the cry of the hundreds of my faces reflected in the green scales of the monster. And I saw that each of these faces was slightly different, as if they reflected the expressions on the monster's faces, ranging from hatred to horror, from mockery to bitterness, from indifference to excitement.

Unusual lightness took hold of me, and I found myself floating in the air. I found myself flying past thundering waterfalls that cascaded with spraying blasts into the depths of the canyons. I found myself gliding along a tumultuous river, following its twisting path among the rocks. I was flying past grassy slopes on which large groups of furry marmot-like animals grazed. Then I began a whistling ascent towards a mountain pass in the clouds. I broke through the freezing fog and emerged on the other side. The landscape that revealed itself to my eyes moved me deeply, even shocked me.

That was the landscape of towering mountain peaks almost piercing the sky, of massive domes of rocks and stones; of an undulating sea of yellow, red and purple slopes on which there wasn't a shadow of life; only the earth and the sky, like on the first day of creation.

My flight didn't end; I continued to swish through the air with sustained speed. In the valleys below I started to notice solitary settlements of square houses, patches of barley fields, glistening snakes of rivers and streams, massive but crumbling forts on top of rocky promontories, lamaseries half carved into steep mountain sides, and rare, very rare people who had found home in this cruel, disinterested world.

Then I rose towards a saddle-like pass and floated over a shining, greenish glacier from which the threads of streams, the beginnings of rivers, descended in all directions towards the barely visible valleys below. I kept rising higher and higher until I noticed, deep below me, snowy peaks arranged in the shape of swastika. The snow-covered peaks formed the twisted arms, which were connected into a recognizable shape by the glaciers spread like a huge spider among tem. I hovered above this wonder of nature in complete disbelief. How can something like that exist?

An invisible force pushed me in the direction of the rising moon. I soon realised that the moon was actually the shining icy dome of a round mountain. I shivered with a warm feeling that this mountain was my true goal.

Then, suddenly, everything vanished and I opened my eyes. I was lying in my sleeping bag next to snoring Yogananda, in a stuffy front room in a house of strangers not far from the river Zanskar.

When the old man woke up I narrated to him in great detail what I saw and experienced in my dream.

He said nothing for a long time. I thought he had fallen asleep again. But then he started to talk. His voice was unusually warm.

I had received a sign, he said. The twelve-headed monster is Yamantaka, the killer of Death, one of the most powerful demon-gods in Tantric mythology. The bull's head represents the god of death, Yama, who is actually the merciful Avalokiteshvara, the master and judge of the dead, who leads people through suffering to the outer edge of illusions and to awakening. On top of the pyramid of horrible faces is the head of Manjushri, who keeps confirming that death, too, is no more than illusion.

He said that Yamantaka represents the dual nature of man: with the bull's head his bodily, instinctive, animal side, and with Manjushri his spiritual side. As body, man is mortal; as spirit, he is eternal. Every man, others no less than I. Yamantaka is an animal, demon and god; a symbol of life's energy that creates and destroys. It is also a symbol of the possibility that during the years of my life I can spiritually as well as emotionally mature and escape the trap of illusions forever.

I had received one more sign, he said. The mountain with the white snowcap is Kailash, also known as Meru, the snow jewel, the centre of the cosmic mandala, whose slopes are the source of four magnificent rivers: Indus, Sutlej, Ganges and Brahmaputra. Kailash, the home of god Shiva, is the centre of the mandala that incorporates all of the secret tantric symbols: the sun, which is the master of days and the peaceful divinities of light; half-moon, which is the master of nights and of the terrifying gods of darkness; and the mountains in the shape of swastika, which is the symbol of creativity with no end.

There is no doubt at all, he said. I have been claimed by Tantra.

What I am facing is Evil. Awaiting me is a passage through the Devil's kitchen to death or salvation or both.

I said that all this sounds very mystical, even poetic, but facts must surely be different. The temptation to use dreams as a guidebook through the wakeful state is of course very strong, but something tells me the interpretation of dreams is interesting only as long as it remains a game; when it turns into a search for instructions it becomes dangerous.

"Why?" Yogananda asked. "When you were dreaming, everything seemed to be real. Now, when you're awake, when you insist that you're awake, you're claiming that only your present experiences are real, and that whatever happened before was a dream. Why don't you want to believe that it may be the other way round? That true reality was in your dreams?"

I certainly couldn't prove that, I said, but I am prepared to swear that what I experienced in the middle of the night was a dream, while the conversation we are having now is reality.

"What makes you so sure? What you experienced in your dream is part of what you're experiencing now. Whatever you experience, you always experience now. The meaning of your dream is completely irrelevant as far as interpretations go. What matters is what you're going to do with, or because of, your dream.

"Dreams exist. They light up the corners of reality that in a state of wakefulness remain in the shade. In the same way the state of being awake brings into light the corners that remain shadowy during dreams. You must connect and intertwine the two sides. You already know how to use the state of wakefulness to your advantage. Why don't you want to use dreams in the same way?"

He laughed. "If you want you can move among dreams just as freely and purposefully as in the state of wakefulness. You can train your dreams to be your spy. To send you warnings of dangers awaiting you on your path through life. Like a blind man with his stick, you can use dreams to check for obstacles on your way."

He asked me to return to the dream of the previous night and dream it again, but this time from the end to the beginning. If I succeed, I can start learning more difficult forms of dream yoga. I can learn how to summon dreams before falling asleep. And how to guide them once I start dreaming. In dreams I will be able to change into animals, rocks, other people. Perhaps I'll be able to experience states of all-knowingness. And finally I'll be able to dream on when I wake up. I will be able to dream in the middle of the day."

I said that dream yoga surely isn't for me. I would find it impossible to subjugate dreams to my will. Even less would I be able to change into an animal or a piece of rock. I believe that this isn't possible. That this is merely a part of Tibetan folklore, just like levitation, reincarnation and *tummo*, warming oneself with an inner fire.

"Right," he said. "Let's forget about it."

12.

Crossing a bridge

We thanked the two brothers and their sexy wife, and continued walking towards the mountains in the north. When we reached the river, I looked back.

The young wife was standing in front of the house – her left leg slightly bent, the right hip provocatively thrust out, her right hand invitingly pressed against it. She raised her left hand to her forehead as if to shield her eyes from the sun. The indefinable longing in the posture filled me with an almost irresistible desire to return.

Just then the tall Indian hunter emerged from the house. My longing subsided and for a brief moment it was replaced by unreasonable fear. I was reminded of the feeling that overcame me when we met: that Fate had chosen this dark-skinned Indian to be not only my judge but also my executioner.

I followed Yogananda's long steps as best as I could, and was glad when after two hours we came to a halt on the bank of the river. The old man performed his usual asana: standing on his head for five minutes. The sun was already caressing the slopes with a golden glow, but the air in the valley was still quite chilly. The thundering water threw up ice-cold spray which penetrated my skin and forced its way into my mouth and throat. It was too cold to stand in one place, so I began to repeat my own exercises.

I was still far from performing them as I should. Although at times I got the feeling that the ligaments in my joints were lengthening and becoming more flexible, at other times I had to admit that my physical awkwardness was increasing. I preferred breathing exercises; they were much easier. Although Yogananda had warned me they were also more dangerous, I felt that they were the only things that kept me reasonably sane. I also performed a brief headstand every morning, although the only result of this effort was a painful erection that wouldn't subside for three or four hours.

We climbed up a steep path that winded along the rocky mountainside above the river. A chilly wind began to blow trough the gorge. It was bitingly dry, smelling of soil and sand. Occasionally it caught the water spray rising from the river below and slapped it into our faces. I knew that by midday the wind would become burning hot, as hot as the breath from the twelve mouths of the demon Yamantaka.

The river made a sharp turn to the right, and so did the path. As we turned the corner I stopped in disbelief. It was as if I had gotten stuck in the dream of the previous night. There, not far away, swaying in the wind and connecting the two steep banks of the tumultuous river, was the hanging bridge I had dreamt about.

"It can't be possible," I said.

Did the old man hypnotize me, returned me to the dream I believed was finished when I woke up that morning? But this was no more than a passing thought – the biting wind on my face was real, and the tiredness I felt in my body was certainly not a dream. I was awake.

But I was standing on a spot familiar to me, and I felt quite clearly that what was happening had already happened!

I closed my eyes. The image of the gorge and the river and the bridge appeared in my mind. They all looked as real as if I had kept my eyes open. I opened them, but everything remained the same. I closed them, yet nothing changed. An invisible link was established between what I really saw and what I merely imagined. As if I had lost my eyelids.

Terrified, I stumbled to Yogananda and fell on my knees before him. I kept clutching at his hands and clothes. "I can't close my eyes! I can't close my eyes!"

He laughed. "You wanted to achieve a higher state of consciousness. Yet now when you're experiencing what you so badly wanted you're terrified. I'm sorry but I can't help you any more. It's too late now. You're alone, completely alone. I'm no more than a silhouette. A shadow of your desires. An echo of your thoughts."

Something snapped inside me and began to wail like an abandoned child. "I can't close my eyes!" I kept shouting and pressing both hands to my face But the hands, too, were transparent. The image of the gorge and the river and the bridge remained consistently real and clear regardless of whether my eyes were open or shut. Filled with true horror by now, I began to strike my head against the nearby rock.

"Darkness, darkness!" I yelled. "Please, God, give me darkness, I beg you on my knees. Make it possible for me to close my eyes!"

God failed to respond. In the eyes of old Yogananda I saw a message that there was no God that could take pity on me. That God was something quite different from the game I was playing with myself and my presence in the world. In his eyes, which were unusually mournful as if my breakdown filled him with grief, but also cheerful, almost roguish as if nothing special were happening. I found the only assurance that a vessel didn't burst in my brain.

Gradually, the feeling of terror began to subside. Anxiety was replaced by resignation. The feeling that everything was all right began to spread throughout my body. Carefully, but with growing enthusiasm, I familiarised myself with the state of mind I was experiencing for the first time in my life.

"This isn't a dream," I said. "I'm awake. I have been awake all the time."

I shouted at the top of my voice: "I'm awake!"

The echo ebbed away down the gorge.

The old man said, "When you realise that everything you think about yourself and the world is no more than a swarm of dream images, it no longer matters what these images mean. When the symbols break you get unstuck from the ground. Wakefulness becomes a dream play. That's why the bridge swaying before us is no more than a bridge swaying before us. And if we tumble off it, our death will simply be what it will be: the fall of two men into the river, nothing more."

The hanging bridge was made of four parallel ropes and of a number of cross ropes roughly a foot apart and side ropes connecting the upper and lower main ropes. To cross it, one needed the skills of a tightrope walker. Every time you placed your foot on one of the cross ropes you had to make sure the rope sank into the hollow of your sole, depending, of course, on the type of shoes you were wearing. Flat soles were the most dangerous, the easiest to slip; if they did you were in serious trouble. You kept your balance by holding onto the side ropes, the "fence" of the bridge.

It only took a few steps for my right foot to miss the cross rope. I lurched to the right, grabbed hold of the side rope which wasn't firm enough to hold me back; in a vertiginous twist I managed to grab it with my left hand as well while my left foot slid through the gap and got twisted between the two cross ropes. And that was how I got stuck: with feet spread apart like a frog, hanging on to the rough twigs woven together, afraid that the weight of my backpack would pull me off the bridge into the river.

If Yogananda hadn't pulled the side rope back with his coordinated muscles, enabling me to assume an upright position, I would have lost my balance for good and that would have meant death.

Through the sound of thundering water below and the whistling wind I could hear Yogananda explaining that the rope wasn't a fence on which I could lean. The side ropes could hold me in place only if I grabbed both at the same time and pull them together.

He was two metres ahead so I thought it would be best if I emulated his movements. If he leaned to the left, I also leaned to the left, if he leaned to the right I followed suit like a pillion passenger on a motorcycle. The bridge was swaying because of the wind and moving under our weight; it swayed from side to side while the cross ropes bounced up and down under our feet. After a violent push which nearly threw us over the side rope, he shouted that I should change my steps.

"When I step with the right foot, you step with the left one!"

Dangerous bouncing soon lessened into a rhythmic series of waves and an occasional shuddering of the whole bridge. The structure was U-shaped, with the middle part so close to the water that the spray wet my boots and trousers.

And then it happened. I lost the awareness that it was the water that was moving while the bridge was stationary, and I suddenly felt as if an invisible force was pushing the bridge over the river below. To reverse this dizzy feeling I leaned to the left at the same time Yogananda, who felt what I had done, leaned to the right, and then I to the right and he to the left, and again right and left… until the bridge began to dance and so did the mountains, the ropes billowing around us like the tentacles of an octopus.

"Keep quiet," he shouted.

The next moment I felt his fingers clenched round the collar of my windbreaker. They remained there until the ropes under our feet stopped moving in all directions at once.

"Stop leaning against the ropes," he ordered.

Slowly and carefully we climbed against the opposite bank. Dug into it were two crumbling tree trunks, to which the four holding ropes were fixed by large rusty screws. As I stepped onto the firm ground my knees gave way in relief and I collapsed to the ground.

"Look." Yogananda pointed back at the bridge.

Coming across from the other side was a slightly built, bandy-legged farmer, carrying a load twice his weight. He was moving with ease as if walking on firm ground, but stepping widely like a duck. Not once did he touch a side rope. He didn't pause or hesitate. The bridge wasn't swaying; it merely vibrated slightly in the rhythm of his steps. When he reached us, he gave a brief smile and walked on without changing the speed or rhythm of his steps. Soon, he disappeared behind the nearest rock.

"Did you see that?" Yogananda asked me.

I said that this certainly wasn't the first hanging bridge the man had crossed; practice makes perfect.

"Well, then I'm astonished that after thirty odd years you're still stumbling through life in the same way you crossed the bridge!"

I said that comparing life to crossing a hanging bridge is hardly serious. Crossing a bridge is a question of skill –

He cut me short. "And life? The man who followed us across was walking straight. He wasn't afraid of slipping, he wasn't catching his balance; he simply surrendered to the rhythm of the ropes. It was that rhythm that brought him across. He didn't come, he floated across. It was all the same to him whether he comes across or tumbles into the river. And because he didn't care, he wasn't afraid. And because he wasn't afraid, he wasn't grabbing at the ropes. Nor did he think he *must* come to the other side. And because he wasn't clutching at thoughts and feelings, his spirit was in his body while both his spirit and body were on the bridge. He knew everything else would be a dream. But you – you didn't carry only your backpack across the river, but also the weight of the illusion you call the past and, in the same breath, the future."

I said that apparently I just wasn't brave enough to see only a dream game in wakefulness. It is very important to me whether I live or not. I know this may be my major problem, but I simply can't help myself.

He turned and walked on along the path. I followed him and tried to explain, almost shouting, that I need more time. I can't just walk past my thoughts, concepts and symbols; I must attack and disarm them.

He did not say a word all day. And all night, which we spent in the wild; I, in my tent; he, wrapped in a blanket not far away.

Then, at some stage in the night, I was visited by an unusual dream. I was an eagle with magnificent wings, hovering above the snow-covered mountains. Then I was gliding over the landscape I remembered from previous dreams: the mysterious mountain range in the shape of swastika, two lakes, one shaped like a full moon and the other like a half moon, dark gorges and sunny meadows, glaciers with herds of yaks making their way across them; and all this was rushing past me like patches of restless clouds. The strangest thing about it was that I knew I was dreaming, yet could not will myself to wake up. Suddenly, a little ahead of me, I saw the round snow-capped top of the holy mountain Meru, known also as Kailash, supposed to be the abode of all the Indian gods. There was a dark speck on the snow and as I sailed towards it, approaching at an incredible speed, I recognised the Indian hunter of blue sheep. He was aiming a gun at me.

No, a voice cried inside me, no, no, no!

But it was too late. I felt a bullet striking my left wing; another bullet perforated the right one. I shuddered and fell like a stone towards the mountain top, landing in the snow at the hunter's feet. The demon

Yamantaka, crouching nearby, looked at me with compassionate sorrow, tears running down the cheeks of most of his many heads. A procession of black-clad mourners appeared from somewhere. The priest heading it kept repeating: "Our Father who art in Heaven, our Father who art in Heaven, be merciful..."

Making up the rear of the procession was a young girl with a submissive shine in her eyes, disappointed, resigned, imploringly looking at the dying eagle on top of the holy mountain. Did they know each other? Were they meant to meet in the future? It was too late. I was growing rigid and cold, slowly entering the eternal winter.

Then a group of very young yellow-robed Tibetan girls came dancing along; all except one had swastikas tattooed on their cheeks. Their dance resembled the whirling movements of dervishes, and at times a choreographed flight of yellow butterflies. The one without a swastika on their cheek detached herself from the group and approached me. She held a sharp knife in her hand. She unbuttoned her robe and revealed her early pubescent breasts. She offered me the knife and waited for me to plunge it into her heart. Helplessly, I twitched my bleeding wings.

Then the girl suddenly changed into an old Tibetan with a black hat, and he too was waiting for me to stab him. There was a touchingly imploring look in his eyes. Too late, I let him know with the last twitch of my dying flesh. I am beyond being able to help anybody.

Suddenly he grabbed the knife and sliced off my wings close to the trunk. And with that he saved me from suffering; I felt no pain any more. A procession of orange-robed holy men approached from another direction. In perfect unison they kept reciting *Om Mani Padme Hum*. The last in the line was Yogananda. While the rest continued, he stopped at my side and bent down. "Om," he said. Then he rose to his feet and shouted at top of his voice: "Ooooooooooooooooooo ooooooooooooooooom!" The sound produced more than a thousand echoes, fading away for what seemed like eternity.

When the last echo died, I became aware that I was lying in my tent zipped up in my sleeping bag, no longer a dying eagle but a traveller who had lost his way in the mountains as he had in his life. I unzipped the bag, rolled over and pushed my head out of the tent.

Before the background of a starry sky I saw, standing on a flat rock, old Yogananda as he filled the night with a fierce, spine-chilling sound. “Ooooooooooooooooom!”

I felt a strange taste in my mouth. It was bittersweet, slippery like fresh blood. I felt a tight knot in my chest.

Where am I? What am I doing?

13.

The language of twilight

The next morning I asked him to tell me a few things about tantra. If he intended to acquaint me with the secrets of this ancient cult, he should give me some guidelines, so I knew what awaited me and what he expected from me.

"I expect nothing from you," he said. "God is a spider and the world is his web."

That was all. He remained silent for the rest of the day, until early evening, by which time we had left behind us three more gorges and one more hanging bridge.

"You tell me," he said, as we found a resting place under an overhanging rock at the foot of a snow-covered mountain pass. "You tell me what you know about tantra."

I told him what I had read and heard. That it is an ancient Asian cult, containing elements of Buddhism and Hinduism, but with a core that is much older, primitive, magical. And there is no single explanation of the meaning of the word tantra, which is of Sanskrit origin. Some say it means body, because tantra emphasizes the physical aspects of life; others say it means rope, because it ropes together man and his god; for some it means harp, because Tantric philosophy is full of music and beauty. Yet others see tantra as the inner kingdom, because its essence is hidden and known only to the initiates.

"Tantra means loom," Yogananda said. "The world is woven from contrasting threads, from two energies, male and female, positive and negative, from two creative forces which, in this part of the world, are represented by a god and a goddess."

"The god is Shiva," I said, "and the goddess is his wife Shakti, known also as the goddess of beauty, Parvati, and as the goddess of faithfulness, Sati, and also as the goddess of hunger and violence, Kali. Shiva isn't known only as Mahakala, the great black god, but also as the master of demons, god of madness, the naked god, deity with an engorged phallus, god with a golden sperm.

"And what do you know about Kali, the goddess of evil?" he asked me.

"Not much," I said. "I know that devotees long ago sacrificed their own children to please her." In northern India there was a band of murderers who used to strangle their victims to gain her favours. Kali is an ugly black woman dancing on corpses. Hanging round her neck is a necklace made of human skulls. In two right hands she holds a sword and a dagger, and in two left hands freshly severed heads from which blood dribbles to her feet. In some parts of India she is depicted with her own head in her hands, her gaping mouth trying to catch some of the blood gushing from her neck.

"We live in the age Kali," he said. "In a time of lawlessness and cold-hearted violence. In the concluding phase of human existence on this planet.

Children no longer respect their parents. Parents no longer deserve the respect of their children. There is no genuine faith any more; God is used as a threat by dogmatic old men. Public and personal relations are marked by hatred, hypocrisy, and distrust. Husband does not trust his wife; the wife does not trust her husband. They are not worthy of trust.

This is the time of spiritual, psychological and physical ills. In his hunger for profit beyond any sensible needs, man has polluted rivers and seas, destroying forever all kinds of fish; it has polluted the air, so that flowers and forests are dying at a faster rate. Relations between nations, allies, tribes and clans have been degraded to cheating and lies. Words have been devalued to cheap rhetorical tricks.

"Has the world ever been different?" I asked

"Yes," he said. "But mankind is unable to remember it. The age of the goddess Kali, Kali-yuga, started five thousand years ago. We are living right at the end of this period. Evil is everywhere, and the majority of people see it as the natural state of things. It has been given important philosophical, scientific, political names. Humanity has evolved into a snake that can kill itself instantly with its own poison. Wisdom has been fragmented into millions of opposing opinions. People go to war with each other because of insignificant differences between their beliefs."

"That's the reason for tantra. If there is no innocence any more and every form of morality is no more than a calculated lie, we must grasp at what rejects false morality. That means you mustn't suppress your desires. You must surrender to them. You mustn't say no to wine and women and other enjoyments of flesh. You must sink into them. Sensual delights must become your deity. You must raise them to the level of utmost devotion. That, too, is a way to freedom. If you want out of the fire, you must first jump into the frying pan."

I must become a servant of tantra, he said. I can't turn back any more; not after swimming halfway across the river. If I reject the path ahead I will remain a dead object on the surface of life, tossed around by the waves. I may return home, but my life will remain immobile, my energy will be consumed by inventing ingenious ways of self-destruction. In the end the burden will become too heavy; I will start screaming and breaking things, they will shut me up in a madhouse and try to keep me quiet with daily injections of tranquilisers. Is that what I want? They will make me peaceful, but it won't be peace; it will be apathy. Is that what I want? I will become a case; scientific essays will be written about me.

The main tantric rule says: Don't reject anything that is an integral part of life and the world. Fulfil all your desires; abandon yourself to the holy trinity of eating, drinking and fucking. But do that in such a way that you remain free, unattached to your pleasures. Don't cling to them but use them only to purge yourself of what they represent. Tantra is a paradoxical method for achieving spiritual growth, suitable only for those in a hurry. But this rush has its costs, so care is needed.

Akbar the Great, the Moghul emperor of India, begged to differ. By his order, practitioners of tantra were tied to elephants' tails and quartered in public. The Buddhists and Hindus, too, were hostile to them.

In Bengal they burned them alive. It is hardly surprising that the cult went underground. It became an exclusive society with secret meetings and special signs by which members could recognize one another.

The practitioners of tantra regard themselves as a society of the chosen. Other spiritual disciplines are like whores, they say, available to everyone, even to drunkards, idiots and syphilitics. Tantra, on the other hand, is like a faithful wife that reveals her charms only to her lawful husband.

"That's why it is available only to those who understand its true meaning," Yogananda concluded. "They know they can't abuse it without being punished."

Half-asleep, I seemed to hear a distant howling of a wolf. But when fear startled me fully awake, all I could hear were the sounds of water rushing along the riverbed. Occasionally a blast of wind brought an echo of the flapping of prayer flags from the small lamasery on the other side of the river. There was a palpable tension in the uneven mixture of sounds and deep mountain silence.

I lay on my back, staring at the roof of my tent. Suddenly I became aware of the soft flapping of wings above me. A mountain eagle? It was followed by silence, but the sound of wings returned from another direction. Again it drew away. I waited, almost impatiently, for the flapping sound to return. It never did. But with my hearing sharpened, I became acutely aware of other sounds. When the wind abated and I pushed the sounds of the river from my ears, I became aware of gentle whispering that I couldn't call sound but rather something that was stealthily entering my awareness as some kind of foreboding. An image of silky softness forced its way into my mind.

When I lifted the flap of the tent and peered out, the image became joined with the whiteness of snow falling in gentle swirls from the sky, covering the rocks and my tent and old Yogananda who was lying under his blanket a few metres away. And when the wind blew snowflakes into my face I once again heard the bone-chilling howl that had thrown me out of sleep. Now there was no doubt any more: Yogananda and I were not alone in the wilderness.

I moved back into the tent and surrendered to the awareness that winter had caught up with us and that wolves were not far away.

And that I wasn't alone, because my protector was there, not far away. He had declined my invitation to join me inside the tent. He preferred to sleep in the open, wrapped in his rather thin blanket, and he fell asleep as peacefully as he would behind the walls of an impenetrable fortress. This free and blessed old man who had in his itinerant life found everything that others seek in vain in hard work, money, friendship and love. There was so little I knew about him; and nothing at all about his past. He responded to all questions about what he did in his younger days with a shrug and a grin. As if that didn't matter.

Judging by the breadth of his knowledge and his way of forming sentences he must have attended a very good university. He may even have lectured at one of them and lived in a comfortable house with plumbing and servants. He may have worn ironed shirts and conservative ties. Or he may have been one of those holy men that the masses worship as reincarnations of long dead saints. He may have been anything or all of that, until he grew tired of it, withdrew into wilderness, changed his name and covered all traces behind him.

The distance between us seemed insurmountable. He was a realised yogi; I was, at best, a pale imitator. He was living everything that I only thought about. He felt the holy nature of the world, and was able to add to it. I was fighting quixotic battles with concepts, symbols, and words: What is holy? What are feelings? What are thoughts? My windmills kept rumbling on and on.

I was blinded by a belief that I couldn't extinguish, however hard I tried, that I am body and soul, body and mind, not one, but two. Thank you for nothing, Monsieur Descartes! Against my better judgment I continued to believe that the spirit is holy and the body is made up mostly of shit. It was this duality that generated my intellect, the self-proclaimed judge of reality. Not the one that feels, but the one that knows and understands on the basis of proof. Instead of touching the world and living it, I kept analysing it. And this cerebral circus, presenting its programmes 24 hours a day, was *hiding* the reality which was the object of my desire.

Relations between Yogananda and me were like a long walk across a marshy plane: whenever I felt I was finally on firm ground, the ground gave way under me. When he saw that I was eager for a debate, he sank into obdurate silence. When it was my turn to sink into a state of withdrawal in which I could not move my tongue, he leapt on me with a sarcastic glow in his eyes, and started to berate me, insult me, and poke fun of me.

If I struck back, he fell silent again; if I turned my back on him and walked off, he came after me and kicked me or struck me in the face. If I started to cry (which I did a few times because I couldn't help myself), he made silly faces and tried to imitate me until he managed (like a mother would her crying child) to pacify me and make me laugh. And when I was again in a good mood, he soon found something to destroy it.

Most cruel about him were his eyes. It was rare for me to see a glimmer of approval or warmth in them. Why didn't I leave him? Largely, I think, because that was what he would have liked me to do. That was the edge to which he was pushing me. Kill yourself. Stop. Jump into the abyss, he kept urging me in hundreds of different ways. Stop trying, it's all in vain. Your efforts are pushing you into the very ground out of which you're trying to dig yourself.

That was the reason he was pushing me in the direction of tantra. The mind engaged in a battle against spontaneity cannot know joy; it is not free. When Eros serves Reason it cannot express itself because reason translates it into theory. And then life isn't a play, it is a working day; and then an event isn't experience but a description on the page of a notebook. I knew I had to free Eros from the chains of Reason. I knew I had to become an animal before I could become a man.

I also knew that something terrible and unknown was happening with me. I knew that in the same way that during one of my journeys in Africa I knew I had malaria before I became aware of the symptoms. And this time, too, my feelings vacillated between despair and resignation. My inner walls were crumbling, fragmenting, caving in; I seemed to be disappearing into naked rocks, unearthly colours of the steep slopes, into the loneliness of the landscape.

Moments of manic excitement were followed by long hours of dejection, when everything, including the breath in my lungs, felt like lead. In between I hovered at a strange remove from myself and indifferent to everything registered by my senses. There were moments when I was assaulted by panic; I leapt to my feet and tried to escape. Or I sank to the ground, tightly shut my eyes and pressed my hands to my ears.

Three times I threw myself at Yogananda's feet and begged him to help me, to pull me back from the hell into which I was sinking, or at least tell me what we were doing in these desolate mountains. Where are we going, when shall we get there, what is waiting for us?

When I did that for the first time he said nothing; he turned and walked away. The second time he reached out and, with a gentle smile, helped me to my feet. Then he forcefully thrust his knee between my legs, causing such pain that I nearly fainted. The third time he quietly said it didn't matter. It doesn't matter if the wind blows, if vultures are circling above the plain, if I'm losing my mind. Nothing of that matters as long as I'm aware of what is happening with me and around me.

"But it must!" I shouted. "It must matter. I must have some kind of goal!"

"Why?" he asked, genuinely surprised.

"Because otherwise I feel like a leaf torn off a tree by the wind and aimlessly tossed about!"

He laughed. "But isn't it pleasant to be a leaf tossed about by the wind?"

"No!" I said. "I'm *afraid* of living without a purpose, and this fear is killing me."

"Because you don't trust the wind," he said. "What you expect from it is a timetable, itinerary, time of arrival, reservation, window seat! I blow you into the heart of freedom, and you call for help. You're so stupid! If you were my son, I would kill you."

He raised his hand to strike me in the face. But he restrained himself. The glimmer of despair and anger I saw in his eyes moved me so deeply that I began to cry, grateful for the compassion hidden behind his anger.

For the rest of the day and throughout the night he did not say a word.

The next morning he said, "Behind those mountains is a temple of the ancient Bo'n sect. A meeting place for people who practice ritual sex with virgins and toothless old hags, and for those who, for religious purposes, consume human blood, the flesh of rotting corpses and their own excrement. Lovers of demons, devotees of evil. They might be able to help you. I can't. But they meet in secret, so we must find someone willing to introduce you into their circle. People like that are few and far between. And if we do find one, he may demand an impossible payment. Now you know what we're looking for. Feeling better now?"

My memory of the days that followed is a succession of random images that keep springing into my mind without any narrative order, tied into crisscrossed conglomerates, hiding behind one another, some sharp, others blurred, but never clear enough to enable me to confirm their meaning or location.

All I remember clearly is that we changed direction and were walking south again. In the middle of nowhere we met a ragged itinerant lama. We greeted one another and sat down for a brief rest. The lama, whose face was as filthy as anything one could imagine, reached into the sack of essentials he carried with him and pulled out a wineskin filled with strong barley beer. Half an hour later we were half-sitting, half-lying among the rocks like drunkards on their way from a wedding feast. The lama, who was suffering from such a bad cold that he couldn't stop sneezing and wiping his filthy nose with the back of his sleeve, was an incessant talker. The stories he kept telling Yogananda must have been very funny for Yogananda couldn't stop laughing. Never before had I seen him laugh so much. They spoke Tibetan, so I didn't understand a single word. In the end the lama switched to rudimentary English and said that we must cross the high pass Cha-cha-la; on the other side we will find what we're looking for: the place of the worshippers of the black Shiva.

I no longer remember how we found out that the joke-loving lama wanted to send us across a five-thousand-metres high pass just for fun because on the other side there was nothing except a similar lonesome valley and plenty of starving wolves. All I remember is that we stayed in the valley of the river Zanskar and continued to walk towards the province of Lunak.

We slept in rare villages that we came upon, in small lamaseries, and under the sky if darkness caught up with us far from any settlement. In the villages we managed to get some food and water to take with us; people were friendly and generous. After the brief snowfall the days were again hot, dusty and lonesome, filled with exhaustion, aching feet, thirst and headache. And increasingly, hunger. Our reserve of barley and butter which we used to make *tsampa* and tea on my portable gas burner had run out and we were facing starvation. Fortunately we reached, just in time, the market in Padum where we bought a sack of barley, a pot of yak butter, eight kilos of rice, a small bag of tea leaves and some dried peas.

All that amounted to quite some weight; how would we carry it? I remember Yogananda having a lengthy discussion with a Balti merchant from Kargil who was selling all kinds of belts, saddles and similar items. I had no idea what they were arguing about, but eventually the merchant despatched his young assistant behind the corner, from where he soon returned with a sad-looking pony for which I had to count out onto the merchant's palm five hundred Indian rupees. When Yogananda and I loaded the provisions and my backpack and tent and sleeping bag, as well as Yogananda's blanket, on the back of our newly acquired possession, the poor beast nearly collapsed under the weight.

"Rosinante," I named the unlucky animal as we left Padum and carried on past crumbling chortens towards the mysterious gorges of Lunak.

14.

The world is my home?

Two days into our journey, Rosinante could take it no more; he collapsed. He is lying on his flank, breathing heavily. But the old man is full of inner peace and outer freshness. When we reached a bubbling stream he asked me for soap, took off his clothes, waded into the water and washed his slender but muscular body from head to toe. Then he washed his trousers, brown cotton shirt, yellow robe and knee-length woollen socks. He put them all in the sun to dry, and then he spread out his colourful blanket. Now he is sitting on it, completely naked.

I keep looking at his slender body, his straight back, the curvature of his neck, the grey strands of his long hair, his matted beard. I keep looking at him and at the exhausted animal, lying and panting, almost gasping for air, not far away. I feel a large knot in my throat. At 35, I'm closer to the broken animal than to an enlightened old man!

I am dizzy with tiredness. I stare at the whitewashed walls of a distant lamasery and wish I could experience this remote world as a tourist. I look at stone-carved images of the Buddha lining the path at fifty-metre intervals and wish I could experience all that is happening to me as mere food for the intellect, as material for an essay, as a means to obtain knowledge and get a degree. I look west, towards home, and long for a peaceful rest in a comfortable room in which Buddha, Shiva, Vishnu, Kali, tantra, yoga, enlightenment, and nirvana would be no more than titles of books I could leaf through, close and put back on the shelf. Or sweep them off the shelves, all of them, throw them out on the street, lock the door and breathe a big sigh of relief!

So tired am I!

It was much easier when it all started. Even if I only imagined I knew what I was looking for; I had some sort of map inside me that provided some orientation. The map, however illusory, gave me an assurance that new places and events were stages of some sort of progress.

Everything I had been doing in the past weeks – the exercises prescribed by the old man; all our discussions and arguments; all his kicks and blows; his mocking of the seriousness with which I carried out my tasks; all my various ways of stilling the mind: attention, "catching flies", repeating mantras, undoing the webs of illusory reality – all that had only one purpose: to convince me that I'm not what I think I am; that I'm merely what I think. That my ego is self-constructed. That perhaps I don't need it.

Yogananda had warned me it would not be enough to accept that intellectually; that way I would still remain inside the vicious circle of *samsara*. I would reach enlightenment only when I experienced it.

Why did I fail?

Because my attention remained egocentric, defensive? Because I tried to subdue the monkey inside me with violence instead of attention or mere observation? Because I invested too much energy in my yoga exercises and expected immediate results? Because I got scared when I peeked into the depths of Nothing – scared of the loss of consciousness, of the fact that there would be no tomorrow, no hopes, no possibilities?

What if the old man is only playing a game with me? What if he doesn't really know anything; what if he only thinks that he knows? What if he doesn't care whether he knows or not – just as he doesn't care how his indifference affects me? Or is the problem entirely mine and it is I who don't know what I want?

Yogananda is looking at me, and there is warmth in his eyes. This is one of the rare moments of closeness between us; we could be father and son, we could be twins.

"You're trying too hard, my friend," he says. "You really are the most dangerous friend to yourself. There're more than a thousand mountain peaks in the Himalayan range. Only one is the highest. Sagarmatha, Everest. From its top you can see all the others. From its top you can see over the others. If you want to climb to the top, you must climb up its slope. But first you must find it. You don't do that. You climb up every molehill. And when you reach the top you say: damn, this isn't the right peak. And you're terribly disappointed. When you reach the next hill or mountain, up you go again. And now you're surprised that you're tired?" There's a mild shadow of merciful sympathy in his eyes. "Which is your mountain? When you arrived, you could see it."

"I would like to see it again," I said. "I don't know how, but it seemed to have slipped out of sight."

"Toss your notebook and you camera into the stream, and your sight will improve."

I look at the stream that could become the grave of my notes (and save me from the conviction that my experience must give rise to a document, testament, become some king of "chorten" on my way into the great beyond). I look at the water frothing around large stones in the streambed and try to imagine life as a calm surface without cross-currents, and without the channel that binds it to a fixed direction.

Is that what I'm looking for? Indifference to everything that surrounds me? I think not. Life must remain a drama, and in this drama I must retain the role of a hero. I must have an audience which, by approval or disapproval of my performance, proves to me that life isn't a dream.

My notes are a part of the connective tissue that gives my drama its shape. They may indeed be the knots of the net with which I keep fishing myself out of the formless sea. But if I weaken my intellect so much that reality will flow through me like water along the streambed, I will lose everything that gives my existence meaning and shape. Everything that makes up the map without which I wouldn't know where I am and where I should go.

"I'm not saying you should live without such a map," Yogananda said. "Your problem is that the map is all you see. It has replaced reality through which it should guide you. That's why you're so tired. You're travelling across the map looking for the land that the map represents."

"What, then, should I do?"

"Stop swimming against the current. Surrender to it."

"But that doesn't mean anything!" I shout. With such words I came to him looking for wisdom, and he dismissed them as the most vacuous kind of poetry. Are they any different if they come from his mouth? How can I stop trying too hard? Against which current must I stop swimming? His advice contains too many contradictions; can't he give me something straight, something concrete?

"But everything I give you, be it a word, a sign or a kick in the ass, you instantly turn into a symbol. To everything you add importance and deeper meaning. Every inch of the real ground I place in front of your feet you convert into a map. You demand something concrete, but when you get it, you start doubting it, checking it, ejecting it. You want something concrete? Right, I'll tell you how you can get rid of tiredness."

He asks me to lie back on the grass, lean my head against the edge of my backpack and close my eyes. I oblige him.

"Now observe your tiredness," his subdued hypnotic voice whispers to me. "How is it present inside you? Like a weight, like a sack of flour? Or like a tension, like excessive air in a balloon? Where do you feel it most, in your head or your feet? In your bones or your muscles? Is it blue, green or red? Stay with it, circle around it. Observe how it beats, how it contracts, how it expands, how it thickens, how it evaporates. How it grows pale, invisible, how it is leaving you. Try to fill the gaps through which it is pouring out of you. Quick, otherwise there won't be any left. Wouldn't that be a terrible waste? Your tiredness is soooo precious; you would be empty without it."

I can feel the lack of energy trying to leave me: first it turns into greenish water, then into an avalanche of sand, then a broken-off chunk of a large glacier, then a grey mist I can't touch; then it becomes a crackling and sparkling ball that explodes into hundreds of little firecrackers, and then it turns into flapping wings of hundreds of black crows with sharp beaks, and finally into a cloud that is getting thinner and drawing away until it is dispersed by the wind. All that remains is a clear windy day at the height of summer.

"It's gone!" I shout. "How is that possible?"

The old man laughs. "How is it possible that a mountain points to the sky, that it doesn't stand on its head? How is it possible that man isn't a rock and has this wonderful faculty to get excited and shout: 'How is that possible?' Possible is everything that is possible."

Even that the exhaustion returns? My excitement soon deflates into fear. And in this fear I already feel like a vessel that will catch tiredness in a similar way a bowl catches rain.

"There is no need for you to be such a vessel," Yogananda says. "Be a bottomless vessel. Knock out your bottom. Renounce your addiction to grave seriousness. Laugh. Every morning for ten minutes laugh as loud as you can. Laugh until you turn into the man you want to be. Despair, exhaustion, lack of will – these three bandits are forever in hot pursuit. The only thing they are afraid of is laughter. When they hear laughter, they flee. So why don't you laugh?"

"Ha ha." I manage to squeeze it out my throat. And: "Hi hi." Then it stops.

"Never mind," Yogananda says. "If you persevere the laughter will stop being forced; it'll become genuine."

And so I laugh. The pony raises its head in fear and stares at me as if seeing a ghost. In the beginning the laughter is forced, deliberately conceived in my lungs and pushed up the bronchi into my throat and from there out of my mouth. It doesn't sound genuine. It sounds faked.

"Ha ha, ha ha." My laughter reverberates like an intruder in the silence of the valley. "Ho ho ho, hi hi hi."

It sounds so stupid it's almost funny. So funny is my laughter that it makes me laugh. I laugh at my laughter, and this laughter is genuine. Then I realize what a trick the old man has played on me, and I laugh at that. Soon, five different types of laughter reverberate inside me, and the first of them, the forced one, is fast becoming inaudible. Eventually I laugh completely relaxed, almost helplessly, as if I had been told a first-class joke. Then it occurs to me: *I* am that joke, my seriousness, my search for my true self is that joke. I laugh and jump up and down, I dance and roll around on the ground, while in my heart I feel something soft and peaceful and warm: forgiveness.

Laughter is forgiveness. I forgive the world for being what it is. I forgive myself for trying to be different than I am. I forgive all who love me, who hate me, who despise me, who adore me, admire me, and all those who remain completely indifferent to me. I forgive them. I forgive Fate (and myself for believing in Fate); I forgive God for instilling in me a desire to believe in him. I forgive myself for being so clever, and I forgive myself for being utterly stupid.

"Dance," the old man says. We join hands and dance on the bank of the stream like two intoxicated fawns; we jump and fool around like two little boys.

"And now shout at the top of your voice: The world is my home, and at home I can do what I like!"

"The world is my home!" I shout as loudly as my lungs allow. "The world is my home and at home I can do what I like!"

Through the whirl of shouting and laughing and dancing, and through the swirling circle of snowy mountains, one particular image keeps forcing its way into the foreground. The image of the old pony, Rosinante. The image of his baleful eyes, of his exhausted, almost tragic posture.

My laughter ceases as if cut off. Suddenly I feel ice in my heart. Suddenly I'm almost sure that the old man is a fraud who is trying to sell me a fake picture of reality.

I gasp. "Laughter is not the answer. I can't believe that everything could be so simple."

After a pause, Yogananda says, "Idiot."

15.

The art of making trousers

The next morning our little caravan was again on the move. Marching ahead as if in a trance was the old *sadhu*, followed by the tottering pony that could barely drag himself along, while I made up the rear. It was around midday when I spotted three women working in a field on the other side of the river. Suddenly a thought struck me: Can you be enlightened without being aware of it? If knowledge in the form of opinions and data is an obstacle on the path to awakening, an average inhabitant of the Zanskar valley should have an advantage.

The average Zanskarian has no idea that reality can be perceived in many different ways. He isn't weighed down by a whole army of ideas. He is self-sufficient, enjoying the fruits of his labour, literally. I, on the other hand, have to be fed by an army of specialists, ranging from the wheat grower and miller to the flour merchant and baker and bread seller, from the pig farmer to butcher to potato grower to wine producer. The Zanskarian keeps warm by burning dried chunks of yak excrement; I must be kept warm by a complicated network of gas installations.

The Zanskarian doesn't need Benetton; he makes his own clothes: he produces his own wool, weaves his own cloth, makes his own coat. The Zanskarian cures his ills with the herbs growing on the slopes of the mountains. If he needs a roof over his head, he makes bricks and builds a house with the help of his neighbours.

My house has to be built by a battalion of specialists. I can't build it myself, I'm not allowed to. I can't grow wheat or bake bread or raise sheep and cows. I can't do my washing in the nearest stream. I can't walk even to the nearest shop. I have to work.

Why? So that I can buy the food I have no time to grow, so I can buy a TV set on which I can watch conserved bits of life I have no time to live, so I can buy a car and don't have to waste time on walking but can use it for playing tennis and other exercise which I could do naturally and for free if I couldn't afford to buy a car!

The time I spend on working is the time I'm trying to save. And the more of it I want to save, the more of it I have to spend working. The Zanskarian sows his seeds when it is time to sow and collects the crops when it is time. There is a balanced relationship between his efforts and the fruits of his efforts. Because he does what he has to do when it is time to do it, he is not in a hurry. For him time doesn't equal money. Impatience is something he doesn't know.

I began to suspect it wasn't only the intellect that stood in the way of enlightenment. I was also held back by my perception of time. By my concept of time as something I either have or don't have; by my conviction that things have to be finished within an agreed span of time. To be late is the greatest of sins. Towards the evening, as we came to a halt at the foot of a granite mountain, I mentioned all this to Yogananda.

He laughed. "Well, there is another concept for you. It's a pity all you can do is think. That you're not at least slightly practical. If you were, you would quickly see what you're doing wrong."

I asked him what he meant by being practical.

"You're practical if you can make a beer barrel. Or plant and tend a fruit tree, sow barley, turn it into flour and turn the flour into *tsampa*. If you can make a clay pot. Or catch a wolf."

I said I was not as impractical as he thought. I can repair my car. I'm an amateur cabinet maker; I have made two wardrobes, a bed, writing desk, some picture frames. I have repaired some windows and doors. "And look at this." I proudly showed him my trousers.

He circled around me to see my trousers from every angle. He felt them, he examined the seams. "Unbelievable," he said. "I had no idea I was walking around with a tailor."

That I am not, I said. The tailor was my father, whom as a child I observed at work. I made clothes for my puppets from the pieces of cloth he threw on the floor. Many years later, when I came into the possession of a sewing machine, I simply couldn't resist the temptation. After two failed attempts I managed to put together quite a decent pair of trousers. As my skills improved I made some more. But when I had enough of them, more than I could wear in a month, I put the machine away and never touched it again.

"Why didn't you tell me before?" Yogananda asked. "Can't you see the state of my trousers? You will make me a new pair."

"That's impossible without a sewing machine," I said.

"We're going to find you one." He winked at me.

A group of ragged children led us to a spacious house on the slope. The friendly owner offered to put us up for the night. Then he grinned and took us to a large courtyard. And there, standing on the earthen floor, was an old-fashioned sewing machine. My excuses about having used only to an electric one and that I wouldn't want to ruin the cloth as well as the machine were cheerfully dismissed.

"Can you sew or can't you?" Yogananda looked me straight in the eyes. When I nodded he said: "You will make me a pair of trousers."

"Can you lend me some money?" he added. "So I can buy the cloth? I will return it when I come to Europe."

"Be my guest," I said, knowing perfectly well he was joking, although he kept a straight face.

The next morning our host brought into the courtyard three bales of cloth. The cloth was thick and rough, woven manually with threads spun from the wool of Kashmiri sheep. The first bale was dark red, the second yellow, the third greyish brown.

"Red trousers?" Yogananda laughed. He chose the greyish brown. The cloth was very long, but it measured only 25 centimetres across. I asked our host if he had anything wider; such a narrow strip was not really suitable for a pair of trousers. "That's all there is," Yogananda intervened, "such is the width of the loom, I'm sure you'll find a way; any tailor would."

The host offered me a piece of string with which I measured the length of Yogananda's trousers on the inside and outside. After some calculation I cut off a long piece of cloth for which the owner, also after some calculation, charged me two hundred rupees. That seemed fair enough. I cut the cloth into six strips of roughly the same length which I sew together first one to another and finally across the entire width on the upper and lower side. This large piece of cloth I folded and then, with a piece of dry dung, marked on it a rough shape of what should become a pair of trousers.

So far so good. But my satisfaction didn't last long. The scissors were not very sharp, the edges of the cloth were frayed, and with a blunt needle I found it almost impossible to make straight hems. The sewing machine seemed to have a life of its own: either it wouldn't move no matter how hard I pressed my foot on the handle, or it suddenly began to spin as if trying to escape from my clumsy hands. And so the seam was very uneven, it was either too far apart or too close together. The cotton thread kept snapping and twice the blunt needle almost broke.

My confidence was being further eroded by the sarcastic comments coming from Yogananda and the owner of the sewing machine.

The news about a visiting "tailor" soon spread. In less than half an hour, almost the entire village came rushing to the courtyard. To have a better view, some youngsters climbed on top of the roof. Under the burning sun, I began to sweat. I became awkward and things fell out of my hands. I began to make utterly stupid mistakes: I was beginning to sew together pieces that didn't belong together, and cut apart those that did; twice I sewed the left trouser leg to the right one, and vice versa; then I realised that the pockets were too shallow; I had to cut new ones.

I was becoming more and more awkward, nervous and hot. It wasn't long before I felt like tearing the "trousers" apart with my teeth and stuffing the pieces into the mouths of the grinning audience. My feeling of helplessness was caused by my stubborn belief that I couldn't afford to acknowledge defeat because that would kill me. I left the needle inside the cloth and muttered that I have to go to the loo. I pushed my way through the crowd of ragged mountain folk and staggered toward a rock rising out of the slope above the house. I threw myself into its shade and buried my face in my hands. I remained like that until I was joined by Yogananda. He sat down beside me and we both remained silent.

After five minutes, he said: "What can you tell me?"

I replied that the making of trousers revealed to me something I didn't know. It seems to me that in looking for enlightenment (as well as in making his trousers) I keep falling into psychological traps that deplete my energy and destroy my motivation.

"Describe these traps," he said.

I said that there were many, but they all originated in my attitude to work. My first mistake was not realising how harmful the influence of the circumstances can be. I knew it was too hot in the courtyard, that the scissors were blunt, that the sewing machine was disobedient, that the thread was brittle. I knew the needle was bent and a little loose. I also knew I was not used to sewing in front of a curious and sarcastic crowd. I should have taken all that into account. I did not; I plunged into work convinced that I would finish a pair of trousers with as much ease as I did many years ago with a faultless machine in the comfort of my own flat.

The second trap was my unquestionable conviction that I knew how to make a pair of trousers. Instead of adapting to the unknown material and the peculiarities of the sewing machine, I tried to adapt both to my experience of sewing, to my memory of events in the past which had frozen into a rigid pattern. I allowed myself to become a victim of the natural fossilisation of memories. That was a trap I should have known how to avoid.

It seems to me, I continued, that I had been led into this trap by another trap which I should have avoided: awareness that people are watching me; that I am *acting* the part of a tailor. Because of that I felt awkward and not a little embarrassed, so I tried to create an *impression* that I was up to my task; and from that moment on it was no longer my true "I" that was doing the work; it was my ego who was watching himself through the eyes of the observers.

When I realised I was making stupid mistakes, I fell into the next trap: the fear that I will fail and make a fool of myself. This fear made me nervous, and because I was nervous I made even more mistakes. When I saw that all my efforts were in vain and that the trousers refused to submit to my will, I was attacked by a bout of impatience, which is the mother of all traps.

Impatience is caused by a belief that each task, each process taking place in space and time must be finished within a certain period. Impatience leads to haste and lack of feeling, both of which sooner or later cause a fatal error. And when the ego realises how terribly it had derailed the project, it takes refuge in helpless red-faced anger that most often takes the form of cynical apathy.

"And not in the form of inner peace," Yogananda said. "Inner peace arises from the identification with the present moment. With trousers, when you are making trousers. You must create conditions in which the trousers will make themselves, with you as a mere assistant. The whole art of making trousers is in the fact that the trousers, while you make them, are the main goal of your entire life. You must believe you have been born for no other reason than to make this particular pair of trousers."

After collecting the remnants of my courage, I returned to sewing. When I finished, Yogananda pushed his spindly legs into my "masterwork" and proudly showed it to the villagers. A tiny man stepped out of the crowd and said that he, too, needed a new pair of trousers. He pointed at Yogananda and said he wanted a pair exactly like that, with pockets and flies that could be unbuttoned. The tiny man was soon pushed aside by an aggressive father who demanded trousers for his three sons. It wasn't long before orders were flying from all directions.

The owner of the sewing machine, the village tailor, wasn't too happy with the turn things had taken. He simply couldn't believe that the nervous stranger, the laughing stock one minute, could turn into a master tailor the next. He smelled competition that could threaten his livelihood.

I was no less surprised by the turn of events. It made me aware how small the distance between success and failure can be. You do something and something happens. You create inner peace, and: hail to the jewel in the lotus!

It occurred to me that I could stay in that remote village and make a living as a tailor. I would live in a rectangular house without window panes, I would own a yak whose excrement I would use for making fire, and perhaps a goat to give me milk; I would marry one of the red-faced girls who were cheekily staring at me from behind their elaborate headgear; I would take her into my house to cook *tsampa* for me and give birth to snotty little Tibetans; I would settle in, settle down so that no one could tell me apart from the sunburned natives; together we would brew and drink beer, I would make trousers, skirts, maybe jackets, and under my breath happily repeat *Om Mani Padme Hum.*

As soon as this vision opened up before me, something brushed at me, whooshing past me, stroking me with feathery softness. Fleeting and uninvited, the possibility of awakening touched my heart. If at that moment I could renounce the kind of life waiting for me when I returned to Europe (and would feel neither relief nor regret); if I could change the vision of a completely different life that offered itself to me into reality without hesitation, but also without undue excitement, I would have done something. And something would happen.

But the realisation that enlightenment was so simple and so accessible immediately filled me with doubt that this would be *true* enlightenment (so simple? so accessible?). The doubt was the striking force of my ego which was reconquering territory that had slipped out of its grasp. And as soon as it reclaimed its power it changed my experience of the moment into a conviction that the simple life of a village tailor wasn't for me and that the whole thing was no more than a silly thought.

There was disappointment in the eyes of old Yogananda. He was expecting that it would suddenly happen; I was as close as never before. I, too, was disappointed – not so much because I had wasted an opportunity that would probably not be repeated, but because there seemed to be nothing special in the awakening that for the first time offered itself to me as a real possibility. Nothing exotic, merely something that seemed to be strangely familiar and disturbingly close.

When Yogananda and I took our leave, the village tailor seemed to be the only one glad to see me go; all the others were disappointed, some even insulted. Finally they accepted the inevitable and even brought me presents: a pot of yak butter, a belt adorned with jewels, a copper water flask filled with barley liqueur. A small group of young people accompanied us to the foot of the mountain and to the path near the river, where one of the pretty young girls pulled the jewel-studded belt from my hands and playfully tied it round Rosinante's neck.

Then we said goodbye. The yogi and I continued our way towards Lunak. The village stayed behind, in the heart of stony loneliness, a grape of whitewashed houses on the hip of a grey-brown mountain, drawing away, in the end no more than a splodge on grey background.

We did not speak. We both understood what had happened (and what did not) in the village.

Something moved inside me: boredom was replaced by uneasiness, which gave me the impetus to start looking for peace again. But instead of returning to the unravelling of my mental constructions I began to devote all my attention to Yogananda. And I thought: here is the man who had achieved the state of enlightenment. Here is the model you can use to turn yourself into something similar!

He really was completely unlike me! He was living in a permanent state of meditation, aware of the flow of reality without effort, without intention, just like that. There was no haste in his gestures, and there was no undertone in his words that he would not be aware of. His actions were free of neurotic tension. I always felt that he was exactly where he wanted to be, always at the point of his destination. In everyday situations he seemed be discovering something that remained hidden to me. I got the feeling that there wasn't a single thing that would remain ordinary for him; on the contrary, the daily life with all its usual trivialities was the main source of his yoga practice. Problems that brought me to the point of anger and even despair were for him sources of inspiration. He never tried to reject or deny anything; in every situation, in every moment he made use of everything that was offered. And because he never tried to reject anything, he never felt threatened by anything. He lived as if every situation was a reflection of his inner state, and because he never tried to become anything, because he merely was what he was, everything that he did or encountered seemed right and natural.

My inner space, on the other hand, was tight and filled to the last square inch with trash that I felt I could not live without. And so with each move I banged against something; with each step I hit an obstacle and got hurt. I was like a blind man inside a shop stuffed to the ceiling with second-hand furniture, desperately looking for a way out, yet afraid of stepping on a sharp nail or lurching into an unsheathed sword. My gestures were not spontaneous; they were careful and deliberate, but blind. I was a blind man in the second-hand shop of my mind, an awkward, unhappy man, hemmed in by the tight load of opinions, convictions, hopes, disappointments, bad habits; surrounded by the fossils of a past I should have learned to let go.

16.

The situation is desperate

I felt as if a dark veil had covered the world. "What's the matter?" Yogananda enquired with a touch of derision.

Call me Sisyphus, I replied. If every day you get close to your goal but can't touch it because you don't see it, because you only feel it is there, while the next step is already a step away from it, then it is hardly surprising if at some stage you begin to doubt that your efforts make any sense.

"The situation is dire," he agreed. "On the one hand, you must loosen your intellect, make it more transparent, so that you'll be able see reality directly, feel it intuitively. On the other hand, you must examine every bit of knowledge you gain by intuition with the very intellect you must first loosen to make intuition possible! Crazy, I know, but that's how it is. There is no other way."

I said that I was now even more confused than before. If I can't trust the intellect because it is tyrannical, and if I can trust only intuitive flashes which the intellect (that I can't trust!) after examination proclaims to be valid (on the basis of what judgement, I wonder), what am I to do? This is a vicious circle that even the Devil would be incapable of inventing. How will I know if I perceive true reality and not only my own invention?

"With the ability that transcends not only intellect but also intuition. The Buddha called it insight. The intellect sees only the map of reality while intuition can sense reality as represented by the map. It is insight that enables you to see true reality."

"Well," I said, "that's all very nice. Insight. But where can I find it?"

"It appears," he replied. "It opens like the lotus flower. It opens when feelings part company with the ego, when the thought is pacified, and when the pacified thought examines the intuitive revelations and purifies them. Insight appears when intuition and intellect finish their work and withdraw."

Towards the evening we stopped near a shallow pond. I put up my tent, prepared tea, added some barley flour and made *tsampa*. By the time we finished our dinner it was already dark; a full moon emerged from behind the clouds, covering the valley with a silvery blanket.

"Incredible," Yogananda said and walked to the pond. I followed him. He pointed at a reflection in the water. "What's that?"

"The moon," I replied.

"The moon?" he exclaimed. "What about that thing in the sky? Are there two moons?"

"No," I said, "the moon in the water is only a reflection of the real one in the sky."

"And look at this." He pointed at a small puddle near the pond. "Here is another moon. And here" – he bent down and scooped some water into his hand – "in these drops you will also see one. How many moons are there?"

I said that all these were reflections. There is only one moon, but there are many reflections. It is reflected by every surface of water, small, big, round, square; the size and shape are of no importance.

"Could we then say that these water surfaces are, in a manner of speaking, receivers?" he asked.

"We could," I nodded.

"They are receiving the moon, which is reflected in them according to their abilities: in a large pond clearly and beautifully, and in a drop of water on the palm of a hand barely visibly."

He picked up a stone and tossed it into the middle of the pond. The splash caused concentric ripples which travelled towards the edges of the pond. The reflection was broken into hundreds of shuddering dots. "What is that?"

I said that the stone caused a disturbance and reduced the quality of reception.

"Right you are!" he exclaimed. He approached the puddle again and poked around in it with his stick until the water grew muddy. "Where has the moon gone?"

I said that the only thing gone was a reflection because of the muddy surface; the moon was still where it was, in the sky.

"Broken receiver," he said. "Some time ago you asked me what one experiences in the state of mind known as nirvana. One of those expressions that you Westerners like to push around in your mouths like a piece of chewing gum and then ungraciously spit out with the words: Eastern rubbish! Is it clear to you now? The Absolute, call it God if you like, is the moon. You are the receiver reflecting it. You say: I would like to achieve the state of wakefulness. I would like to reflect the Absolute with maximum clarity. Do you understand what I'm talking about? I am talking about the fact that the pond must be cleared, the mud and the sediments must be removed."

He walked away into the night.

I could feel sudden warmth spreading around my body.

"Yogananda!" I shouted. "What's wrong with the receiver?"

I could see in the moonlight that he stopped. Then he turned around and slowly came back. He didn't say anything; he walked to my tent, spread out his blanket right next to it and waited. I unrolled my sleeping bag, climbed inside it, zipped it up to my chin and manoeuvred myself into a sitting pose. And waited for my dangerous friend to speak.

I waited an hour. I waited two.

Then I began to fall asleep. Just as my eyes were about to close, the old man rose from his meditation and spoke in a tone of voice that seemed to be floating around me and wrapping me into an ever tighter embrace.

"You cling to the forms that are transient and exist as forms only in your mind. As long as you cling to them, each wish fulfilled only creates a new wish, and each answer to a question merely gives birth to a new question. Fixed forms are the mud in your pond. Your nervous system has been muddied by the sediments of *maya*, illusion. Clean the pond. Only then will it reflect the moon, the Absolute. It doesn't matter what you call it: emptiness, hollowness, Brahman, God, Spirit, Being; call it XYZ if you want to. When metaphysics reaches its outer borders and psychology fails to give you satisfaction, that's not a deception. You're left with the receiver which is material: your nervous system, your brain."

I asked him, afraid of the answer, if that meant I could clear and sharpen my receiver only with yoga, meditation, mental exercises.

"There are hundreds of methods," he said. "We already know that the most common type, hatha yoga, is too dangerous for you. You have no patience. Remember your stint as a tailor? We discovered, not only once, that you're by nature inclined towards tantra, which is sensual and cathartic. That is what suits you. You're not an ascetic. You enjoy hunger as long as it gives you the feeling that you've just had a good meal. You enjoy discipline as long as you can relax and be yourself in its framework. That's what you're like, why pretend? Still, tantra will not be enough. We know that you also possess the gift of dreaming. In the world of dreams you're very flexible and inventive. Surely you're clever enough to exploit that. You have had reasonable success with meditation. So this is your trinity: meditation, dream yoga, tantra."

I felt great relief.

"Right," I said. "Meditation, dream yoga, tantra."

My trinity.

"But do you know its purpose?" he asked me.

To repair the receiver, I said. To calm the surface of the pond, to make the mind quiet. The senses that are on guard must be put to sleep; the army of ideas, memories, concepts, worries and defence mechanisms must be demobilised. Only then will the surface of the soul be quiet and crystal clear. Only then will the moon be reflected in it with all its power. Only then will my individual consciousness be connected with the Absolute. And I will reach the state that will be neither sleep nor dreams nor ordinary wakefulness, but insight.

17.

Meditations

During the night we received another package of snowfall. Because the path towards the high pass is dangerous we decided to remain in the valley and wait for the snow to melt. The wind and sun are hard at work and maybe in a day or two we will be able to carry on. But there is no certainty, only waiting.

All of a sudden nothing is happening.

The feeling is highly unpleasant. It is suffused with restlessness, all the time grasping after the shadows of past events. The mind refuses to accept that nothing is happening, so it changes boredom into a problem and occupies itself with the pain of waiting for something to happen. The mind requires entertainment; if there is none, it amuses itself by longing for it, by the sensation of missing something essential. It grabs at every passing idiocy, and if there are no problems it quickly invents one. As long as it can deal with something, however trite, it doesn't have to empty itself.

When the last breath of hope that something might happen evaporates; when it ceases to matter whether it will or not; when the time simply passes and that is all there is; when you just sit, crouch, wait without really waiting (like the Indians for trains; hour after hour, without impatience or anger, without glancing at the timetable), when you simply sit and wait without a desire for stimulation; when you just wait for nothing and you're empty and bored without being angry or frightened, then – then something happens.

I sit, I observe, I waste time.

The mind is still restless, boredom distracts me. I can't surrender to it without putting up at least a semblance of fight. But the fact that boredom distracts me no longer disturbs me; I have accepted that as something that just happens. Boredom is not very pleasant, the mind is restless, but I have accepted that. The mind is restless, but it does not seek rest.

I sit, I observe, I waste time.

This is the state of natural mindfulness. I slip into it without trying. I see Rosinante rushing into the wealth of thick grass on the bank of the river. At first he is astonished at the amount of food. As if afraid it would vanish before he gets the chance to assuage his hunger, he eats impatiently, vociferously, moving from one end to the other and back to the middle. It isn't hunger, but gluttony. However, it doesn't last; when he realises that there is enough grass, that it would always be there, he relaxes. Then he slides to the ground and falls asleep.

And so I, too, stop seeking peace. It's all the same to me that I'm restless and bored. The energy causing my restlessness has enough space, it can expand as much as it wants to, the grassland is endless, there is enough food for centuries; it keeps growing back. When I realise that my restlessness has enough space, I stop being afraid of it. The space is so large that restlessness disappears in it. And because there is no need to keep the mind on a leash any more, the mind forgets itself. And is at rest!

When the wind turns into a gentle breeze and the cloudless moonlight spreads over the valley, the cold silence fills me with the hope that it won't snow any more; in the morning the pass will be open, we shall climb over it into the valley beyond, and then, hopefully, we will reach the secret tantric lamasery.

Suddenly I am shattered by the realisation that soon all this will end. Whatever happens, except if I die, it will be over and I will have to return to what I call home. Back to Europe, to the world of TV, technology, economy, looking for work, uncertainty, wars. From the heart of loneliness I will have to return into the heart of the society. And what will all my experiences mean in the multitude of different preoccupations? Won't they quickly (far too quickly) fade into something “traveloguish”, interesting epically but without any binding message for me and my world?

Wrapped in his blanket, Yogananda sits next to me. “Something is bothering you.”

Yes, I nod. Knowing that sooner or later I will have to leave these mountains forces me to evaluate what I am doing. The world in which I live has neatly ordered drawers for mental gains with which I will return. Even before I get over the jet lag, everything will be classified and shut away. The process will probably start in my mind during the return flight. I fear that everything that’s happening to me now will become a faded painting on a wall of my museum of memories.

“These are the fears of your ego,” he says. “For ego everything must be useful: truth, God, everything. Ego doesn’t know what to do with useless things. Why meditations, why freezing in the mountains, why tantra, why all that? The answer is very simple, but you’re afraid to confront it. What guides you on this path is the desire to reconnect with the rejected half of your nature. You’re not ashamed to admit that. It sounds psychological. What you’re afraid to acknowledge is the fact that this is a desire for God. You’re looking for God. When you will find the courage to admit that, you will remove the greatest obstacle on your path.”

That is true, I reply; my world is rational, evolution-based, scientific. Although it is clearly one-sided I’m afraid to admit that it is God I find missing in the whole picture. If I could find space for God, a rational justification, then maybe he wouldn’t be the missing part of the picture. My instincts tell me that a purely rational approach isn’t enough; but an equally powerful instinct prevents me from accepting a concept that is not scientific.

“Why should God be unscientific?” He laughed. “Is he at odds with the tenets of evolution? Life is a fight for survival, reserved for those who adapt to the environment most successfully. How successful at adapting was Man? Not very. Blind reliance on Reason has brought him to the point where he can wipe his kind off the face of the Earth by pressing a single button. We are standing on the threshold of the end of history. Those who still don’t believe that only God can save us belong to yesterday’s generation.”

I realise that, I reply. I admit that –

"That's not enough!" he cuts me short. "You must make a step. Who is going to make it if everybody is waiting for someone else to make it? A step in the right direction. It must be practical, it must be an action, words have lost the power they had. God must return, open your windows and doors, let him in. Only God can cure you. You're not suffering from an ordinary illness. A madman doesn't know he is mad. To a psychopath his world appears logical and correct. And that is the truth of the world at this moment. Everything is logical and rational. But this is a state of psychosis. Man has suppressed half of his nature and gone mad. Have you heard of the star Sirius?"

I said I did. It's very unusual. A twin star, Sirius A and Sirius B, circling around each other. Their gravitational fields are equally strong; they attract and repulse each other with the same force.

"You have a similar system inside you. One star is the ego. The other is the soul. Let's call it that, for want of a better word. As long as their forces are equalised they circle around each other and your mind is balanced. But in man this system no longer works. The ego has been blown up, become abnormal; it has pushed away and overshadowed the soul. What you miss is the soul. Only when ego and soul are equal again, circling around each other, only then will you be normal again. Where is your soul?"

Where is my God?

I began to sink into the realm of dreams, flying through empty space towards a mythological world. I landed on the bank of a river. I negotiated a deal with a boatman to take me across to the other side, which was covered in mist. But the mist was penetrated by the glow of an inviting light. The boatman was Yogananda. The boat was small, the bench very hard. Yogananda offered me a paddle. "I must do it myself?"

"Of course." He laughed. "I'm only your steersman; the work has to be done by you."

I started to paddle. I paddled and paddled and paddled. But the opposite bank refused to come any closer. The mist remained as thick as before, and the light shining through it equally inviting. I paddled every way I could, but the bank I tried to leave remained right behind me, almost as if following me. I put the paddle away and lay down in the boat.

"There is no progress," I said.

It's all right, I thought, falling asleep. There is no need to fight.

18.

Henry Napoleon Alexander

I was woken by subdued voices. Someone seemed to be walking past my tent, moving away. I heard a man's laughter. All was quiet again. A palpable tension lay at the heart of the morning silence. Dreams, I thought and began to slide back into sleep.

Suddenly a beam of light shone into the tent. The unshaven face of a native appeared behind it; he held a torch in his hand. I twitched in fear and rose on my elbow. The man opened his mouth, let out a puff and withdrew. I could hear laughter and boots, softly squeaking away.

I pushed my head out of the tent and was almost blinded: everything was soft and white; snow had fallen during the night. The mountain slopes were enveloped in fog.

On the bank of the river I spotted a herd of yaks. Standing in the snow twenty yards away was a multicoloured tent with three pointed tops, five times bigger than mine. In front of it, four yaks with timber saddles were being loaded by a group of men wearing heavy woollen coats.

As for Yogananda and Rosinante, there was no sign of them.

"Hey," I shouted and staggered towards the loaders; I was almost convinced they had stolen my backpack and my provisions. But among the baskets and boxes they were fastening to the yaks' backs I looked in vain for the sacks Yogananda and I had bought in Padum. One of the loaders, an old silver-haired Tibetan in worn leather trousers and wearing a wide-brimmed black hat, looked at me haughtily and said something. His companions broke into derisive laughter.

“My backpack,” I shouted in English, “my backpack! Where is my backpack?” They laughed again. Six pairs of dark eyes set in deeply lined suntanned faces were looking at me as if I were a madman.

I circled the rock where I had meditated the day before in the hope that Yogananda and Rosinante were hiding behind it with my luggage.

Nothing. My little tent, standing in the middle of the snowy plain, was the only proof that I wasn’t dreaming.

A tall hook-nosed man emerged from the large tent which had appeared overnight out of nowhere. He was wearing a thick red windbreaker and black woollen trousers. His mountain boots reached all the way to his knees and his thick nest of black hair half-obscured his forehead. He approached the loaders, checked their work and said something. The haughty mountain men lowered their heads and rushed to the yak which was already fully loaded; they began to untie the ropes to rearrange the load so it wouldn’t lean to one side.

Then the man pushed his hands in his pockets and walked towards me. There was something comforting in his posture. Not only because the wild mountain men evidently obeyed him but because in the midst of fearful surroundings he was something familiar. He stopped in front of me and aimed his velvet-brown eyes directly into mine. A friendly smile appeared under his thin moustache.

“How are you,” he said with an American accent, “my name is Henry Napoleon Alexander.”

I shook his hand with a little more vigour than necessary and told him my name and where I was from. Unable to hide surprise, he looked me up and down.

“Your mule driver left last night,” he said.

“My mule driver?” I gaped at him.

“The old Indian in yellow frock. He said he was returning to Padum.”

“Rosinante was a horse, not a mule!”

“Can’t really trust these people. As soon as they discover your weak point they start cheating and exploiting you. That’s why I treat them in military fashion; one slip, and I sack them without pay.”

“What about my backpack?” I asked hoarsely. “I had a backpack.”

Henry Napoleon Alexander put his arm round my shoulders and led me towards his tent. "It was lying in the snow. So I moved it into my tent."

He entered and returned with my backpack. I could see at once that the straps were pulled tighter than usual. Someone had opened it and went through the contents. I did not doubt for a moment that this was Henry Napoleon Alexander.

"Before I forget," he said, hastily entering the tent again. He re-emerged with a pair of brown trousers, neatly folded. He pushed them into my hands. I could see that quite a few stitches were already undone.

"This is what he gave me," he said. "And he said something strange. That he can't see the trousers having a chance to make themselves. Something like that. Peculiar guy, this mule driver of yours, where did you find him?"

I tucked the trousers under my arm, grabbed the handle of my backpack and dragged it towards my tent. I crawled inside the way an injured animal crawls into its lair. I buried my face in the sleeping bag like a child who closes his eyes and believes no one can see him. But in the darkness a light was shining, and in its beam I could see the face of old Yogananda.

In his eyes I noticed disappointment, almost anger. I'm sorry I can't get excited about the results of your efforts, his eyes seemed to be saying. You tried and you failed, and now I have to attend to other things. But in the gentle smile under his moustache I could read something different: tolerance, inclining towards understanding and empathy. Not everything's lost, his smile appeared to be telling me. By leaving you I'm giving you one more chance. Don't waste it as you have wasted all the others.

I sit, I am mindful. What's happening inside me? What do I feel? Humiliation because he had returned the trousers I made him ten days ago? I'm not a tailor, so why should I take this as a disgrace? Is it the seeker within me that feels humiliated? Because in the making of the trousers I see a symbol of my self-realisation, and in Yogananda's refusal to wear them a rejection of my efforts? We are both humiliated: the tailor who made the trousers and the tailor seeking freedom from given models. But I am neither one nor the other.

Who feels the fear that paralyses me, the fear of a child lost in the woods and deprived of the warmth of its mother's hand? Of a child who doesn't know the way and is afraid of dangerous beasts? This child is inside me, afraid as never before. He has lost the guiding hand that he had come to depend on. Yet I am not that child. I can see he is inside me, I know his feelings, but I am outside his feelings, I am somebody and something else.

And who is the one feeling betrayed, this moral merchant who, in the spirit of partnership, had signed a contract (or so he thinks) and now feels anger because his partner withdrew his capital and know-how, leaving him stranded? Is that me, that inflexible ethical freak who expects others to behave the way he would like to behave toward others (although he can always find an excuse why he can't)? That merchant is also inside me, but I am not him.

Who, then, is feeling rejected – if not I, who? And if not I, what do *I* feel?

In the solitude of the snow-covered valley I suddenly saw the image of my inner world. The mind shines on the outside world the way the sun shines on the land, making it lonesome if it feels lonely, and frightening if it's afraid. Each mental state can only be a reflection of what I can connect with by being mindful: anxiety if I am anxious, fear if I am afraid, rejection if I feel rejected. That's the herd of my ego, looking for pasture. There is no point in trying to drive it away. It is hungry. If I prevent it from finding food and relaxation it will stomp all over me.

The pain did not subside, it continued to boil inside me without overflowing; I became a trough in which it frothed. I climbed out of the tent and looked towards the camp of the mysterious American.

I could see only three things in the middle of the white plain: my little tent, my backpack, and myself. Henry Napoleon Alexander and his caravan of yaks had vaporized as if they were no more than a mirage.

Coughing and feverish I remained alone in the valley. With no food, no direction, no strength. A wolf began to howl close by.

I pulled out my Swiss army knife and waited, tense like an animal, for the sound of paws in the soft snow, hoping to hear it before a shadow could leap towards me. I was determined to defend my life to the last shred of flesh on my bones.

My mind was as sharp as the knife I held in my hand. Ego has left its centre, deserted the battlefield. I could still feel its violence, but it was distant and subdued, unimportant. I alone was waiting for the wolf – I, the inheritor of the world, the world itself. I became the moment, and in this moment at peace, tense but at peace, observed and observant, an event and conscious of the event unfolding, almost as if performing a play and watching my own performance, without being aware of myself or any audience, watching it without value judgments, without projections.

I was overwhelmed by a burning feeling of freedom.

The world is my home, I felt. Good or bad, the world is my home and everything that is happening (with me, to me, without me) is happening at home. Everything is all right, acceptable, merely a fantastic adventure, filling me with expectation of what else may happen; everything merely a magic fairytale, read to a child before sleep.

Instead of a wolf, a rider on a short-legged pony emerged from the mist. It was the grey-haired Tibetan in leather trousers and with a dark-blue hat on his head. He had brought with him another pony, no doubt for me. He pointed towards my tent and uttered one single English word, "Come!" I wasted no time, although the word sounded more like a rude order than polite invitation. It took me less than five minutes to fold the tent and the sleeping bag, tie both to the backpack, drag the backpack to the pony's side so I could step on it and climb onto the animal's back, bend down with some difficulty to lift the backpack off the ground and manoeuvre it on to my back, and already the old Tibetan, who reminded me of the actor Anthony Quinn, turned his pony into the direction he had come from, with my pony following, and already we were riding across the wet snow into the heart of the thick fog. The tall American had obviously had a change of heart and decided to take me with him.

Or lend me one of his yaks to go my own way.

Suddenly it struck me that I had no way any more. Yogananda was my way *and* my direction. I felt a surge of terror. I was alone – not only in the snow-covered mountains but also in myself, lost in the wilderness of my mind (and my soul), without direction, without support, with wolves on my trail. I felt dizzy. I toppled over and landed with a thud in the snow.

The first thing I saw when I came to was the inside of a large tent. I was lying on a deckchair, and I wasn't cold any more. The warmth was coming from an unusual gas heater gently hissing not far away, filling the interior of the tent with bluish light. Sitting on a folding stool nearby was Henry Napoleon Alexander, scribbling notes into a thick dog-eared notebook.

"Ah." He gave me an encouraging smile.

He got up, made two steps towards a linen bag on the other side of the tent, pulled out a tin mug, moved to a gas burner on which stood a red metal teapot, filled the mug with steaming tea and brought it to my bedside.

"Drink," he said. "And after that, pills."

"What pills," I objected, "I'm not ill!"

He placed the back of his hand on my forehead. "40°C. Pneumonia."

Suddenly I broke into a fit of coughing. I felt a stabbing pain in my back. I realised I was swimming in sweat. Oh God!

"Don't worry," he said, pouring some more tea into his own mug. Then he sat down again on the stool, which squeaked under his weight. Watching each other, we sipped tea, I on his deckchair under a double sleeping bag, far superior to mine, and he with his elbows on his knees, leaning towards me.

"Thank God for the fog," he said. "Today I wanted to cross the mountain pass, but the yak drivers refused. It probably *is* too dangerous. I hope the fog will lift overnight."

He reached into a leather bag on the ground behind him, pulled out a bottle of whiskey and poured some into his tea. Then he passed the bottle to me. "Have a sip," he said almost impatiently.

I leaned on my elbow and held out my mug; he poured some of the golden liquid into my tea. When I tried to withdraw the mug, he pressed the top of the bottle against the inner side of the rim to hold it back, pouring some more whiskey into my tea. "Best medicine." He laughed and took a swig from the bottle.

I wanted to ask him what he would have done if the fog hadn't kept him at the foot of the pass. Would he have left me, alone on the snowy plain, although he knew I had no food? But such a question was out of place, considering that he had, after all, decided to take care of me.

We drank and chatted away. Finally I sank into a feverish sleep not longer than a couple of hours. When I opened my eyes I found Henry Napoleon kneeling beside the deckchair, getting ready to give me a large injection.

"What's that?" I shouted and moved away.

"I don't know what you do about pneumonia in your country, but in the US we use penicillin."

"I don't have pneumonia!"

"Not at the moment, but would you like to have it?"

"No."

"All right then, show me your sweet behind." He winked at me.

I turned around and pulled down my trousers to expose my buttocks. I could feel the needle penetrating my skin and gently sliding further into the flesh. Then it was deftly pulled out, all without pain or even discomfort. Was Henry a doctor?

He laughed and left the tent. I could hear him talking to the yak drivers, who immediately started to drag and push something around; one of them suddenly appeared inside the tent and placed a large bag on the ground. He gave me a peculiar look before he withdrew. Henry Napoleon returned, rummaged inside the bag and fished out two cans. He opened them and put them on the ground next to the deckchair. The first one contained spicy Mexican beans and the second one something I hadn't eaten for years: chicken livers. "Here." My benefactor offered me a small metal spoon.

"It's not caviar," he said, "but it's American. And all of it kosher, in case you're Jewish."

I had no proper appetite, but the food was so tasty that I emptied both cans in no time at all; I even felt a little embarrassed by the speed with which I swallowed every spoonful. Henry Napoleon watched me with fatherly approval. "Good. And now some more of this, for digestion." He reached for the bottle of whiskey. "It doesn't matter if we finish the bottle; I have five more."

We chatted late into the evening. A few times he stepped out into the open to check if the fog was lifting, but every time he came back with a frown on his face. "Anyway," he said, "by tomorrow it'll be gone. You should be grateful; you'll have a good rest and get back on your feet, so you won't cause me too much trouble tomorrow.

I asked him where he was going, but he just shrugged and remained silent. Perhaps he didn't trust me. Perhaps he was a spy.

"And you?" He gave me a provocative smile.

I had nothing to hide. I said that Yogananda and I were waiting for the sun to melt the snow on the pass in order to cross it and descend into the valley on the other side. We were looking for a tantric lamasery; the old man, my guru, wanted to initiate me into the lesser known secrets of tantric yoga.

I got the feeling that my words put Henry Napoleon into a rather bad mood; he evaded my eyes and busied himself by cleaning the can opener. I asked him if he had heard of tantric yoga. Still he didn't say anything. Then he dropped the can opener into the leather bag, got to his feet and began to talk.

Was I really so vain as to assume I was the only Westerner interested in Tibetan Buddhism? For ten years he had been coming to these mountains, he had had gurus in India and Nepal, he had lived in Hindu ashrams and Buddhist lamaseries, he had studied at yoga centres in India and the US. At home, in New York, he has a library that contains more than two thousand books on all aspects of Eastern wisdom. He had tried everything, and still he came; not a year went by that he didn't come to Ladakh and Zanskar to collect data and impressions and sit at the feet of enlightened men. Still he didn't lose hope that one morning he will wake up "awake". Every year he would spend seven months in his pharmacy on East 23rd Street; then he would leave it in the hands of his assistant and fly off to the foothills of Tibet. He had started ten years ago. This time, however, he had a more practical aim: he had come to look for yeti, the Himalayan snowman.

In that case, I said, he was way off the mark; as far as I knew this creature had never been seen except in eastern Nepal.

He looked at me sharply. "Nonsense. How do you know? Anyway, I will take you across the pass, there are villages on the other side."

Abruptly, he turned and left the tent. It was evident that he could be quite touchy. I decided to be more cautious next time I talked to him. I didn't believe he was looking for the yeti. That he was looking for something was obvious. Why else would he have come to these mountains with a load for eight yaks, a tent for five people, and a gas heater that would look much more natural in a New York living room than it did on a snowy plain in the Himalayas?

19.

Crossing the glacier

The next morning, with only patches of fog left, the caravan set off. Heading the group was the old Tibetan with a grey-bluc hat (the "Anthony Quinn"); he led a pony loaded with Henry's binoculars, photo and film cameras and other expensive equipment. He was followed by Henry, who had tied his scarf round his head in the upright position, with the two ends sticking up like a couple of large rabbit ears. I followed behind, still feverish, and dreadfully cold, especially round the ears, until I, too, wrapped my scarf around my head in Henry's fashion. Following me was a line of loaded yaks and their drivers.

The ground, hidden beneath ten centimetres of crunchy snow, began to slope upward into a gentle incline. Ascending the mountain made me feel warm, and soon my frozen soul thawed as well and worrisome premonitions ebbed away, leaving room for hope and trust. These yak drivers, I thought, must have crossed this pass hundreds of times, and many other passes besides.

We slowly zigzagged our way up an ever steeper slope, looking for a path among a scattering of large blackish rocks. The valley was already deep below us, with the other end far away, yet clearly visible in spite of the clouds. A small reddish lamasery crouched on a hill under a massive mountain. And suddenly it came to me like a blow: Where is Yogananda now?

Our progress was very slow. Although we were already high above the valley, the saddle-like pass didn't seem any closer. There were no paths, so each of us followed the leader according to his judgement, with special care across snowdrifts, where the drivers walked in front of their yaks, testing every patch of ground under the snow with sharp sticks, and just as carefully among the gaps in the ground through which we could see eternal ice.

Half an hour into our climb, the clouds suddenly parted and the sun revealed the whole glory of the white mountain peaks, so magnificent in their silent solitude, yet so self-sufficient and un-lonely that something broke inside me and I began to cry: alone and lonely in the midst of the cold indifference of the universe.

Oh God, I caught myself sighing, oh God! The vast silent distances forced me to close my eyes. I felt as if I had been extended all the way to the horizon; as if the entire visible world had settled inside me: the cold shining skeleton of the mountains, with ice in my veins, immovable and eternal.

Then the fire which suddenly sprang from my heart melted the petrified world into a glowing porridge of swarming particles which began to revolve around me in concentric rings, faster and faster and faster, as if some centrifugal force were pushing them farther and farther away into the depths of the universe. A sound began to vibrate in the heart of my consciousness: ham-sa-ham-sa-ham-sa-ham-sa-ham-sa; in its rhythm the swirling ring of the world grew paler and paler and finally vanished. I ceased to exist in space and time, I was merely a vibration of energy, until hamsahamsa was reversed in my mind and became sahamsaham, and the vast ring of the world came swirling back from invisible infinity and began to revolve in the opposite direction, faster and faster and faster, approaching me like the walls of the sea after an earthquake, as if a centripetal force inside me were sucking the entire material creation into me, with the world sinking with a thundering noise ever deeper into the centre of my mind, and then disappearing through black holes in my consciousness into inaudible absence and finally into the silence of the Universe.

Suddenly a sharp light appeared above me. I noticed the shape of a strange monster with something resembling rabbit's ears sticking out of its head. I realised it was Henry Napoleon who had once again tied his scarf round his head.

"What's the matter with you?" he said, shaking me. "Don't pass out on me here, man."

With great effort I pulled myself up on my knees. "It's nothing," I said, "I just feel a little unwell. Everything will be all right." Heat was emanating from my body as if I were on fire.

"We're waiting for you," Henry said in a clear tone of reproach.

He was right. Heavily breathing yaks, standing among the patches of snow, were gazing with their moist eyes directly at me as if they too were reproaching me for slowing down the climb towards the top of the pass. Their drivers, leaning on sticks, stood in a group a little lower down, their silhouettes on the background of the sky reminding me of sinister vultures.

We carried on. Gradually the steep slope evened out into a jagged rocky plain, covered in a thin layer of frozen snow. Rising out of invisible depths behind the edge of the plain was a jagged ridge of white-blue mountain peaks, behind which I sensed a blue-white infinity of similar mountains, a granite sea of silence in which in his time (as the legend goes) vanished without a trace the venerable Lao Tzu, and also the saint Bodidharma who had brought Buddhism from India to China, and in which (it seemed to me) I, too, was going to vanish without a trace.

I could already feel myself sinking into a foggy ravine as dizziness returned. The events took on the quality of a silent movie in slow motion. Again I was lying on the ground, surrounded by the yaks and their drivers with their mocking eyes, and everything seemed as distant is if it weren't happening to me. Then for a long time nothing, only darkness and a dreamlike feeling of painful rocking.

When I came to, I found myself sitting against a large rock. The yaks, half-unloaded, foraged among the snow patches for rare tufts of grass. The drivers had stacked flat pieces of dry dung into a pile and made fire. Crouched nearby, Henry Napoleon was taking something from his bag of provisions.

Then he came to me and offered me a piece of pale yellow cheese on a toast. "Cheddar," he said. "You should've eaten something for breakfast. I'm not surprised you got sick playing at being a mountaineer on an empty stomach."

"Thank you," I whispered, moved by his generosity.

"Don't worry," he made a dismissive move with his hand. "That's what we're here for, aren't we, the Americans, to help developing countries with bank loans when they catch economic fever and become dizzy."

I didn't have enough strength to laugh, not even politely; I sank my teeth into the cheese.

After two bites, I felt my stomach revolt and rise. I stumbled behind the rock and began to throw up. Even after my stomach was completely empty, the cramping did not stop. Henry's words and the taste of cheese triggered a memory in my mind: a moment in my childhood when I was also leaning on my knees and hands, trying to clear my stomach of "Cheddar cheese, donated by the People of the United States of America" – cheese that I, with Mother ill and unable to bake bread, had hungrily stuffed into a large capsicum and wolfed down.

My eyes fell on the stiff fingers of my hands which I was pressing against the frozen ground. And it struck me: these are the hands I was leaning on in the orchard behind our house as a little boy! These are the hands of the child I was and of the old man I will be.

And the time in between, where is it? The time in which my life should have been fully realised, where has it gone to? And where is my life? What was (if it really was) my life? I'm still that child who, in desperate hunger, had stuffed himself full with foreign cheese. What I'm trying to throw up now are the ideas that disagree with my spiritual stomach. I am trying to throw up Yogananda. He is too heavy, too fatty for me. Mother Europe had fallen ill and couldn't make bread for me. But I was hungry, very hungry. Yogananda was my capsicum filled with cheese. He had stuffed me with a mass of ideas that my system couldn't absorb and turn into energy – perhaps because I didn't take enough trouble to chew them over. Oh God, I moaned silently to myself.

I was answered by a protracted thunderous sound which came from somewhere among the mountains and slowly drew away with a series of fading echoes.

"Avalanche," Henry explained. "Lots of snow this year." He pointed over the edge of the rocks. Deep below us, in a large mountain hollow, a blue lake was glistening in the sun's rays that had just penetrated the clouds. Reflected in its surface were the surrounding mountain peaks.

Suddenly the reflection became uneven, wavy, then it broke up and reintegrated into the face of an old bearded man. There was no doubt: grinning at me provocatively out of the lake was Yogananda. "Get lost," I shouted. He laughed, and his laughter reverberated among the mountains like a series of snow avalanches. I rose to my feet.

"Mistagog!" I shouted.

"Mista-gog-gog-gog…" The echo slowly withdrew, leaving room for his evil laughter. I was gripped by sudden fear that I had ruined my life. "Leave me alone, leave me, leave me, leave me alone!" I continued shouting to silence his laughter. "Leave me, you're not my friend!" I kept clutching at my hair as if trying to pull it out. "Damn you!"

In a surge of rage I ran towards the edge of the cliff, determined to jump on the laughing face of my guru and tear it to pieces.

Again it was as if watching a silent movie in slow motion. I could see the faces of the yak drivers looking at me with amazement and then disbelief and finally with fear. I could hear Henry shouting something, and then I could see the old Tibetan, the caravan leader, moving with long jumps across the snow to restrain me. I could see how his hat slid off his head in the speed of his first jump; and then a strong pair of hands grabbed me from behind and pulled me to the ground. And I could feel another needle being pushed into my buttocks.

The mad laugher below me withdrew.

20.

The song in the mountains

When I came to, the world seemed normal again. The surface of the lake was again reflecting the surrounding mountain peaks, the sky was clear; the sun was shining on my face.

A shadow appeared above me, blocking the sun's rays. "Have a sip." Henry was offering me a bottle of whiskey.

I was lying on the ground, a prisoner zipped up to my chin, arms and all, in a sleeping bag; I couldn't take the bottle even if I wanted to. Henry laughed.

"Let me out," I said. He waited another few minutes before freeing me. The yak drivers were resting in a group nearby. The ponies and yaks were being fed, one by one, by the old Tibetan. Henry, binoculars in his hand, was sitting on his folding stool next to me.

"And how does the wild man feel after his outburst?" he asked.

I carefully rose to the upright position. "Much better," I said, surprised that my head was suddenly clear. I reached for the bottle and took a few sips. Pleasant warmth soon began to circulate through my body. "A miracle," I said.

"And I'm responsible for it," Henry said. "At first I thought it was pneumonia, so I gave you penicillin. During the climb over the pass your strange behaviour made me think it might be typhoid fever, so you got a dose of chloramphenicol. But up here, when you started to rage like a madman, I knew at once: malaria! So I filled your behind with two massive doses of chloroquine."

"Malaria?" I laughed in disbelief. "Four thousand metres above the sea?"

Then I suddenly remembered. Four years earlier, in Africa, I had caught the deadly falciparum malaria, the only one that doesn't return if your survive it. But this dreaded disease masked the symptoms of the simultaneous infection with the far less dangerous plasmodium vivax, known as tertiary malaria, with attacks every third day. Unless you are a small child or a frail old man, it doesn't kill you, but the parasites hide in the liver and may, when your immunity drops, break out into the bloodstream again. It had happened before. And now, so it seemed, again.

"You slept for a while," Henry said, "then you suddenly leapt to your feet and started to exorcise the devil again. Don't you remember?"

"No," I said. "What devil?"

"Yogananda. You wanted to throw him up, pull him out of your stomach with your hand. That's good. That's natural. When a relationship like that reaches the critical point and there appears a danger of dependency, the guru must sever the umbilical cord. If he is good, he chooses the best possible moment."

"He wasn't good," I snapped. "He was bad, very bad!"

A teacher who can't or doesn't want to be consistent, is a dangerous teacher. If he uses his hands to guide you and his feet to trip you; if he laughs when you fall; if today he tells you something that completely invalidates what he told you yesterday; if he accuses you of mistaking the map for reality while everything he tells you remains an analogy; if he tells you to get rid of your mental constructions while his own "wisdom" reverberates with the echoes of Vedanta, Tibetan Buddhism, Taoism, Zen-Buddhism and even some half-modern scientism, then at some stage you can't avoid asking yourself: Who and what is this man? Where and how did he obtain his ideas? Who was his teacher?

"No, you can't," Henry agreed. "But what did you expect from him? Answers on a plate? A nicely backed theory?"

No, I said. What I did expect was a greater coherence of his ideas.

"That's your second mistake. Guru is not a teacher. Having a teacher is a lot easier. He imparts knowledge and thereby increases yours.

You have more data, more skills; you excel in academic debates, and make more money, perhaps. That is the role of the teacher. But the guru doesn't teach. He tries to wake you from your slumber, tries to open your eyes, wrestle you from the grasp of your fake identity. From the dream you call reality. The only way he can do that is by resorting to tricks and violence. You come to him for heaven, and he gives you hell. The teacher confirms what you are; he expands the knowledge you already possess. But the guru destroys. His task is to tear down the world of your false projections and force you to confront what you really are, what the world really is."

I said I can't forgive him for leaving me without advice on how to proceed.

"Why should he? That's your problem. He has torn you down like a house built by amateurs, he has given you material for a new one. It's up to you what to choose and what to reject. What do you expect from him? To reassemble you? Would you then still be a man? You would be a monster. Yogananda's Frankenstein."

"A ruin should reassemble itself?" I asked in complete disbelief. "Its own architect, it's own designer and builder? How?"

"But you know that," Henry said. "In your delusions you were thrusting your hands at me and saying: these are the hands of the child I was and the hands of the old man I will be. That's not true. All the cells in the body change every seven years. Not all at once, one after another. The body is changing all the time. So is the mind. From moment to moment. I'm not the Henry you met in the valley below. You, too, are different. We are all part of the flow. This is the answer to your question about how to proceed. Yogananda has crashed into you the way an avalanche crashes into a river. The current is strong, piece after piece will be pushed along the bed and taken away. Finally everything that has crashed into the river will become part of its flow. In the same way, gradually, you will discover meaning in everything Yogananda has told you – for some things tomorrow, for others years later. And for some, maybe, never."

An unusual sound floated towards us through the barely discernible breeze. At first I thought that I was imagining it, but Henry also rose to his feet. The drivers stopped chatting and turned their heads.

Below us, in the silent solitude of the lake, a gentle girl's voice sang a melancholy song, rising above the accompaniment of indeterminate Himalayan instruments, strings, flutes and drums, rising and falling, sinking back into silence and returning. As if turned to stone we stared into the depths, holding our breaths. A siren, I thought. Block your ears, Odysseus, tie yourself to the mast!

I looked at Henry. In rapture, his Jewish face seemed strangely beautiful, solemnly melancholy, in harmony with the tone of the song. For the first time since we had met, he seemed astonishingly human. I looked at the drivers; in the outlines of their tousled heads, in the tension of their half-turned torsos, in the arms frozen in mid-gesture I read an anxiety that was no less stifling than mine. They felt it too, I thought – each in his way transitory, each silently hopeful that the ebbing would cease and the high tide return, each looking for the illusion of certainty that the present is more than it seems; that we are more than just transient pieces. The song stripped us of the protective layer of warmth and deceptive hope. And we were skeletons, on the path from dust to dust.

The only everlasting thing is transience, the endless waves of dust and rock beyond the nearest peaks. Mountains also pass away, more slowly than we do, but no less irrevocably. They, too, get old and disintegrate through endless freezing and thawing, endless cracking and crumbling, endless erosion. On their slopes, even the south side, there is increasingly less forest, less soil, less growth, fewer people, ever more dust and silence.

Beyond the horizon, in Tibet, are isolated, abandoned, crumbling towns. Old civilisations have disappeared, often without trace. The source of life on earth, the sun's furnace, a balanced nuclear explosion, is weakening and burning out. In a million years it will collapse and be extinguished. Space itself also rises and falls.

Why then be afraid of what is, of all there is, of what there can only be? Why this quenchless thirst for false certainties that the journey from dust to dust will stop at convenient points or begin to repeat itself or at least end with a meaning greater than the bare fact that it has happened? We love a little, laugh, hurt a little, then we expire.

When the song finished, we hung our heads and looked for things to do. And when we finally headed towards the valley, the commands sounded restrained, almost apologetic: the yaks will also collapse and return to dust.

From the hollow below the pass there rose a gentle incline. On it we saw scattered greyish brown houses like molehills. There led up to them rows of battered, red and white painted chortens already abandoned by the sun, and in the deep shadow they resembled crested pigeons. It seemed that on this side of the pass no snow had fallen. When we came a little closer I saw that on the lower slopes there were fenced, terraced gardens. In the early evening silence, the settlement gave the impression that it contained no living soul.

From the first house, a dog on a long chain barked wildly and hurled itself in our direction. Saliva sprayed from its bared teeth as it growled. An old Tibetan threatened it with a stick; the dog snapped at it, ripping it from his grasp. The other drivers ran up, waving wildly and shouting, forcing the attacker to retreat.

From the roof, the owner of the house watched sullenly. It never occurred to him to calm the growling beast; he looked at us with suspicion, almost hostility. When the old Tibetan called to him he turned his back and vanished.

A little further on, the caravan halted. Henry Napoleon waited for me to approach.

"Friend," he said, patronisingly putting his arm around my shoulder. "I'm glad we met. It was interesting. Sadly, we must part here."

My gaze flew across the unfriendly houses where shadows were already thickening into dusk, and towards the gloomy ravine, becoming lost beneath the overhangs. I was overcome by an urge to throw myself on the ground and beg him not to leave me alone in this sinister place, utterly exhausted, without food, without a guide; to at least take me with him to the first road, to a bigger village.

"The best thing is to spend the night in one of these houses," he said, "then in the morning offer one of the indolent natives a modest sum to lead you to somewhere more civilised."

"And you?" I said with difficulty.

“I have my own path to follow,” he replied drily. “But I’ll leave you some food so you don’t starve.”

He began to rummage through a bag on a yak’s back. He pulled out a tin of beans and a packet of rusks.

“Thanks,” I said, with bad grace – I had expected something more from him. I thought that with this small gesture he was also trying to ease his conscience for abandoning me.

“Good luck,” he said, giving me a quick hug and pat on the back. “Keep on searching and – Om Mani Padme Hum.”

He turned and said something to the drivers; two rushed up to one of the yaks and took my rucksack, tent and sleeping bag from its back. I stood and stared at the departing caravan until it disappeared round the bend and everything fell silent except for the pulse in my throat.

21.

Little Dolma

I threw my rucksack on my back and went up the slope. My knees were trembling from terrible fatigue, but the burning willpower in my soul dragged my body behind it.

At the first house a mastiff attacked me. Fortunately, its chain stopped it two metres in front of me, where it thrashed around and went wild like a mountain demon; ggggrraarrr ggggrraarr resounded his fury through the twilight.

Soon more barking started up from the other houses, even the most distant; the valley beneath the pass echoed with the infernal noise of canine indignation. On the other side of the pass I had often seen Tibetan mastiffs, massive hairy creatures with fangs that could frighten even a snow leopard, but the creatures on this side were almost unearthly in their bloodthirstiness.

I circled the house and followed the stone wall to the next. There, too, I was greeted by a hoarse ggggrraarrr, accompanied by the whimpering of puppies. I thought it would be better to return to the foot of the mountain, find a suitable pitch for my tent and spend the night in my sleeping bag.

Then I heard a sharp call and the dog in front of the house obediently fell silent.

A man with a strange head covering stood on the roof, staring at me. It seemed unlikely that he would speak English, so I just stood and waited to see what he would do. He stared back, waiting for me to say or do something. In the end, I awkwardly waved in greeting.

The door opened and from within shone a pale light. In the frame of the doorway appeared a silhouette of a woman in a long skirt. A little boy, rushing past her, ran towards the dog, lifted the chain and fastened it more shortly to a nail in the wall. The woman moved back from the threshold and invited me into the house. As I passed her, I was surprised that her features were more Indian than Tibetan. She wore a nose ring and massive jewel-encrusted earrings. She was amazingly beautiful.

The boy lead me through the entrance and up a ladder to the next level. The spacious room was lit by the restless flicker of butter lamps. A grey-haired old crone, eagerly stirring a glowing copper pot, sat before the fire. The heat stunned me so much that I almost threw myself on the floor; I took off my rucksack and leant it against the wall while a yellowish mist floated before my eyes.

When the mist cleared, I found a smiling girl with slanting eyes before me, offering a dish of steaming liquid. “Solcha,” I said gratefully, taking the tea from her.

Leaning against the wall, I sank into a sitting position and began to sip. My eyes searched the room through the steam. On the floor there were mattresses covered with woollen rugs. On one sat the beautiful woman with the earrings and the man I had seen on the roof. What I had taken in the dark to be an unusual head covering was in reality a bushy nest of plaited hair. On the other mattress sat three girls, two with necklaces of red coral, one with a small jewel in her left nostril. None of them were more than thirteen years old.

Their dark eyes were turned towards me without embarrassment. The old woman by the fire half-turned to take a better look at me. The man rolled a cigarette with long, thin fingers, never once taking his eyes off me.

I shuddered at the thought that in this house, in this village guarded by mastiffs, something was not quite right. In the stupefying heat I started to be overcome by extreme tiredness and realised I could not resist it; I’ll sleep right here, I thought, right here, by the wall. My eyelids started to droop. The few times I forced them open, I saw all their motionless eyes still fixed on me.

Then I sank. Once more I was cast into a half-sleep. I felt a touch; one of the girls was removing my boots. Two of them were trying to remove my jacket. One of them took my hand and pointed to the nearest mattress. I crawled towards it on all fours and rolled over onto the rough rug. Before I finally fell asleep I saw that the girls had returned to their places and were watching as motionlessly as before.

After three or four hours I was woken by strange noises. The room was lit by a single butter lamp. The girls were asleep by the opposite wall. On the mattress in the middle of the room I saw a scene that almost made my heart stop beating. In the flickering light, the beauty with the jewels and the man with the bird's nest of uncombed hair were entwined in an erotic embrace. In a yoga-like pose with their nine limbs, idyllically slim and tanned, they rhythmically swayed in time with his measured thrusts. In front of the mattress kneeled the toothless crone, burning sweet incense in a copper bowl and chanting a monotonous mantra.

The lovers stopped for a moment, slightly untangled themselves, changed position and continued. The woman turned her head to me. She stared at me, eyes wide; she saw that I was awake, watching. From the depths of her eyes there blazed an ecstasy that filled me with an untameable, pounding strength; for a long time I could hear only my restless heart, beating almost in rhythm with the thrusts of their love, *bum, bum, bum*. Then my head began to spin, I was falling into those eyes that were sucking me in, falling into the silence of space and unconsciousness.

When I was woken by the barking of the grumpy mastiff, the sun was streaming through the shutter. In the merciless light, the room that seemed romantic and mysterious in the glow of the butter lamp, was shabby, dirty and dusty. The mattress on which the lovers had carried out their ritual exercises was leaning against the wall; someone's head covering was airing on the window sill. From the fireplace, where the old woman was once more stirring the pot, came the mixed odours of pigswill, while from the mattress in the corner there wafted a smell of piss. And on me things were crawling: my trousers, my hair, my armpits swarmed with flea-like creatures.

I went over to the window. The houses looked less intimidating than in yesterday's dusk. The pitted walls, the naked sandy earth among the gardens, the low trees and the monotonous colours exhaled the mountain poverty to which I was accustomed. Here too there was no room for aesthetics or other kinds of luxury; here too life had to be torn out daily from the cruel earth. At the foot of the slope I saw a few reddish green patches. What grew there? The valley floor was ruptured by the steep greenish grey wall of the mountain on which, two hundred metres up, were carved the Tibetan prayer letters "Om Mani Padme Hum". Below them grazed a scattered herd of yaks.

I leaned out of the window to look at the pass over which we had come. Instead of the pass I saw the man with the nest of hair, sorting twigs and clumsily tying them in bunches in the courtyard. He was helped by the woman with the earrings. Wrapped in a sheepskin coat and with her head covered, she did not appear beautiful. It seemed impossible that the highland peasants impassively preparing stores of firewood for the winter could have anything in common with the pair of naked lovers that had last night, in the glow of the butter lamp, demonstrated almost the whole repertoire of the Kama Sutra.

Around the chortens on the nearby hillside two urchins chased a bleating goat. Everything is still the same, I thought. I'm still in Zanskar. The only difference is that I have no intermediary, no Yogananda. That was why the world seemed so strange, so present.

I heard someone coming. Embarrassed, I hopped back to the bed and pretended to be asleep. An unkempt girl with a cheerful face climbed up the ladder, holding a small basket of peas in one hand. When she saw me, she opened her mouth and emitted an astonished "Eh?"

She stared for a while and then came up to me and touched my left ear. Then she tugged my beard. Finally, she took hold of my nose and gave it a good pinch. She laughed and said something in a language I did not understand, probably: "Hell, you're not a ghost."

Or something like that. Bravely and curiously, she stared straight into my eyes, as if waiting for me to say something. She laughed. She was different from the others.

“And you’re pretty,” I said to her in my own language. She responded immediately in a rippling voice. Becoming more serious, she narrowed her eyes and looked carefully at my rucksack. She pointed towards it and said something that sounded like a question.

“You want to know what’s in it?”

She shrugged, then nodded.

I unzipped it and pulled out Henry’s tin of beans, then the rusks. She cast her eyes over them, then came a flash of anger, she even blushed, a torrent of words fell from her lips, it seemed she was rebuking me, that she was telling me something. She put down her basket, grabbed the tin and packet from my hands and shoved both back into the rucksack. Then she rushed over to the fireplace with her peas, put them down and started rummaging among the pans and dishes.

The old crone bristled and started to scold her in a shrill voice. The cute little weasel suddenly turned to face her, put her tongue out and blew a raspberry.

The old woman fell silent and turned her back on her. The girl grabbed a splint from the fire and lit the incense in a copper bowl, then she rushed over and placed it in front of me, rushed back to the fireplace and returned with the basket of peas, rushed back once more, found a wooden dish, reached into a pot, scooped something up and brought me some steaming porridge. Then she kneeled in front of me and with a solemn gesture bade me to eat my breakfast.

“Thank you,” I said and reached for the porridge. I sniffed it and it smelled almost pleasant. I licked and slurped and the porridge ran into my beard, while the girl watched me with a satisfied grin, full of herself for appropriating such a hairy toy. “What is your name?” Pointing to my self, I said, “Evald.”

Her eyes lit up. She repeated my gesture and cried out, “Dolma!”

The old woman got up onto her knees and once more started to scold her. Dolma turned to her and once more put out her tongue and blew a raspberry. Once again the old woman fell silent. When Dolma saw that I admired her skilful tongue, she laughed out loud. She then watched me eat with the eyes of a faithful dog.

How old was she? Thirteen?

When I'd had enough I smacked my lips and rubbed my stomach. Then I said I would like to wash; I raised my arm, sniffed my armpit and grimaced. "Phew!"

She laughed. Jumping to her feet, she grabbed my hand and began to drag me towards the doorway. "Wait, wait," I said. I put on my boots, then took soap, a towel, trousers, a shirt and socks from my rucksack.

She led me to the ladder and down into the courtyard. The mastiff rushed towards me growling, but in a flash Dolma swung round and hushed him with the same trick of the tongue she had used on the old woman. The shaggy beast obediently put his tail between his legs and slunk round the corner.

The courtyard was empty. She took my hand and led me along a wall, behind which were some crooked trees. She hurried me along the path of beaten earth by the neighbour's house and past two chortens up the steep slope, where a stream rushed from the heights, pouring across a rock shelf like a waterfall.

First, I thought that I would strip to the waist, but then thought this is stupid, the waterfall will wet everything. Why should I be embarrassed in front of this child of nature, I thought as I undressed. I wondered whether she would be embarrassed. She was not. When I stepped under the freezing shower and started to gasp and shout, she jumped about excitedly, encouraging me. I did not stay long. I quickly soaped, splashed and scrubbed myself, then jumped onto dry land and started to rub myself vigorously with my towel.

"Phuuuh," I breathed. "Phuuuh."

"Phuuuh," Dolma repeated. "Phuuuh."

As I put down the towel and reached for my trousers, my eyes strayed to the top of the slope.

My heart stopped. A cliff stretched high above me towards the sky and on it – half cut out of the rock, half built – were the white buildings of a dreamlike lamasery. Carved into the rock face above it was a left-facing swastika.

22.

The master of the diamond vehicle

Behind the first chorten the path wound its way through a passage between the rocks to which two fierce-looking mastiffs were chained. One was howling from the right, the other from the left; both could have ripped me apart. But Dolma put out her tongue and blew a raspberry, first at one, then the other. The creatures obediently withdrew to a safe distance.

We stopped at the highest chorten. The cliff grew out of the ground and rose vertically towards the sky. A gigantic cave yawned inside; whitewashed buildings sprouted from the darkness and poured on terraces across the rocks.

Dolma took my hand. In her touch I felt a need for human contact, as if the magnificent lamasery awoke in her a feeling of vulnerability and transience.

Then my heart was pierced by both heat and ice. From one of the roofs or balconies high above, came the sound of strings, joined by a flute, then the beat of drums. The voice I had heard with Henry and the drivers on the path across the mountain pass rose above the music. A gentle girl's voice trembled above the accompanying instruments, rising and falling, succumbing to the wind, withdrawing, returning, becoming lost in the valley. *The siren*, I thought.

At once I understood it all: the dogs guarding the houses and path to the lamasery, the mistrust of the people, the ritual act in the glow of the butter lamp and the presence of so many girls.

This was no ordinary settlement.

The feeling strengthened when we turned towards the entrance to the lamasery and ran into a group of villagers coming down the slope with empty dishes and baskets. Dolma took my hand and pouted. When they saw that she was taking me to the lamasery they, the men in particular, began to scold her while the women shook their heads in disbelief at her effrontery. The general anger intensified into outrage and words began to rain down on poor Dolma like stones. The moment I decided to drag her back down the path and save her from her tortuous dilemma, she suddenly thrust her head forward and screamed so loud that the stunned men and women were thrown backwards. Now she was the one railing against them and protesting. She did it with so much zeal that she was trembling; I got the feeling that she would leap at them in turn and scratch out their eyes. First the women withdrew, then the men.

She dragged me behind her. When we had already passed them she put out her tongue and blew one of her insulting raspberries. For a moment they were all struck dumb. Then one by one they turned, muttering indignantly as they hurried down the path. Dolma gave a deep sigh, looked at me and burst into peals of laughter, almost as if to say: "Well, that was easier than I thought."

In the courtyard of the first building we were stopped by a young monk in a russet-coloured robe. He was clearly thrown by my presence. He looked at me suspiciously and then finally turned to Dolma, asking for an explanation. From her tone, I judged that she was spinning him a yarn and showing surprise that he dared to interrogate her. I do not know how she succeeded, but after a few moments the monk who apologised, saying he had not meant anything by it. She punched him playfully in the stomach.

We began to climb towards the heart of the lamasery. We climbed ladders, stairs, felt our way through gloomy vaults, rose from one roof to the next, ever nearer to the buildings that crouched in the gloom. I was getting more and more short of breath, even as I grew more and more amazed and astonished.

The monastery was so big it reminded me of a medieval town. It seemed to go from one level to another in line with different activities. At the bottom, there was laundry drying. I heard hammering and, when I peered through a door, saw a blacksmith, beating a white hot piece of metal. A little higher were storerooms for firewood and food, above them kitchens. There was no shortage of mastiffs, but they were different from those down below: lazy, yawning, nonchalant. There were only a few monks in the lower areas; I saw mainly women in long skirts and men in costumes as ethnically varied as in the village.

And I saw girls. Girls with earrings and colourful necklaces, peeking out from doorways, moving about inside windows, sitting in corners, acting bored, playing with their hair or dozing: like temple servants enjoying a moment of idleness. Their eyes, soft and catlike, some melancholy, others lazily seductive, accompanied me. I was greatly disturbed by their hands which, in contrast, were the hands of grown women. Their faces also radiated maturity, almost to the point of weariness and premature ageing. No naivety or youthful cheerfulness, just experienced, watchful, slightly amused eyes. And here and there a creased forehead.

Towards the top, there were more monks in russet robes, more rooms with *thangkas* on the wall, more statues of Buddha in different poses as well as statues of assorted gods and monsters. Some walls were covered with vivid mandalas. On one of the terraced roofs, a circle twelve monks sat reciting holy texts which reminded me of a Gregorian chant.

Then we came into the damp shade and I saw the roof of the cave arching above us. Bats were squeaking in its gloomy depths. On the terraced roofs, greyish white doves sat or strutted. A small stream meandered from the depths of the cave and disappeared into a hole in the rocks. Dolma bent down, scooped up some water and bathed her burning face. Then she scooped up some more and drank. She repeated the motion and held out her hands towards me: I drank from them. Her small, dirty hands touched my heart.

We climbed up to a room where a very old monk sat meditating before a statue of Buddha. We tiptoed past him and were already at the door when a shout rang out and we froze. When we turned, the monk has opened his eyes and was looking at us in a strict, fatherly way. Dolma started to introduce me and explain something. She spoke with respect. The old monk shook his head and bowed to continue his meditation.

I heard Dolma take a deep breath and feared that she would kick up a fuss and start screaming. I doubted she would get her way like that with the old man. Luckily, she knew this herself. Once more she patiently made a request, then she rushed over to the monk, grabbed his hand and kissed it three times. At first sight this did not seem to move him, but suddenly he smiled, pinched her cheek, got to his feet and went into the next room.

She grinned at me triumphantly. Although I had no idea what awaited us beyond the door, I could not help but admire her persistence.

When the old man returned, she turned to him looking concerned. He spoke briefly. Her features suddenly radiated relief and happiness. Then she was serious again and went towards the door, indicating that I should follow her.

The room was full of heady incense. On the opposite wall, an altar was illuminated by the sun shining through a loophole. In front of it, on a red cushion, a man sat in the lotus position with his head bowed. He was dressed in a white silk robe. He was wearing four round black pendant earrings and three necklaces – red, white and black. In front of him stood a small, low table on which a diamond-studded sceptre or *vajra*, a symbol of spiritual power in Tibetan Buddhism, lay beside a copper bell and a vase of mountain flowers.

Dolma fell on her knees before him and prostrated herself three times. She softly and respectfully made her request and plea. Then, hanging her head, she waited.

From beneath the robe a beringed hand reached out, picked up the bell and shook it. An old monk appeared, took me by the elbow and led me from the room. Through a side door he led me on to a sunny terraced roof. He said something; I understood I was to wait there.

I went over to the edge and looked down at the roof below.

Nearby I sensed more than saw a familiar figure: a tall man in black wool trousers, in high mountain boots and a mass of untidy hair. He slowly turned.

"Hello, Henry Napoleon Alexander," I said.

He could hardly believe his eyes. "What the hell are you doing here?"

"What about you?" I responded in kind. "Looking for the yeti?"

"Why didn't you tell me you were coming here?" he asked accusingly.

"I didn't know I was," I replied. "You did, so why didn't you tell me?"

He walked up and down the roof with his hands in his pockets. I could see him biting his lips. He looked at me out of the corner of his eye and asked, "How much did you pay?"

I told him not a penny.

"I transported a ton of food," he said. "I gave them a thousand dollars in cash. I brought filming equipment, which they seized and will probably sell in India for another thousand. And you think the Master will receive you just like that, without anything?"

I was going to reply that I didn't care whether he received me or not as I had no intention of staying.

At that moment, the old monk called from the doorway. I followed him back into the incense-heavy room. Dolma had gone; the Master, who represented the lamasery, sat amidst the incense smoke. With a barely perceptible movement of his eyes, he bade the monk leave and then stared into my eyes.

"Sit down," he said in a melodically-accented English. I obeyed. He looked at me penetratingly for some time. I did not avert my eyes, I wanted to give the impression that I was not afraid of him. Then he said: "Welcome to the Temple of the Diamond Carriage."

I said thank you. "Unfortunately, I have used up most of my resources and only have enough to pay for my return home. I cannot repay you for this privilege."

"It is not a privilege," he said. "Nor is there any need for any payment. At least, not in the way you mean."

"How, then?"

"Do something for Dolma. She chose you and requested a place for you."

"What about the people down in the village?" I asked. "They were not very enthusiastic about my arrival."

"You are like the Australian who was with us a year ago. Tantra drove him crazy and we had no choice but to leave him to the wolves. I wouldn't want that to happen again."

He smiled and looked at me: with no curiosity, with no intolerance, with no desire to convince me of anything.

After reflecting, I said, "I have experienced things that have disturbed me terribly. Although I'm extremely interested in tantra I am uncertain as to my real motives. It would be smarter to leave and return some other time."

He watched me for nearly five minutes in silence. The incense tickled my nose and slowly intoxicated me.

"Dolma has chosen you," he said. "If I had turned down her request, her energy would have become destructive. So I consented." He was silent a moment. "And so I cannot permit you to leave."

Only when I rose and said that I would go back to the village for my rucksack did I begin to understand he was not joking.

"Why all that effort?" he said. "I'll send one of the young monks."

"No," I replied, "I'll go myself."

I only got as far as the door; a strange force paralysed my legs. I wanted to move forward, I had the will to do so, but my body no longer obeyed me. It was as if I had strayed into a field of invisible energy. I turned my head and through the haze of incense it seemed as if the Master's eyes were flashing. The next moment he looked as dignified and friendly as before; the feeling that I was gripped by a force field passed. But as soon as I tried to leave, it returned, and this time I felt it even more distinctly.

I was so horrified that I had trouble staying upright.

"I'll send one of the young monks," repeated the Master.

Then the panic turned into resignation, that I would be able to leave this place only at the discretion of the Master of the Diamond Carriage.

Tomorrow, if that was what he wished, or never.

Very well! I gave in. Let him do what he wants with me. It was incredible, but the feeling of submission brought a sense of freedom; without difficulty I wandered into the entrance room and from there onto the wide terrace where greyish white doves were walking. With the sudden sense of relief, I was again gripped by a desire to leave, but after only one step the mysterious force fettered me as irrevocably as before.

When I told myself I would look for Henry or for Dolma, there was no obstacle – I could move. But as soon as I thought about leaving the lamasery, my body became paralysed.

What was this force?

A number of times I tried to trick it: I would tell myself that I was going to look for Henry, then started to head out. But as soon as my real intention reached my consciousness, my legs froze. I tried everything. I said to myself, "I'm going to the foot of the mountain to take another look at the lamasery from the front." And I tried to believe this. But it was as if someone had promised me immortality if in the next minute I did not think of a white horse.

The Master had hypnotised me; I could not find a more plausible explanation. At first it seemed highly improbable, stupid, silly. It seemed impossible that, with my own will, I could resist my own will. I would tell myself that I was leaving, that I felt the will, the determination within me, but I could not move.

I was overcome by a desire to return to the Master and beg him to remove this psychological padlock, in return I would promise not to leave. But I could not do this either. As soon as I thought about going to the Master with this intention, my legs were paralysed. I was unable to leave, I was unable to return to him until he called me himself; he had killed two birds with one stone and then pushed the whole thing from his thoughts.

This Master was no fake.

I felt relief. In being dependent on a will that was unquestionably greater than mine, I sensed a freedom that was comfortably framed. The reduced possibilities meant I no longer had to decide about basic things. From a sense of being lost, in which everything was open, everything dependent on me, everything freely composed of unknown wilderness and mysterious people around me, I had moved into a world of rules, customs and indisputable authority.

23.

The girl with a knife

I was tempted to talk to Henry about what had happened. It quickly became clear that the Master was the only one in the lamasery who understood English. I asked above, I asked below, I peered through every door, I described Henry with gestures and words, but everywhere I encountered only shrugs, stares and mockery. Once at the bottom of the lamasery, I figured he had returned to the village and headed for the way out.

I took only three steps before getting fettered by an invisible force field.

I slowly made my back up towards the top. From shady corners among the buildings, from thresholds, from behind shutters the monastery girls observed me. They followed me with half-closed eyes like those of a wild cat observing visitors at the zoo. What did the novice monks do with them? Were they servants of evil, temple prostitutes, or attendants in tantric rituals?

Returning to edge of the roof outside the Master's house, I took off my jacket, rolled it up and shoved it under my head before lying in the sun. Thus I dozed off.

I was woken by an out-of-breath, smiling young monk who had brought my rucksack, tent and sleeping bag up from the village. I followed him across the terrace and into the cave. He led me alongside the stream towards the buildings that disappeared into its jaws. Turning left, we went through a narrow tunnel and came to the underground rooms excavated out of the cliff. They were divided into individual cells with low ceilings and small windows. The entrances were low arches without doors.

The monk stopped in front of one of the cells. I bent over and crawled into the square little space in which there was nothing apart from a bare mattress on the stone floor. The monk pushed the rucksack after me, bowed and waved goodbye.

My home, I thought.

I pushed open the shutter and the magnificent mountain on the other side of the valley shone before me. The window sill was covered with a thick layer of bird droppings.

At least, I won't be completely alone.

I unrolled my sleeping bag, placed it on the mattress and sat on it. Dampness breathed from the stone wall. With the window facing east, the shade in my cell indicated it was one o'clock. Let it be. I closed my eyes and leaned against the wall.

About an hour later my little weasel came laughing though the entrance arch.

"Dolma," I cried.

I was bathed in grateful warmth; she had not forgotten about me, the cheeky little devil who had done everything in her power to get me into the lamasery and ensure that I stayed there.

When she squatted in front of me and looked me over with ownerly pride, my heart was chilled by the thought that perhaps her enthusiasm concealed some far from innocent intention.

"It's not that you're in love with me," I teased her.

She laughed and babbled something in Tibetan. That was how we conversed – without having the slightest idea what the other was saying.

"It seems to me that you're a bit too young for such things," I said, and she went, "Bru-bra-ngrye-nagrroum-lung-chem-nagryong-pru-grrien-tong-bang-beng."

"You have caught me," I said. "What do you intend to do with me?"

She said something in reply.

"It's a comfort that these are only the winter holidays, a break before returning to the world I know and have even begun to miss."

She nodded and laughed and babbled animatedly.

"I'd like to teach you my language," I said. "You're a cutey."

She looked at me with surprise for a while. Then she said, "Cooty." My laugh delighted her. She leapt up and jumped around the cell, repeating: "Cooty, cooty!"

And then, as if suddenly struck by something, she narrowed her eyes and started to berate me in her mother tongue. We went over to the rucksack, reached into it and began to take my things out. She discovered my dirty socks, raised them to her nose, rolled her eyes towards the ceiling and grimaced. "Phew."

She carried on until she reached the bottom. Each time she discovered some dirty clothing she "phewed" and "ughed" as if she had never smelled the like before. She collected quite a pile, as almost everything I had with me was dirty.

She gathered my clothes into her arms, winked at me and left. A little later I found her at the stream. She was enthusiastically soaping my shirt, socks and underpants, wringing them, rinsing them and banging them against the stones like an experienced washerwoman; some items she had already laid out in the sun.

"Dolma," I called to her. She was taken aback when she realised I was surreptitiously watching her, blushed angrily and chided me, her meaning unmistakably clear: How dare you! I blew her a kiss and in reply she stuck out her tongue and blew a raspberry.

Then she laughed, as if to say she didn't really mean it.

I went across the terrace to the Master's house. The old monk glanced at me curiously, but did not stop me. The Master was still sitting on the red cushion, half-concealed by clouds of incense. The altar behind him was in shadows, the sun had moved to the small table where it was reflected in thousands of sparkles from the diamond sceptre.

He raised his eyes, which were warm but without any recognisable feeling, and they shone at me.

"I can't find my friend," I said. "The American, who arrived yesterday evening." He continued observing me and didn't reply. "In which part of the lamasery can I find him?"

"I don't know," he said.

"Why did Dolma ask for a place for me?" I asked suddenly. "What do you expect of me?"

"I don't know," he responded.

We sat in silence, looking at each other. He was interested to see whether I had any other question and I wondered whether his behaviour was intended to make me start shouting and breaking things.

"I'd like to know what you expect of me," I repeated. "I'd like to know the rules, so I know how to behave. What do you expect of me?"

"Nothing," he replied, looking at me with surprise.

I got up and opened my mouth to ask why he would not let me leave, but before I could say a word my mouth went numb. The Master looked at me and smiled encouragingly. Dizzily, I staggered outside and spent five minutes on the terrace taking deep breaths.

Later, Dolma came to my cell, bearing a dish of rice and vegetable stew in which – miracle of miracles! – swam a piece of meat. I hadn't eaten meat and rice for such a long time that I wolfed everything down. Dolma squatted in front of me and imitated my slurping.

She took away the dish but did not return. I stared through the window towards the mountains, where the sun was giving way to the evening shadows. The night will be cold, I thought. Extremely cold. A dove fluttered onto the window sill. It stepped lightly here and there, lowering its head and looking at me with surprise. It shat, looked at me once more as if to say that's for you, then it flew off.

Through the underground passageways there swam towards me muffled sounds from the distance: choral singing, drumming, ringing, reciting. Then all was silence. A biting wind began to blow across the valley floor. I closed the shutter and wrapped myself in my sleeping bag. I felt so bad inside that I felt like crying.

Then do it, I thought. No-one can see you. And it burst over me. I sobbed until the sleeping bag was wet through. And then I slept.

When I awoke the moon was shining through gaps in the shutter. I realised someone had covered me with a thick blanket. Underneath it, snuggled against me and with her thumb in her mouth, there was little Dolma. She was breathing as calmly as if she lay beside her father.

A feeling overcame me. Gratitude that I was no longer alone? Happiness arising from the warmth of our friendship? Disturbance that I was lying under a blanket with a thirteen-year-old girl? I only knew for certain that there was nothing sexual in my feelings. And yet she would only need to be three years older.

Poor Dolma. Poor me. Neither of us knew what awaited us. Safe in the warmth of our bodies we knew only the sense of relief and trust of two people who had found each other, created a space that belonged only to them and become allies.

I hugged her and returned into the inviting depths of sleep.

And onwards into the realm of dreams.

They were vivid like never before. Everything that I had been through poured into me like water through a funnel, coming from all sides, mixing together and thickening and flowing though me into the dark of unconsciousness: wandering with Yogananda, climbing rock faces, walking across hanging bridges, snow, freezing in the tent, Yogananda's face, his eyes, his scolding, the radiant mountain; it all flowed through me like the simultaneous projection of hundreds of films.

It was as if I were revisiting memories, clearing the decks, so that I could deal with everything new without old baggage. The images faded as soon as I was done reliving them, only then did I discover breaks among them through which I managed to slip back to wakefulness.

The sun shone through the loophole. It was already ten, but there was no sign of Dolma.

I did not see her all day. The sun stayed with me until evening, accompanying me as I mooched about the lamasery, adapting to its daily rhythm. After a breakfast of tsampa offered to me by the friendly old toothless ladies in the kitchen, I was joined by a red-cheeked boy monk by the name of Dorje who – miracle of miracles – "knew" English. He knew about twenty words.

That does not mean that we understood each other at all, for when I asked him where Dolma was he replied, "Up there below the birds." He was thinking of the doves. And when I asked where the girls who were sitting around the lamasery yesterday had disappeared to, he laughed as if I had said something awfully funny. Then he adopted a meaningful expression, leaned towards me and whispered, as if giving away a state secret: "In the evening on the other side."

I lost hope that we would become embroiled in a sparkling debate on tantric yoga. He had probably learned a handful of words from the odd guest or two without knowing what they meant and he always responded to my questions with whatever came into his head first. In spite of this I tried again. I said that there was a tall dark-haired American called Henry Napoleon Alexander in the monastery. I described him in great detail and asked Dorje if he could he take me to him.

"Yes, yes," he nodded enthusiastically, "in the evening on the other side." And he looked at me as if waiting for me to commend him.

He dogged my heels the whole day. I tried to get away from him a number of times, sneaking round the corner, slipping out of some room through a side door, hiding behind a chorten when he looked the other way for a moment. But every time I bumped into him around the next corner. I decided not to let it bother me any more.

I was captivated by the brilliant sunshine. Everything the sun's rays touched shone, not with surface light, but with a radiance that came from within; as if the material world was a mirror in which the sun was reflected.

I was intoxicated with the wealth of colour. The greyish white pillars of the chortens on which fluttered red, green and yellow prayer flags, restless tongues of colour against the backdrop of the decorative cliff walls and the white blue sky; the russet robes of the monks on carved wooden balconies; squares and circles of light in the shrines and meeting halls where the sun broke through an open window; flickering yellowish red butter lamps in dark corners, to which the contrast with the sunlight gave an unearthly feel; the dignified faces of hundreds of Buddha statues in meditative poses on illuminated walls, surrounded by red, yellow and green aureoles; twelve-coloured mandalas among which shone silk-bound holy books, some turbidly in the light of butter lamps, some vividly in the sunlight; the hazy glow of copper kettles in the kitchen when the sun broke through the smoke rising from the fire and through the steam rising from the kettles; the greyish white plumage of the doves dozing on the roofs; the stunning colourfulness of the tapestries in the rooms smelling of heady incense; the tapestries showing horrendous pictures from the *Tibetan Book of the Dead*; and the sounds of prayer and incantation echoing from meeting halls; all this filled me with an indescribable gratitude to fate, which had brought me to this place, and apprehension at the thought that I would leave it as a different person.

After a lunch of rice and peas, Dorje Blockhead led me into the dark interior of the cave, from which the stream flowed and through an unlit tunnel into a stuffy corridor that led deep into the cliff. The first hundred metres were so dark that I could barely see beyond the end of my nose and had to follow the sound of the monk's clogs. Then there was light: through holes drilled into the rock face from the outside every ten metres there came thin shafts of daylight.

Soon the corridor widened into an arched tunnel supported on the right by brick pillars; behind them, in the rock, were carved out cells and shrines and altars with wall paintings. In some of them butter lamps flickered, in others the daylight poured through a loophole, while some were in darkness. In some I glimpsed the outlines of monks in meditative poses.

The tunnel led to a wide terrace that offered a stunning view of the snow-topped mountain range.

"The other side," said Dorje and gestured as if to show me what he had discovered or created himself.

We were on the other side of the cliff in which the lamasery was built. The main part of the monastery looked towards the north-east. From the terrace we looked southwards, towards India, towards the warm monsoon winds. The mountain range was probably an extension of the central Himalayas.

The terrace measured thirty metres across and twenty deep. It was paved with granite stones and surrounded by a protective wall. When I reached the edge something glittered far below me. There, five hundred metres down lay the blue lake I had seen from the pass!

From its shores a steep terraced slope dropped down to the verdant valley floor with its houses, fields, trees, streams – in stark contrast with the valley floor on the other side, as if I had strayed onto the southern side of the Himalayan massif. It struck me that this miraculous lamasery was the economic, religious and spiritual centre of two different worlds, a meeting point of opposites – a dusty wasteland to the north and green abundance to the south.

"There other side," said Dorje. "Here this side."

The boy knew what he was talking about and I felt ashamed for labelling him an idiot.

We turned towards the cliff. Below the red swastika on the vertical rock wall above us there extended a series of arched viewing loggias cut into the rock. Arched doorways below them led into a spacious subterranean hall.

He pulled me towards the entrance.

In the glow of the butter lamps I saw twelve monks with bowed heads sitting in a circle reciting mantras. A stone lingam, the representation of Shiva's sexual organ, stood in the centre of the circle. Its base was embraced by a stone ring or a yoni, symbol of the female sex organ. Both were surrounded by copper bowls from which swirled heady incense.

I scanned the walls. They were covered in vivid pictures of gods. A strange force drew me to the back wall, on which hung the grimacing face of a monster known to me.

I stopped in front of it.

The picture poured into life, the monster huffed and puffed. Its body was covered in greenish scales that reflected my face hundreds of times. Its multitude of arms waved with a forest of fingers that both enticed and repulsed me. The monster had twelve heads. It danced before me in hideous glittering colours that flowed into each other and in it shimmered reflections of my face.

This was the demon god Yamantaka, my supposed patron. Yogananda had told me about the "destroyer of death", one of the most terrifying demons in tantric mythology. His bull's head represents the god of death Yama, who is in reality the merciful Avalokiteshvara, the lord and judge of the dead, who leads people through the torments of suffering to the edge of illusion and from it into freedom and awakening.

The monster of my nightmares had become real. He twisted and smacked his lips and muttered and panted and pounded his hooves on the floor, drooled, threatened me, comforted me, cried for me, grinned at me.

I don't know how long I was caught up in this dance of the imagination. When I returned to my normal state the underground hall was heaving with people. I pushed my way to the exit and onto the terrace, which was also full.

The crowd was in a strange trance; old women with rosaries in their hands rhythmically swayed and sang in monotonous tones, girls with turquoise earrings absently repeated ritual verse, the men stood around chatting and waiting for something. Monks served tea. Here and there a baby wailed. Older children sat around in groups or played with lazy dogs.

Then from the viewing loggias could be heard the brass trumpets known as radongs. Their monotonous tones created a carpet of sound into which drums and melancholy flutes began to weave bewildering musical patterns. The crowd at the entrance to the cave broke up.

Through the gap came the Great Lama, the tantric master, the head of the monastery, wrapped in a yellow silk scarf. He was accompanied by two monks wearing tall ceremonial hats. Two younger monks laid a carpet on the ground, on which the Master kneeled. He put his hands together above his head and prostrated himself three times: towards the south, towards the west, towards the east. A monks' choir began to sing melancholy melodic psalms. Overhead the trumpets sounded ceaselessly.

The Master rose and with his retinue moved towards the carved steps that led up to the largest, central loggia. He sat on a decorated throne and raised his hand. The choirmaster began to declaim a liturgical text in a deep bass voice. The choir joined in and accompanied him with a sound hierarchy of baritones, tenors and boy sopranos. The ritual floated upwards.

And I too floated. I had already seen, experienced all this on the roof of Nawang's house in Zanskar, when Yogananda threw me into a telepathic trance, during which my spirit floated above the mountains and into the future. The awareness that the details in my dreams were coming true disturbed but did not frighten me. I still hoped that I was wrong and that it was similar, not the same. In spite of this I remained enraptured, completely paralysed.

The ritual was followed by the dramatic dances of masked demons and fortune-tellers. Those present applauded and laughed, children shrieked, dogs barked; even the Great Master was smiling good-humouredly. Only towards evening did the terrace begin to empty.

They all left, I remained alone: rapt in the silence that had replaced the racket, rapt in the moon that had replaced the sun. Late into the night I squatted on the terrace, without thought, connected with my surroundings.

Then, in the loggia above the terrace, strings were plucked, joined by a flute, then the dull sound of a drum; the night was filled with a girl's gentle voice singing a wonderfully melancholy song, rising and falling and sinking into the silence of the night, rising again and trembling above me; the voice that I had first heard from the slope of the pass and which I would never forget. Then some Tibetan girls in yellow robes appeared, dancing; the girls I had encountered in my dreams on the summit of Mount Kailash. They took me by the hands and danced around me in circles; their tousled hair leapt in the air in a circular rhythm of relaxed beauty; and the moon shone milkily on the jewels that adorned them.

The dance ended and one of them approached. She stopped right in front of me, watching. In the moonlight, I recognised Dolma. In my dreams, she was always the one who brought a knife, uncovered her breast and asked me to stab her. I thought that in the same dream I had also met the old Tibetan who was Henry's lead driver and who brought us over the pass. In my dream he also offered me a knife and asked me to stab him.

Dolma returned to the girls. They danced another circle and then ran into the tunnel. The music stopped.

I was alone.

Horror filled every fibre of my being. Now I could no longer blind myself. I had to admit that in my dreams I had experienced fragments of the future before it became the present. Late into the night I squatted on the terrace, shivering with cold, but with fear even more.

I pleaded with God, the old Christian one, to take pity on me, lift me up and carry me home, to rescue me from the depths of confusion into which I was falling.

24.

Sly as a fox

Next morning I ran into Henry Alexander in front of the Master's house. We were both glad to see each other.

"I don't know what's happening any more," I lamented. "I can't leave; the Master has hypnotised me. I've been adopted by a sweet girl of thirteen who sometimes mysteriously disappears. Other times she washes my clothes, brings me food and sleeps next to me. I keep asking the Master what he expects from me, but he keeps saying he expects nothing. You must know what's happening. What are we going to do?"

"Sleep, eat and drink," he said. "Listen and observe. Wait for someone to come, take us somewhere, or tell us something. The more impatient we get, the longer nothing is going to happen. Last night I spoke to a guy from Switzerland who's been here a month. On the surface nothing is happening. Only rituals, dances, congregations, incantations. Teaching of kids and novices, meditations, renovations of faded frescoes. A typical life in a typical lamasery. But the thing is: if this isn't enough for you, then this is all you're going to get. If the Master suspects you're trying to force your own tempo on him, he will leave you out in the cold. The Swiss guy told me they set a test for you the moment you arrive, and if you pass it, they set you another. You're initiated into the secrets of the cult gradually as you pass a series of tests. You pass a test if in a certain situation you react the way they think you should. We are both being tested, but my tests are different from yours. This is the biggest trap of all. You never know when one test is finished and a new one begins. You don't even know what the tests are. At every step you can make a mistake. You may have made one already. The same goes for me."

I said I was tired of word games and paradoxes; I was interested in actual tantric practice –

"Don't be a fool," he admonished me. "What do you think all this is: the impatience you feel because you think that nothing is happening; resentment you feel because they refuse to tell you what they expect from you; the fear you feel because you're hypnotised and cannot leave? This is not tantric practice? As soon as the Master sets a test for you, you become part of the process, part of practice; already you're given a chance to react the right way. Tantra is, from beginning to end, a series of tests, nothing more."

I said I was quite willing to accept tantra as a risky way of psychological transformation. What bothers me are its occult, magical aspects: mythological monsters and the whole superstitious medieval folklore. I described to him the horrible expressions of tantric deities I saw painted on the walls of the underground corridors: vengeful monsters wielding bloodied swords and human skulls; demons vomiting fire; gods in various poses of copulation with goddesses; all that, I said, gives me the feeling that I am dabbling in some kind of primitive erotic magic, in some kind of witchcraft. That's not for me, I said. That isn't me.

Henry laughed. "You remind me of a little boy I met in a remote village in Bolivia. I offered him a walnut. He had never seen one. I said it was good to eat. Without breaking the shell he put it in his mouth and, biting hard, nearly broke all his teeth. He gave the walnut back to me as if to say: that's not for me. Just like you. You're in the mountains on the periphery of Tibet, a land with many ancient traditions. Every form of wisdom has the shell of its culture. You must break the shell before you can taste the wisdom."

I asked him if that meant that tantra was first and foremost a kind of psychology.

"Not only," he said. "The essence of tantra is the secret knowledge to which only the chosen few can gain access. This knowledge presupposes that man is an unfinished product. That he isn't what he can become. You can change from a neurotic to a demigod, from a servant of your own ego to someone who can head, with the chosen few, the evolution of the human mind."

And how can I gain access to this secret knowledge, I asked. I'm undergoing trials and nobody is going to tell me what's going on. Must I learn Tibetan, read thousands of tantric texts, hoping that wisdom will jump at me from between the lines?

"Have you noticed how stupid some younger monks are? Give one of them a pocket calculator. He'll be pressing the buttons all over, ting ting ting, and he will believe that you have given him a funny toy that makes funny noises. With the same calculator I can work out the mathematical basis of quantum theory in minutes. The monk, hearing the same noises, will think I'm playing with the same toy. Tantra in your hands is like the calculator in the hands of the monk. You must start with simple multiplication and go on from there. And that's what they are doing. They are teaching you multiplication and setting trials for you. Hoping that at some stage you'll exclaim: I see!"

In the middle of the night I was woken by a howling wind which rattled the shutter for half an hour as if trying to blow it away. A little later I heard, in the depths of the lamasery, distant sounds of a gong. Dolma wasn't there; alone and lonely I trembled inside my sleeping bag. Every now and then exhaustion saved me from wakefulness, but the cold and the unusual sounds quickly brought me back to unwilling attention.

Towards the morning a woman's laughter began to reverberate in the labyrinth of underground passages. At first it was playfully shrill, then it grew helpless and drawn out, and finally tremulous, fading into painful moans. These were joined by a man's voice which at first sounded comforting and gently persuasive, but soon became abusive and screaming, then persuasive again, and finally it turned into laughter. It was joined by other voices, male and female, and the laughter began to sound like a congregational prayer, I could hear jingling and drumming. Then, abruptly, everything went quiet.

Secret rituals were taking place in the underground halls, God knows what kind, God knows for whom. I sank back into sleep and dreamt that I was sitting at the feet of the Great Lama who was watching me through narrow slits under his eyelids.

I opened my eyes and realised it was already late in the morning; sunshine was streaming in through a small window. Sitting before me was indeed the Great Lama, watching me half-amused and half-worried. At first I thought he was still a dream vision, for he was in no way different than in my dream. I couldn't be sure that I was actually awake; the Master, such as he was, merely grew step by step more corporeal.

"Good morning," I said, slightly confused and embarrassed. He smiled and waited. His eyes were strangely vacant, yet at the same time penetrating; I felt he could read my thoughts.

"You're full of uncertainty," he said.

I sat up and leaned back against the wall. "I'm afraid of games with subconscious forces. If my soul does need washing and ironing, I'd prefer to do that in the old, tested way, not with an unknown process which might tear and discolour it. My doubts are merely an expression of caution. Before I take a leap, I'd like to know where I'm going to land."

The Master twitched and smiled. "You claim that you don't know what tantra is, yet you're a tantrist without being aware of it. You want to know where you're flying and where you're going to land. That is tantra. You don't want to waste your time."

I said that time rarely obeys me; most often I'm its slave. I know that this isn't to my advantage, but I can't find a way to domesticate time.

"You have expressed the second principle of tantra," the Master said. "You know it is possible to live in two ways: to your advantage and to your disadvantage. If you live to your advantage every waking moment, you're already a master."

I said I was far from being that; mostly I live to my disadvantage. I live in a world of social norms and conventions that suffocate me, but I adapt to them to some extent to make life easier; rebellion for the sake of rebellion would be useless and childish.

I live in a world in which I need money to survive, and this money I must earn, and I can earn it only by doing work that often isn't as valuable as I would like. I live in a world of daily conflicts and contradictions that would destroy me if I didn't know how to make compromises. And although I make fewer compromises than most people I know, and only such that are not immoral, I still feel that the "I" who lives my life isn't my true "I", and that I remain a victim of the world in which I live most of the time the way I can and hardly ever the way I would want to.

But the world is what it is; I can't change it. All I can do is change myself.

"You insist you don't know what tantra is, yet you keep explaining its principles. You're aware that dreaming of a different world would be harmful escapism. As a tantric master you are a warrior who is always ready for everything while never expecting anything. Your response is always appropriate to the challenge. You are aware that you cannot abandon the battlefield. It is your life, and you are a warrior. But you can't be a real tantrist here, in this lamasery. This isn't your world. Tantra is the art of life in your everyday world. When you return home, then and only then can you be a tantrist. Here you can only watch, learn and practise."

"Thank you," I said. "I have been paralysed by the fear that I'm getting entangled in something that will prove to be useless on my return home."

He remained silent for quite some time. Then he said: "Tantra is the worship of gods that reside inside you. These gods are your energies. You are divine. But if you believe that without knowing the true nature of things you are mad. The true nature of things is Nothing. Your true nature, too, is Nothing. Even your gods are Nothing, only symbols on your path to the realisation that everything is Nothing."

I said that slowly it was beginning to dawn on me that I may actually know what he is talking about, but still I wish that his words were a little more concrete.

"Right." He smiled. "You said that you remain a victim of the world in which you live most of the time the way you can and hardly ever the way you would want to. That's not true. You're not a victim of the world. You are a victim of your interpretations of the world. The world is at every stage your opponent. By that I don't mean the society and its demands, or the material necessities, or your cultural, intellectual environment, or the conditions of life in the modern world. I mean you. Your thoughts and your feelings are you true world. Your desires, your ambitions, your moral principles, or lack of them, your expectations and hopes, your fears, all that is your world. Even what you think you are, your self-created "I", is your world. These are all energies with which you are in conflict. You are in conflict with yourself. Tantra is the art of harmonisation of these energies."

He was looking at me with a sly smile.

I said that now, finally, things have become clear to me. Tantra is definitely something I need. I said I was grateful to Destiny for leading me to the feet of the unsurpassable Master.

He laughed and nimbly rose to his feet.

"Come," he said.

I followed him through dark passages until we reached an underground room made visible by a ray of daylight. In the middle of the room there stood a large wooden puppet with a grinning dragon-like face, wide and rounded at the bottom, narrow and pointed at the top.

"What did you call me?" The Great Lama laughed. "An unsurpassable master? That I am not. The unsurpassable master is standing before you. Kick it. Throw your weight at it and topple it."

He aimed a strong kick at the puppet, which moved to and fro, but soon regained its upright position and stabilised. Its centre of gravity was under its middle. I grabbed its head with both hands and pulled it down so that the head was touching the ground. As soon as I removed my hands, the puppet swung up, centred itself and stared at me with an evil grin.

"This is the true tantric master." The Great Lama laughed. "You hit it, you kick it, it doesn't resist, it gives way. It bends and adapts. Then it bounces back to its usual position. It isn't in conflict with itself. Nor is it in conflict with the world. It is the master of the moment."

During our next conversation the Master asked me to describe my feelings to him.

Surprise, relief and excitement, I said. Surprise because tantra appears to be something quite different from what I expected; relief because I suddenly know what exactly I'm trying to achieve; and, finally, excitement because I know that my goal is achievable.

"At every moment you and the world are in conflict. How are you going to solve it: to your advantage or disadvantage? That's the only question worthy of attention."

He said that only three words were important for a tantrist: attention, attention, attention.

"When you're attentive, or mindful," he said, "you're in the heart of the moment. And in the heart of the moment you see that you're not alone, that there are two: you and the world. That means that these two are you and your interpretation. Your opponent is your interpretation of the situation at any given moment. You do something; something happens; that is the practice of tantra. When you are totally mindful, your judgement is correct, your reaction is appropriate, and the effect is to your advantage."

I said that, after all this, I think of tantra as a form of friendship with myself. Instead of reigning in and suppressing my nature, I must harmonise with it, surrender to the strength of its currents, flow with them if I can't stop them, and in a suitable moment take control of them using their own strength. I must learn to dance with myself. With everything that I am, with everything that I carry inside me. I must become light and nimble, resourceful and artful; sly as a fox, attentive as a rabbit, swift like a striking cobra.

"Become a fox," the Master said. "Become a rabbit. Become a cobra."

25.

Handball with an invisible ball

In the first days of practice I determined the space in which tantra would have a meaning. I realised that this space is the moment. The moment is a situation that is a problem. The situation is the form in which the moment reveals itself; the problem is my judgement. If my reaction is appropriate to the challenge, I have mastered the situation, and I'm a master of tantra. But I can fail, of course. It may happen that I react too quickly, too slowly, too weakly, too strongly. Tantra is the art of an appropriate response.

I talked to the master and described to him the rules of the game of handball. That's how I see life, I said. The playing field is the present moment, the ball is a challenge that needs a response, and how to choose the right one is the problem. I explained that the point of the game was simple: to seize the ball from the opponent and fling it past his goalkeeper in such a way that he can't stop it.

After a brief reflection his face suddenly lit up, he rose to his feet, joined his hands as if in prayer and bowed to me. "Thank you," he said. I followed him to the terrace at the southern end of the cliff. Along the way we collected Henry Napoleon and Manfred, the Swiss man. On the terrace the Master lined us up, stepped before us and announced: "We are going to play handball."

When he saw us exchange disbelieving glances, he added, "The ball is invisible. We can only imagine it. Eventually we will realise that the ball doesn't exists at all and is always something that we imagine."

He turned to me. "You described tantra as the art of controlling the moments. I like that. Tantra is a game of handball with an invisible ball, and now we are going to see which of you is a bigger master."

He removed his sandals. He placed one on the ground near the wall of the terrace. He made three steps to the right and placed on the ground the other one. Then he stepped into the middle and said, "This is the goal and I am the goalkeeper. You three are players."

He took up a position with his legs apart and waited for the first "ball".

When he saw our doubting faces, he laughed. "Come now, you know the game! You said you played it at school."

We said that handball had different rules; what he was suggesting was something else altogether.

He straightened up.

"That wasn't tantra, gentlemen. We said that the response must be appropriate to the challenge. The first principle of tantra: the rules of the game can change without warning. Most often they don't, but very often they do. If you stand there like pieces of wood, believing that you're exceptional and life must adapt to you instead of the other way round, you've lost the game before it began. The current of life is relentless, yet you are trying to negotiate with it. That isn't possible. Here, gentlemen, rebellion is not an appropriate response. You have to be wily, open, and ready for everything. You have to empty yourself. I don't mean that you must chuck away all your knowledge. I mean that you mustn't use it as a protective wall, you must push it behind you and stand in front of it innocent, naked. Once you find out what is facing you, experience *can* be of help, but not before. Because the rules of the game are changing so quickly you need a snappy judgment; without it your response will be stupid and blind. Shall we begin?"

He spread out his legs again and waited for the "ball".

We looked at each other and made a telepathic decision: Manfred "caught the ball" and passed it to Henry, who kept dribbling it for a while, then he passed it to me. I caught it and threw it to Manfred, who made a quick turn and flung it towards the Master. The Master "caught it" and threw it into the middle of the terrace. And so we continued. After a few minutes we all got bored and said that this wasn't a real game because there was no real ball.

"There is no real ball," the Master said and left the goal post. "Your turn to be the goalkeeper." He beckoned to me.

I took my position between the two sandals. The Master picked up the "ball" and passed it to Henry. He passed it to Manfred, who also kept dribbling it in a way that suggested he was going to dribble it for some time, but then he suddenly sprang towards me, rose into air and aimed the "ball" into the right corner of the goal. I threw myself to the right, but the moment I did that Manfred flung the ball into the left corner.

"Goal!" shouted the master and slowly approached. "What happens when you see the problem where there is none? The ball went to the left, you went to the right. There is no ball, but we all saw that it went into the left corner while you threw yourself to the right. You got together all the energy you possess and threw yourself in the wrong direction. Is that tantra? No! The attacker saw what you intended to do. You responded before he made up his mind what to do. Try again. Wait, and don't be afraid you'll be too late. Don't think of your response; pay attention to the attacker. Watch him quietly and with full concentration. React only when he extends his hand."

Manfred took another run at me. I pushed any thoughts about intercepting the ball out of my mind. All I did was watch Manfred, following his moves and the movements of his eyes as if I couldn't care less what he was going to do. When he lifted his feet off the ground I could see (feel more than see) that he was still checking possibilities, anticipating a gap in my defence. He aimed the "ball" in his right hand at the right corner, but then quickly transferred it to his left hand and flung it towards the left corner. I stopped his shot with a gesture that seemed a little too nonchalant to work, but it did; and I wasted no energy at all.

"What have you done?" the Master now turned to Manfred. "You betrayed your intentions. You knew you couldn't fool the defender with the same trick twice in a row. This confused you and reduced your self-confidence. Afraid you wouldn't succeed, you wanted to succeed at any price. In your effort, ten times exaggerated, you grasped at anything that might come in handy. Your attack wasn't straight; you tottered about as if you were drunk. When the ball finally left your hand, it wasn't your hand that threw it; you were somewhere else altogether. That isn't tantra. While examining possibilities, remain quiet. If you act before you know what you intend to do, and try to choose your target with your feet off the ground, the target has the chance to move. When you attack there is enough room for only one thought in your mind. There will be no replay of one and only opportunity. There never is. Now you try," he said to Henry.

Henry Napoleon caught the "ball" and started to play with. He threw it in he air, caught it as it came down, twisted his torso and kicked the ball over his head with his right heel, dribbled it for what seemed like eternity first with the left and then with the right hand, he rolled it on the end of his thumb like a circus juggler, then he threw it across his shoulder, catching it with his other hand at the back; all that to distract me, no doubt. Then he leaned back, raised his right arm, aimed at the right corner of the goal, and jumped towards me. I threw myself to the right, but as I did so Henry transferred the ball into his left hand and started to play with it as he did before. As for me, I landed on the hard terrace floor with a thud. The Master and Manfred laughed.

Embarrassed and with a grazed elbow I stepped back into the goal, determined not allow anyone to make a fool of me again. I was watching Henry as he nonchalantly dribbled the ball with the fingers of his right hand, occasionally glancing at me as if trying to gauge my mental state. Suddenly he bent down and pushed the ball with both hands towards me; I got ready for interception, but Henry changed his mind and continued to dribble the ball round the terrace. For more than five minutes he played with me like that: jumping towards me, preparing to shoot, aiming at this or that corner, but never actually shooting. I kept twitching and leaning this way and that, ever angrier, ever more tired. Finally he turned his back to me and flung the ball across his shoulder directly into the goal.

"Excellent," the Master commended him. "That is tantra."

He approached me with a sarcastic look. "You have shown us what tantra isn't. You're so tired you can hardly stand up. Hard to believe.

There was only one shot, but by that time you were too exhausted to defend the goal. You were reacting to shadows, to empty threats, to monsters in your imagination. If that is the way you play the game of life you will suffer a nervous breakdown. And now you." He turned to Henry.

Henry positioned himself in the goal. I was brimming with a desire to avenge myself. I felt that he had deliberately made a fool of me; the harder I tried, the less I was able to suppress my resentment. I kept passing the imaginary ball from hand to hand, throwing it over my shoulder and kicking it back over my head the way Henry had done (I wanted to show him that I, too, could do it!), I dribbled it round the terrace in circles and from one end to the other.

Henry watched me without any signs of tension, completely relaxed. He seemed not to care one iota whether his defence would succeed or not. That confused me. And angered me. Anger was all the greater because my desire for revenge was quite immature for a man like me. I was angry with Henry, I was angry with myself. I found myself in a state of emotional paralysis, unable to shoot because every attack would be an act of revenge. Anger quickly blew up into despair in which I flung the ball straight at Henry as if hoping that the force of the throw would knock him out of the goal. He redirected the ball past the goal post with a barely perceptible twist of the wrist.

"You made two mistakes," the Master told me. "You were angry, which you found unworthy of you, so you tried to suppress your anger. Because you couldn't, you tried to hide it, which was pretence, and every form of pretence is an abuse of energy. When you're angry, *be* angry! Anger is energy. But don't act it out. If you do, your anger has gained upper hand and you've lost the freedom of choice: the reaction is no longer yours, it is your anger, one single emotion of yours that has reacted. Aggression breeds aggression and worsens the conflict. That isn't tantra. To be a tantrist is to be the master of the moment. How will you subdue your opponent if you cannot subdue yourself?

"Enough for today," he concluded. He "demolished" the goal post by putting on his sandals. Without another word he walked towards the entrance to an underground passage.

Henry bent down, picked up the imaginary "ball" and flung it after him.

I will never forget what happened.

In a lightning move, the Master spun around, caught the non-existent ball and threw it towards me. It hit me straight in the stomach. I felt crushing pain. And I almost lost my balance.

The Master bowed and disappeared inside the passage.

26.

Tantric master

Every morning I take a bath in the cold stream first. Then I walk to the terrace in front of the Master's house, look at the sun, close my eyes, fill my lungs with air and push it out through my mouth. "Haaaaaaaaaah!" I shout. And again: "Haaaaaaaaah!"

I am learning to breathe. All my life I have been breathing incorrectly, without paying any attention to it. My breathing was shallow, non-rhythmic. The cleansing thrusts of oxygen rarely reached the lower parts of my lungs. I was either catching my breath or my breath was trying to catch up with me.

As a tantric master I will use breath to control my thoughts and feelings. Breath will be a weapon in my battles with the world. Without controlling the breath you can't control the mind. Without controlling the mind there is no concentration. Without concentration I cannot be at peace. And if I am not at peace – how can I be happy?

As a master I will always be at peace, because I will always inhabit the space I have taken control of. And I will always be happy, although happiness will no longer be what I think it is. Happiness will be nothing more than the complete awareness of the present moment.

I am still an apprentice. A master's moves are unconscious and effortless. As an apprentice I'm striving. But because the aim of my practice is tantra, I'm striving to learn without any effort. Tension isn't tantra. My best, my only true friend is effortless relaxation.

When I cleanse my lungs, I slowly breathe in and imagine that I'm breathing in infinite peace. When I breathe out I imagine that I'm banishing the uneasiness from my body and soul. Then I imagine breathing in infinite power; it is flowing through my arteries, nerves and fibres, into every little corner of my bodily presence. Then I breathe out and imagine that I'm pushing all my fears out of my lungs.

Then I imagine that I'm breathing in infinite joy and breathing out suffering, melancholy, and dejection. Then I breathe in cosmic energy. It is flowing through me like a fast river, cleansing me. When I breathe out, I imagine pushing out all the rubbish and sediments of ignoble thoughts, confused ideas, negative feelings and stupid desires.

Then I imagine that I'm no longer breathing with my lungs but with my heart, skin, eyes, hair; that I breathe all, that I breathe all there is. I imagine that I'm breathing in white mist of pure vital power. I draw it in and feel how it pours down my bronchi into my lungs, from where blood carries it to all parts of my body. I imagine that I'm breathing out a black mist that contains everything unclean and harmful inside me.

There is more and more white mist inside me, and there is less and less black mist. Finally I'm empty of blackness; I'm filled with a warm light. Everything is all right, there is no conflict; the world and I are one.

But the feeling doesn't last very long, the blackness returns, and again I am in conflict with the world. With my regular practice I try to lessen it and finally get rid of it for good, so that the world will be a riverbed along which I will flow effortlessly like water.

The essence of tantra is concentration on the moment, because goals are in the future, and when you're in the future you're not here and now. Thinking about the past fills you with regrets that drain you of energy. Thinking about the future is full of illusions that hide the present the way morning mist hides the landscape. No energy is wasted only if what you're doing is precisely what you're doing at a given moment.

The reason objects. The reason claims that you can't live like that. Not to think about future, about plans, possibilities? To reject memories, to shut oneself into a tight cave of the present? Thinking about the future may indeed be full of illusions, but it is also a source of hope without which living would be mere vegetating. Thinking about the past may indeed be full of regrets, but it is also a source of experience without which there would be no courage to face the days ahead.

That is what reason tells me.

But only reason which is still in conflict with the world. The tantric master also thinks about his past and future. He hasn't renounced his memories, and he isn't living obtusely from day to day. The difference between the master and an apprentice is that the master summons his memories when he needs them, whereas I'm ambushed by them. And almost never by those that may be of use to me. Associations drag me into opposing directions. And that goes for my thoughts about the future as well. I surrender to worries about the things that *may* happen to me. I surrender to dreaming about the future as I would like it to be. And in these dreams I settle accounts from the past, take revenge for slights and disappointments, correct mistakes, mark victories where I have failed. When dreaming about the future, I always pay back what life has inflicted on me. Or, more often, on my self-image.

I'm like an animal trainer in a zoo: on my left, there is a group of brown monkeys – these are memories; on my right, there is a group of grey monkeys – these are the desires I would like to have fulfilled. The brown monkeys come rushing at me from the left and drag me into the past; the grey monkeys come rushing from the right and drag me into the future. They drag me now here, now there, making a horrible noise and fighting for me as though I were a limp, tattered puppet made of cloth.

When I achieve tantric mastery, everything will still be the same: the brown monkeys on the left, the grey on the right. And I between them. Where will be the difference? I will line them up and order them to do what I want: to jump up and down, or stand on their heads. I will order them to dance, keep quiet, or fall asleep. And they will obey me without a word of objection.

I have drawn a black spot on the wall of the Master's house. I stand in front of it at the distance of 20 centimetres and stare at it. The spot is a magnet drawing into itself everything that's inside me. It keeps emptying me. Concentration is not aggression; it is not an invasion of the black spot. Concentration is surrender. The effort and strength are inside the spot; all I am doing is surrendering. As soon as a thought is born in my mind, the spot draws it to itself and swallows it. The black spot is relieving me of the burden of thoughts and feelings. It relaxes me. Concentration is rest.

After three minutes of staring at the black spot I imagine that I'm breathing in the air breathed out by the spot, and that the spot is breathing in the air I breathe out. I imagine that the spot is alive. We make love. I imagine that the black spot is giving birth to me, that by breathing it is actually recreating me.

Then I imagine that I'm a large eye from head to toe. My existence is visibility; the block spot is the only thing I can see. Slowly, I keep shrinking, the eye is getting smaller; in the end, it is no bigger than the black spot. Then I imagine that I'm even smaller than the spot. I approach it and burrow like a worm into its blackness, emerging on the other side, where I turn around and look back through the hole in the spot – through the hole I made – I see my body, my eyes which are staring at me. My concentration is perfect.

For success I need the power of controlled imagination. Without it, the concentration would remain plain staring at the black spot. The Master calls this method visualisation. To begin with, he advised me to close my eyes and try to imagine a yellow field of barley. I should wade into it and imagine the stalks gently moving in the wind. At the same time I should imagine that a little earlier it had been raining and that the blades of barley were covered in raindrops sparkling in the sun. I should imagine that wetness penetrating my trousers all the way to my skin.

He said that this was the first stage of tantric practice: a rudimentary exercise. No wonder I was incredibly disappointed when I realised that my imagination refused to obey me. Everything that I should *see* as though it were *alive* remained in the realm of thought. Instead of *seeing* a field of barley and *being in it*, I merely *knew* about it.

I was too aggressive. I used too much effort to create a vision in my mind. I tried to fashion it out of thoughts. That's why the thought remained a wall I tried to remove, instead of looking through it or over it or past it. I wasn't the wily fox I should have been: I was relying on power, on pressure.

Tantric master is neither a wolf nor a bull nor an elephant. He doesn't growl, or spear, or squash things under his feet. Tantric master is a fox and a rabbit and a cobra. He is aware of the fact that cunning is superior to brute force, that flexibility is more effective than rigidity. He controls things by surrendering and adapting to them, and by exploiting their energy. That's why he is invincible. When you fight against him, you fight against yourself. You fight while he rests.

My greatest relief is the Master's assurance that I will never become a tantric master because of my efforts, but in spite of them!

He told me a story about an impatient Australian who came to the lamasery a year before and immediately demanded to know how long he would have to practice to become a tantric master. "Five years," the Great Lama replied.

"And if I put twice as much effort into practising?" the astonished disciple asked.

"In that case ten years," the Great Lama replied.

"And if I practice day and night without a moment of rest?" the Australian demanded to know.

"In that case twenty years," the Great Lama said.

When the Australian humbly admitted that he did not understand how this was possible, the Master explained to him the basic law of tantra.

The more energy you invest in concentrating *on* your goal, the less you have left for concentrating on the way *to* your goal. The way is everything. When you are on the way (and not elsewhere at the same time) you have almost reached your goal. But if you allow your thoughts to dwell on your goal, you are not yet on the way.

27.

Not with the eyes, but through them

Yesterday we once again played handball with an invisible ball. I scored five times, and intercepted the ball five times as a goalkeeper. Twenty-two times I failed to score. But that didn't depress me; Henry and Manfred didn't do any better. The Master said that we should be satisfied with that sort of result even on the playfield of life: fifty-fifty is the best we can hope for.

He added that the game of handball with an invisible ball had evidently activated our latent energies: We were young, all of us relatively robust – and a few sacks of barley flour had to be brought from the village to the lamasery.

After breakfast we walked down to the village and set about our task. The sacks were not invisible. And they were heavier than we expected. And there were twenty-one of them! The way uphill was very steep; every ten or twelve metres we had to unload the sacks and take a rest.

I was the worst off. Compared to Henry, who was a giant, and to Manfred, who appeared to be made entirely of broad shoulders, I appeared more of a boy than a man with my youthful and slender body. After weeks without proper diet I lacked the strength for heavy physical work. It's true that I carried a heavy backpack round the mountains; but the sacks were twice as heavy. And they had no shoulder straps! While I was still carrying my second sack uphill, Henry and Manfred were already returning for their third.

With the fourth one I collapsed under the walls of the lamasery. The blinding sun was embracing my sweaty head. The visible world had condensed into a vortex of fragments which were coming at me, flattened and threateningly deformed, as if penetrating a broken window.

I could feel blood rushing along my arteries. Inside my skull I could feel my brain. I could feel it as a mass of grey cells and a complicated network of capillaries. Inside them I could feel tension that had been following me for weeks: the feeling that I must press a little harder and the dike which I was trying to dam up chaos would be washed away.

I realised that this wasn't the first time I was in such a situation. In various disguises it had been following me since childhood: I began something and ran into an obstacle. If I overcame it, I continued to the next one, and so on until I succeeded or ran into an obstacle that I couldn't overcome. Sooner or later I almost always reached the point when I realised that there's only one way ahead: by knocking down the wall with my head.

Isn't that the basic tantric situation? Isn't that the ground from which sprout neuroses, psychoses, depressions, manias, suicides? What to do when you realise that you're not as able as you hoped you were or as you think others believed you to be? Persist anyway? Withdraw and acknowledge defeat? Pretend?

Eventually I managed to drag the fourth sack to the lamasery. Out of breath, I approached the Master. Describing my dilemma to him, I added, "The process of life is a series of trials. I'm faced with situations in which the outcome depends on the extent of my abilities day after day. If the path is smooth, I'm not even aware of it; obstacles give me a sense of direction. As long as I'm able to overcome them, life is a pleasure; I have the feeling that I'm moving along and actually going somewhere. The problem appears when I come across an obstacle that can't be removed. Sometimes the hold-up is temporary; with a suitable move (rest, or reflection, or a small trick) I can soon continue. But sooner or later, in most situations, I come across an obstacle that I'm not up to because I don't have enough strength. Or enough guile. Or enough knowledge."

Without sufficient strength, I feel impotent. I stop happening, the flow comes to a standstill. I believe that such occasions are the most dangerous moments in life. Why? When we slip and fall, our instant judgement of the event is almost always wrong, and our response to it too fast and emotional (not action, but reaction). I believe that even a tantric master isn't all-powerful. Even he occasionally faces a wall that he finds too high. When that happens, what does he do?

The Great Lama stared at me as though he had just been forced to listen to a load of senseless babble. "The sack is too heavy and you're too weak; that is the problem?"

I nodded. And quickly added that I don't mean so much the concrete sacks I have to drag up the hill, but more generally: How does a tantric master behave when he realises that he is powerless?

"The problem is not where you see it," he said. "The problem is the point from which you observe it. The sack you find too heavy is inside you, you have created it with your non-tantric mind. This invention is the burden that makes you feel powerless."

I asked him to tell me what I had done wrong. I know that something isn't right; I feel that I'm reaching for a ball that doesn't exist, but something inside me blocks my view.

"Your view is blocking your view," he said. "Directly you can see only *through* the eyes. If you look at things *with* your eyes, you're disabling your ability to connect with observable things directly. The eyes become a screen, like a misted-up window pane, and what you see is a projection of your mind on the screen. Through the eyes you see what really is; with the eyes you see what you would like to see. That's why a tantric master looks at the world through his eyes. You may get the feeling that he is staring at you, that he is penetrating you with his gaze. And because he looks at everything with his mind, *through* the eyes, he always knows what to do."

After a moment of silence, he continued, "You have a goal. What kind of goal? You'd like to be better than your two companions; and if not better, equally good; or at least not too far behind them. Why? Because you don't want to admit to yourself that there are things in life that others are more capable of than you are. What connection does this have with a sack of barley flour?"

He stared at me. "None. All these are projections of your mind on the screen of your eyes. All this is the usual game of your ego, which can't see the sack as a mere object, but instead sees it as part of its neverending game of self-confirmation."

He advised me to look at the problem *through* my eyes.

I tried.

"What do you see?" he asked me.

"Only the sack," I said.

"There *is* nothing else. The sack is your only opponent. You saw the obstacle in your two colleagues, in their strength which surpasses yours, in your competitive attitude. Strength and the lack of it are merely expressions of comparison. Only when you see *through* your eyes, and see what really is, can tantra be of help to you."

"How?" I asked.

"What you have here is a sack of flour. Play a trick on it. Physical strength is limited; the power of the mind is infinite."

He advised me to imagine that the next sack I had to bring to the lamasery is three times heavier than the previous one. When I lift it on to my shoulder I will be relieved by the fact that it's three times lighter than I had imagined. That will give me courage. It will fill me with trust. It will make me believe I'm equal to the challenge. Before I start climbing the hill I must imagine carrying the sack twice as far as the previous one; to the terrace on the other side of the cliff.

Then my walk to the store room at the foot of the lamasery, my actual goal, will require only half the effort I've prepared to expend and only half the energy I've reserved for it.

I returned to the village. Manfred and Henry were sitting on the steep slope trying to recover their breath. I got the feeling that they had started too fast and had run out of energy.

I followed the Master's instructions. The result was astonishing. With no more than three short rests on the way, I managed to transfer the remaining three of my allotted seven sacks to the storeroom at the foot of the lamasery. Then I returned for the last two – one Manfred's, the other Henry's. They stared at me in complete disbelief.

"Tantra," I explained.

28.

The secrets of tantra

The days were full of blinding sun; filled with flickering multi-coloured strips of light and dancing of shadows thrown onto the roofs of the lamasery by flapping prayer flags. Their slapping sounds filled me with a strange burning sensation, with a tightness in my throat – was I feeling homesick?

In a way. But I wasn't longing for home. I was longing for the place in which I was, for the things that were happening, for the time that was running out. I could sense the inevitability of departure, and this feeling was so strong that I felt the present as though it were already the past, and longing for it as though I had already lost it.

Paradoxically, I had achieved the state of mindfulness that always evaded me. In my desire to hang on to the present I turned my back to the future and reoriented myself to each and every moment. Every moment I wanted to be where I was, that is why – magically – I felt that every moment I was at my destination. Every particle of experience was as precious as the previous one.

Isn't that how a man waiting for execution feels – or a man who is mortally ill and knows he has only a few months to live? Here and now is the only place in which you are truly alive. And when you are fully present in the moment, you get the feeling that *you* don't exist; that you're merely the sum of what's happening. No more crushing and painful collisions of ordinary mental states; there are only two, you and the world.

And you and the world are one in experience.

Everything had become a ritual. The awareness of what I felt, thought and did wasn't following what I felt, thought and did; it was simultaneous. Everything was sharp, crystal clear; no more swarming of vague shadows and shapes that inhabit ordinary mental states; even the shadows and brief flashes of light I was able to register were at the centre of consciousness.

This is it, I thought – and trembled. This is the mental state in which a tantric master dwells.

How different was everything that I saw, smelled and heard now! How different the water I splashed over my body before breakfast every morning; how different the taste of butter tea! It was as if I were tasting and feeling everything for the first and the last time.

Because of the stream burbling out of the rocks, the settlement was without the unpleasant stench so common in mountain lamaseries. The monks washed themselves every day (and even sunbathed on the southern terrace!) while the village women took care of their laundry. Even the mastiffs enjoyed splashing about in the stream when it became too hot. Inside the temples and prayer halls there hung an alluring smell of incense, strengthened by the smells of the rotting paper of yellowed books and of the vaguely rancid scent of the butter lamps.

Even dust had a pleasant smell: the brittle grey-brown mountain dust that covered the ground, the roofs, the endless stairs, and was present even in the underground passages. It came from the perpendicular cliff above the lamasery, with the strong winds removing layer after layer of brittle surface, turning it into tiny grains of dust that hovered above the roofs like a barely visible cloud.

But the sweetest smell of all belonged to Dolma. When she climbed next to me into the sleeping bag late at night, her hair had the smell of freshness and wind, her skin smelled of warm milk, her clothes of the healthy sweat of a young girl, still a child, her hands of peas or onions or other things she had handled during the day.

She never removed her clothes, not even a woollen jacket; all she took off were her boots. Inside the sleeping bag we would first box and tickle each other, then we would pull each other by the hair to see which one would first say, "Ouch!"; then we would amuse ourselves by imitating the sounds of wild animals. She always fell asleep abruptly, without any warning; in the middle of cheeky laughter, she would take a deep breath, assume a comfortable position and start to breathe rhythmically and peacefully.

The nights were terribly cold. I never slept soundly; I was reliving the events of the day even in dreams, as if trying to reassure myself that they hadn't slipped from my memory. Often it seemed to me that I wasn't dreaming at all: so clear and sharp were the images. I wanted to stay where I was. I wanted to live the way I did. I wanted to retain the incredible feeling that in every moment I was exactly where I wanted to be.

With the change in me, the world changed as well: it became open, inviting, forgiving. I was welcome in all parts of the lamasery, and when I wasn't doing my exercises I wondered around the place, explored the temples and underground halls (more often caves), admired mandalas and statues and wall frescoes, sat around silently with groups of monks, watched them in their meditation poses, meditated with them, listened to their conversations without understanding a word; and to the spine-chilling sounds of ritualistic music that started up five times a day in various parts of the lamasery.

With the change in me, people changed as well. They became accessible. Henry Napoleon, Manfred and I – three foreigners, three apprentices – stopped competing; we became friends. We still played handball with an invisible ball, but without any tricks or the intention to outdo one another. Our competitive urge was replaced by a desire to use the game for exploring and discovering new ways of tantric behaviour. We were able to share our most intimate thoughts. By tearing masks off our faces we had achieved an incredible feeling of freedom.

Our confessions revealed a surprising similarity among us. All three of us were victims of spiritual materialism; of greedily pursuing ideas that would help us live more fruitfully and less wastefully; of hoarding knowledge that would lead us to the secret of existence and the meaning of life, and at the same time decorate our spiritual palaces with precious metaphysical art. At a certain point we realised that the piled-up weight of our spiritual gains was becoming an ever greater burden; we panicked and threw ourselves into looking for ways of escape: in religion, psychoanalysis, Marxism, and finally, on the edge of despair, all over the place, blindly, even in mysticism, in the occult.

And we all in the end realised that only a direct path could save us. The path that would not be a further gathering of everything that is on offer, of taking pills, different and newer ones, increasingly damaging to our mental health, but a rejection. A rejection of medicine and our treatment. We realised that only one thing could cure us: the acceptance that we are not ill, that nothing bad is threatening us, that we are all right and the world is all right, and that the situation, such as it is, is more or less manageable. We realised that we needed a psychological shift, a change of viewpoint.

But that shift was the hardest thing to achieve. Only children know how to experience life and the world directly. In later years most of us abandon the world as it is, draw further and further away from it, and invent an alternative one, getting entangled in ever more complicated web of personal and social constructions. The real ground is replaced by a map, and the map becomes our reality. We all felt that only something brutal, sudden and irresistible could force us to rediscover the world as it really is.

Tantra.

When you seize the moment, everything gains a ritualistic rhythm. And that was what life in the lamasery had become: a ritual. When the sun was shining, it was the sun that was shining; when it was snowing, it was the snow that was falling; when the gong sounded and we walked towards the dining hall, we walked towards the dining hall; when, each clutching his or her metal bowl, we stood in line in front of the cauldrons of *tsampa*, we stood in front of the cauldrons of *tsampa*; when we sat on the benches eating, we sat on the benches eating; when we kept repeating prayer mantras, that was what we were doing, only that, nothing more, nothing less.

The day before it was snowing, and the snowflakes hovered above the valley like goose feathers from a perforated heavenly quilt, slowly descending onto the terraced roofs, muffling the sounds and enveloping the lamasery in silence. Henry had spent some time with one of the *trapas* (monks who have not yet achieved the status of lama) and warmed up with a few glasses of barley gin, which lifted his mood to the level of philosophical-mystical passion.

"We're going to be snowed in!" he kept exclaiming despite the sober, even cynical man he usually was. "And next year, when the snows start to melt, we will all be tantric masters!"

Manfred said that a wife with three kids was waiting for him in Switzerland; I said that hundreds of different obligations were waiting for me; but we both knew that these were mere words; we, too, were hoping for a sea of snowdrifts that would save us from thinking about departure.

We talked about the origin of swastika, which is one of the oldest symbols of creation, unknown only in sub-Saharan Africa and Australia. In Germanic mythology it was the emblem of the god Tor. It was known to the ancient Greeks. Ancestors of the American Indians brought it to the New World; and it had come to India (together with the Vedas) with the Aryans, conquerors from Central Asia. It became one of the Hindu religious symbols; eventually it was adopted even by the Buddhists. In Tibet and the surrounding areas, the left-facing swastika was known even to the pre-Buddhist religion known as B'on.

During the night the snowfall abated and in the morning the sun all too quickly licked it off the slopes and the roofs of the lamasery; only in the valley there remained a few white-blue patches. The dogs in the lamasery became restless; they kept pricking their ears, sniffing the air, barking occasionally. Henry told us that during the night an itinerant "naljorpa" had arrived in the lamasery. Naljorpa is a monk who had succeeded (with a decade-long practice) in mastering the art of warming himself with an inner fire (*tummo*), the art of walking in the air (*lungom*) and the art of materialising his thoughts (*tulpa*). He can also control the weather and bring the dead back to life. The only reason it stopped snowing was that he didn't want to fight his way through snowdrifts. The dogs were restless because they felt his demonic power.

More guests arrived at the lamasery: a group of Indian tantrists from the south, among them some strikingly beautiful girls. After arrival they ceremoniously washed themselves in the stream and received the blessings of the lama assigned to welcome them. Henry is convinced that something is going to happen. They are preparing something, some kind of event. There was indeed a palpable tension in the air.

"Something is going to happen," Henry said. "To us. Or with us."

29.

Krishnalila

The sounds of gently brushed strings floated towards me from one of the upper loggias. They were joined by a melodious flute; then a little drum shyly entered the audio picture, discreetly staying in the background. The night was suddenly filled with the tender voice of a girl singing a melancholy song, which kept rising and falling, moving away and returning, trembling above me; the voice I had heard as we crossed the mountain pass; the voice I will never forget.

A group of yellow-robed girls came dancing out of an underground passage. Holding their hands, they danced around me in a circle, with their hair bobbing up and down in the circular rhythm of their relaxed beauty. The moonlight sparkled gently on the jewels that adorned them. One of them detached herself, danced towards me and stopped.

"Dolma," I said.

She took my hand and pulled me into the dance: into a series of bows, turn and twists that I tried to imitate as best I could without understanding what, if anything, they meant. They reminded me of elaborate, measured flapping of an eagle's wings, the swaying of tree branches in a midnight wind, the giving of presents, and smoke slowly rising up to the sky.

When we revolved clockwise holding hands, the circle of other girls revolved anticlockwise; when they changed direction, we changed direction; and again, and again. Then a few girls detached themselves from a large circle and formed a smaller one inside the larger one; and when the large one revolved anticlockwise, the smaller one revolved in the opposite direction; with Dolma and I revolving in line with the smaller one or against it, changing direction all the time to be in line with either one or the other.

This was the erotic dance that the Indians call Krishnalila. Krishna is the eighth incarnation of the god Vishnu, the "eternal youth", surrounded by dancing cowgirls vying for his attention. Everything tantric is symbolic on three levels: the material (body), psychological (soul), and cosmic (spirit).

On the first level the symbolism is unashamedly erotic: cowgirls milking cows, squeezing their udders, pressing out milk, churning it into butter. On the second level their revolving dance represents the whirling of sexual energies in psychic centres; and on the third the revolving movements of stars and galaxies.

Krishnalila is a ritual representation of the transformation of sexual energy into spiritual one. The male archetype is manifested in various roles: as a hunter, defender, warrior, father, husband, lover, businessman, artist. With tantric practice he can distil these roles into one purified and potent form of existence: he can become a tantric yogi. For a yogi who is a tantric master, life is a fashion show where he can appear in hundreds of disguises: on the outside in any shape that suits him, or is required; on the inside always one and the same, and always in his centre.

In a similar way a woman can (with appropriate practice) multiply her archetype into numberless manifestations of femininity: mother, wife, lover, virgin, prostitute, and so on. On the tantric level she can play these roles consecutively or simultaneously but always at her will and as part of the game with a man who, on the tantric level, is the personification of Krishna. A woman can become all women for a man, while for her a man can become the only one: she for him a personification of the infinite diversity, and he for her the representation of the unity which is the source of diversity.

The dancing girls became a visual expression of emotional erotic energy. Tantra teaches that without an emotional surge it isn't possible to break through the barriers of social conventions and manifested duality. A power created by erotic desire is needed to achieve such a breakthrough.

In the legend, Krishna multiplies into identical images of himself and makes love to all the cowgirls at the same time. Each one is convinced that Krishna is hers and hers alone. Is this a betrayal? No, because the cowgirls, too, are only aspects of the goddess Lakshmi. Krishnalila, "Krishna's game", is a symbolic expression of divine love. Vishnu and Lakshmi are eternal lovers and their love is tantric because it is casual and unforeseen: since they play different roles, their union is new and fresh every time, and their energy is inexhaustible.

When the music came to an end, the smaller circle of girls melted back into the larger one which divided and extended itself into a straight line dancing towards the entrance into the nearest underground passage. Dolma reached for my hand and led me into an underground hall faintly lit by flickering butter lamps. It took me a while to see, sitting in a circle around a large stone lingam, twelve very old women who, rocking backward and forward, kept muttering barely audible mantras. From copper pots close to them the bittersweet smell of unusual incense rose towards the ceiling.

Then the yellow-robed girls returned. They emerged in a row from a side passage, one reached for Dolma, another for me, a circle was formed. We began to revolve round the lingam and the mantra-muttering women who were all over eighty; now this way now that way, and back again. The old women raised their heads and grinned at me with their toothless mouths. They leaned forward and extended their arms towards the stone lingam. They fell, all at the same time and not one of them a second late, into a sort of trance, their emasculated bodies twitching and shuddering as if they were about to die. Only later did I realise that this, too, was Krishnalila. Woman was revealing itself to me in the multiplicity of her roles: as a virgin, a dancer, a wrinkled hag; as a child, as a mother, and grandmother, as a gaping mouth of Death. All that is woman; all these are the phases of her blossoming and gradual waning. But under her changing exterior camouflage, she remains forever the same: the opposite pole, the opposite sex, the other half of the whole.

Tantra begins with a union: the whole comes alive when two become one. The woman who taught me that came to me in the role of a lover.

She came in the semi-lit underground room where Dolma took me after the worship of Shiva's lingam by the dozen old hags. On the earthen floor in a circle of butter lamps there lay a soft carpet with coloured patterns that represented a flowering lotus. Dolma led me into the heart of the flower. She pushed me down on my knees and began to undress me. Her movements were measured and ceremonial. I had no idea what she intended to do with me. When I was naked, she crossed my legs into the usual sitting Buddha position. Hail the jewel in the lotus! Then she took a few steps back and looked at me from a distance.

Dolma is a tantrist, there is no doubt about it. It's the way she looks at you that gives her away. When you're embraced by a tantric look you feel as if you had been nudged by a powerful force; as if something had drawn you into the embrace of energy that is not only greater than yours but also more natural, less ambiguous. You feel as if someone had reached out for you and pulled you into a lifeboat; you feel indescribable relief. The Great Lama has a look like that; Yogananda had it. And Albert Einstein. Children until the age of five have it without exception. And lovers, before they feel the first cool breath of disappointment.

The tantric look is innocent and wily, naughty and comforting, penetrating and gently stroking, full of near-wanton challenge and reassurance, full of irony and warm laughter. A great contradiction. When you're swept up by it you feel the presence of a spirit that is neither defensive (it has nothing to defend) nor aggressive because everything is already his (you can have everything without possessing it). The tantric look is a look from the heart, from the centre of awareness of things as they are, of the great paradox that is life.

The tantric look is irresistible; it embraces you like a warm wave at the moment you feel terribly cold; like a gust of fresh air when you're suffocating. Instead of resistance: surrender. Alliance. Even if the look expresses reprimand or anger (which it rarely does) you respond with gratitude. You feel that anger and reprimand are no more than information about a weather disturbance in your psychological space, a friendly warning. The tantric look expresses a question and an answer at the same time, and also implicit trust that you agree with the answer. It lifts you off the ground; it draws you into the greatest conspiracy in the world: the realisation that life isn't a burden you have to carry around, but a present that can be a source of delight until you die.

When Dolma saw me sitting inside the circle of butter lamps like some kind of Budha, she touched the ground with her forehead and repeated three times, "Om Mani Padme Hum!"

And then it happened. I just couldn't stop laughing. For a brief moment I saw the scene from a distance and I found it childish and slightly stupid. I realised that it really was childish and stupid. It was empty, the way all rituals are essentially empty: a succession of words and gestures to which only the feelings of the participants can give (a desired) meaning. At that moment the Buddhist concept of *shunyata* (emptiness) was closer to me than ever before. I felt that everything is empty of essence; the only contents of emptiness are our mental projections.

There was complete silence in the underground room. The grey walls emanated a damp, earthy warmth. I closed my eyes. The first thing I heard was a soft tinkling of tiny bells in the underground passage, followed by gentle rubbing of bare feet against the smooth stony ground.

I opened my eyes and there she was, standing before me. Her striking beauty filled me with deep anxiety. Next to tiny bells round her ankles and wrists, and jewels in her hair, all she had on her was a transparent sari through which I could see the shape of her body, the gentle curves of her hips, the roundness of her pointed breasts, and the dark shadow of her pubic hair. Her long black hair was tied into a large knot, and on her forehead there was the crimson sign of the god Shiva.

She was Indian, not Tibetan, and I recognised her as one of the girls who had come to the lamasery two days earlier with the group of Indian tantrists. She joined her hands and bowed to me. Then she began to dance. Her movements were alternatively soft and abrupt, symmetrically opposed and joined into a sexual invitation that was simultaneously shy and aggressive, addressed to me but also to a supernatural ideal of man; to me as an incarnation of the principle of cosmic polarity. Her dance expressed a synthesis of opposites: it was sensual and yet also priestly and spiritual; provocatively, almost roughly lewd and yet also deeply mystical; as though through the erotic charge of her movements she tried to manifest the heights of spirituality.

Her dance, too, was Krishnalila. The dancer with no name, the Nameless One, offered herself to me in a succession of roles: she was a snake, a soft kitten, a sweet-smelling flower, a helpless child, a boisterous child, a wily seductress, an understanding mother, a sinful adulteress, a comforting nun, a drunken slut, a gentle but passionate lover, a shy virgin, a curious explorer of male anatomy.

Dolma approached with a small pot of scented oil. The dancer threw off her flimsy covering and kneeled on the small carpet, with her knees nearly touching mine. I could see that hers were perfectly shaped and mine were knobbly. She dipped her hands in the scented oil which smelled of nutmeg and jasmine. With her fingers she began to massage the oil all over my body. There wasn't an inch that she left out. During this highly arousing ritual Dolma was kneeling outside the circle of butter lamps, burning incense in a small copper bowl. She kept repeating a mantra and performing unusual ritualistic gestures. She looked enraptured and strangely happy.

She stayed in the room, watching us, greatly excited; even encouraging us. Although encouragement was the last thing we needed.

The lovers' bodies are energetic instruments; love positions are the elements of sexual harmony. The usual act is a duet; the two musicians perform, skilfully or less skilfully, a composition they know by heart. They may be talented, they may play with feeling; they may enrich the performance by being inventive. But because what they play is a piece of set composition, their rendition will never be more than a high form of repetition.

Tantric act is improvisation; a performance of two musicians that compose their piece as they go along, discovering ever better possibilities to achieve harmony. They perform spontaneously; their lovemaking flows from opportunities offered to them by the succession of moments. At the same time it is (by the paradoxical laws of tantra) ritualistic, for they are guided by the awareness that what they are doing isn't incidental but follows a succession of opportunities most suitable for achieving their aim.

Tantra means thread or loom, and so a tantric sexual act is the process of weaving the body and spirit together, the natural and supernatural, the possible with the most proper, physical pleasure with transcendental ecstasy. With a synthesis of all these elements the sexual union becomes a mandala, the source of incredible power which the lovers can use to achieve their tantric aims: to rise above the purely sensual to the super-sensual, and above their daily internment to absolute freedom.

30.

The great trial

She too, I thought, as I looked at a wizened old woman sitting in front of one of the doors; she too had tried to connect with the primary sound of the universe when she was young. But now all the honey is gone; only pale traces of once sensual beauty can be seen on her sunken face. Her eyes are no longer naughty and challenging; they are motherly and forgiving. Compassionate. I walked past; her eyes followed me. What was she thinking? Of her own younger men, when she was younger? There were many old women in the lamasery, and they all loved to sit in the sun; this wasn't the first time we saw each other. But it was the first time that we connected in a strange way.

As I walked past and her eyes followed me, something happened. A palpable feeling of evil wafted towards me. She ceased to be a mother and turned into a witch; she became a personification of femininity in decline, an evil deity, "dakini". I felt as if she wanted to pull me close to herself and suck the life out of me like a spider out of a fly.

The rhythm of life in the lamasery had changed. Unusual tension filled the air; in everyone's eyes there was a shine of indefinable expectation. Little Dolma often gave me a look that seemed to say: finally it will happen. Even the rhythmic sounds of flutes and drums emanated tension that had never been there before.

Then, in the middle night, it started to snow very heavily, with large snowflakes tumbling from the sky as if they, too, were in a hurry to catch an event they did not want to miss. In a few hours everything was feathery white, everything muffled and silenced. The inhabitants of the lamasery withdrew into their corners and into warm underground caves. It was obvious that this snow was there to stay: the long-awaited winter had finally arrived. An old monk by the name of Dorje (there were few monks in the lamasery with a different name) gave us "ganja", hashish in the form of coarse ash. Even Henry Napoleon Alexander was astonished by its effects. Suddenly we were genuinely happy that it didn't stop snowing and we wouldn't be able to get away before the next summer. The world had found its home in us; it was snowing inside our skulls, with the snowflakes covering all traces of fear, doubt and uncertainty.

The next morning after breakfast the young monk by the name of Dorje (the one who "spoke English") led us towards the central underground hall.

In the pale light of hundreds of flickering butter lights we were confronted with a view that nailed us to the ground. In an arched cave we found over a hundred people. They were sitting or kneeling in four concentric circles: young yellow-robed girls in the inner circle; in the next, older girls and middle-aged women; in the third, very old women (among them the "dakini" who the day before had given me a look of evil). In the outer circle sat boys and men, mostly from the village but with many monks among them, probably all that lived in the lamasery. Sitting in the centre of the inner circle was Shiva, the short chubby Indian who had arrived a few days earlier with the group of Indian tantrists. On his right sat the Great Lama, who was holding the *vajra* in his right hand and a copper bell in the left one.

Next to them, on a raised stone with a flat top that was covered with a wolf's fur coat, sat Dolma, dressed in a pure white robe. She was sitting with her knees pressed to her shoulders and with her heels pressed against her buttocks. When we entered she gave me an expectant smile.

In the vague light of the butter lamps we saw more than a hundred pairs of eyes staring at us.

Suddenly giant horns, the "radongs", came alive in the corners of the underground hall. Joining the music one after the other, they created a deafening roar which filled the space like thunder that can't escape its own gravity and keeps returning like an echo of its own echo to its source before drawing away again. *Ah-ha-ha-ha-ha-hum*, the rhythm intensified into an explosion that was cut short almost as soon as it started.

Shiva got to his feet and walked over to Dolma. In his left hand he was holding a large shell. He dipped the fingers of his right hand in whatever was in it and sprinkled Dolma with the drops of yellowish liquid. He circled around her and sprinkled the liquid over her from all sides.

Then he joined his hands, took a deep bow and shouted at the top of his voice, "Shakti!" Little Dolma had become an incarnation of the goddess that expresses the dynamic principle of the birth of the world; she had become the centre, and the congregation had become a living mandala. More than a hundred heads were lowered in a solemn bow. There followed another crashing sound of the radongs.

After a moment of pregnant silence, the Great Lama shook his copper bell and pressed the *vajra* to his chest. He turned and aimed his eyes directly at me. His look was followed by more than a hundred pairs of other eyes.

Dorje, who was standing with Manfred and Henry behind me, nudged me ad indicated that I should move into the centre of the mandala. A feeling of horror swept through my body; I shook my head.

Shiva suddenly walked towards me. Sitting bodies leaned left and right to enable him to pass. He grabbed me by the hand and literally dragged me into the middle of the hall. He pushed me in front of Dolma and said: "You're a lucky man, you've been chosen by a virgin. Impregnate her, so we can worship her as Shakti, the goddess of creation."

He moved away. The Great Lama tinkled with his copper bell; then silence enveloped the hall. Dolma was looking at me with eyes full of tense expectation. She was afraid of what was supposed to happen, and yet she would rather die than let the opportunity pass.

I wanted to tell her that I had dreamt about this: on top of the mountain Kailash, where I had first met her, she detached herself from a circle of dancing girls and offered me a knife; she bared her breasts and asked me to stab her. I wanted to press her little body to mine, the tiny body of a child-friend, and whisper to her: “Let’s go somewhere where nothing of what is happening here has any meaning; where we can escape the fear that we are the victims of Fate that is greater than the sum of coincidences. Or let’s go somewhere where we will *know* the meaning of all this, and *do* what is expected of us the way water adapts to the curve of the wave arising from it.”

But I could not.

Because at that moment, in a way all its own, I died.

Something snapped inside me, something broke. I realised that I was standing at the centre of the mandala, at the heart of the possibility that I surrender, without any misgivings, to the moment and get rid of my shadow.

But my shadow, my ego, would not let me go. Its grip became even stronger. I knew that I was standing at the centre of the cosmic mandala, but through the eyes of my shadow I could see only that I was at the centre of attention; merely a projection of the ways other people saw me.

When the ego realises that it is faced with obliteration, it revolts and shouts, “No, no, no! I really am such as I would like you to see me!” And so my ego ruined the opportunity at the very moment I realised that I had it.

How on earth could I possibly do that? Take off my trousers in front of a hundred people and deflower my sweet little friend who was only twelve, thirteen years old with a member that had retracted into its house like a terrified snail?

I looked at Shiva and said that I couldn’t. Sorry, but there was no way I could do it. And I turned to go.

Behind my back, Dolma let out a shriek as if I had just stabbed her with the dagger she had offered me in my dream; she jumped off the stone and fell on her knees before me. She clutched at my legs, threw back her head and aimed her tearful eyes into mine.

I could feel her pain; I suffered with her. I had betrayed her. In quick succession I caught the eyes of other people as well; their disbelief, astonishment, fear. But most of all I was hurt by the eyes of the Great Lama. What I saw in them was benevolent compassion, suppressed disappointment.

I was a good apprentice.

What a pity that I had failed the last trial.

Shiva came to look for me in my cell to which I had run in order to have a good cry. I was so overcome by emotions that I kept banging my head against the wall. Shiva said that the Great Lama, in his benevolence, was willing to give me one more opportunity. I can redeem myself if I want to. I can correct my mistake and avoid excommunication.

"Anything." I sobbed. "Anything."

He led me back to the hall. Everything was as I had left it: the four circles of people, the Great Lama with the *vajra* and the copper bell, a hundred pairs of eyes staring at me. But Dolma was sitting in the front row, fully dressed and still with tears in her eyes. I must have broken a greater taboo than I could imagine.

Sitting on the wolf's fur in the centre of the mandala was now the old woman in whom a day earlier I had sensed the personification of feminine waning; the "dakini" who had looked at me with the voracious appetite of a lustful witch.

Shiva led me to her and said: "Empty your seed into this woman so we can worship her as Shakti, the goddess of Creation."

The old woman, who must have been at least eighty-five, if not more, stared at me provocatively, but also, it seemed, with motherly encouragement. *Ah-ha-ha-hoo-hoo-hoom*, the radongs sounded again.

No, something cried inside me. No! No! No!

I ran out of the hall, vanished into the labyrinth of underground passages, staggered, gasping for breath, along one after another, knocking my head and shoulders against the walls, trying to escape the demons that seemed to be following me. Out of breath, with blood streaming down my cheeks, I found my cell and threw myself on to my sleeping bag.

This is the end, I admitted to myself.

An hour later, two monks I had not seen before came to collect my things and stuff them into my backpack. One of them rolled up my sleeping bag and pushed it into my hands. They seized me by the elbows and dragged me out of the underground into the open. On the terrace in front of the Great Lama's house I was approached by Shiva.

"You have rejected Shakti," he said. "She has many faces. Also the face of a virgin who had fallen in love with you. Also the face of an old woman who may die tomorrow. You have rejected both of them. But don't worry. Every man gets three opportunities to become a tantrist. Shakti is also Kali, the goddess of death. Go, she is waiting for you."

He turned and disappeared back into one of the underground passages. The two monks dragged me to the lower end of the silent and strangely empty lamasery. Near the first chorten they sent me reeling into the snow.

A dark shadow stumbled towards me through the feathery dance of snowflakes.

"Vhhrrrraaaf." A large mastiff showed me its teeth.

31.

Today I am going to die

The mastiff followed me, half-trudging, half-rolling down the snow-covered slope, growling and flashing its teeth at me. It drove me past the seemingly uninhabited houses that nestled behind the veil of snowflakes. It drove me past the chortens topped with pointed snow hats and through the stinging cold of the damp snow all the way into the valley. There it got stuck in a snowdrift. It growled and thrashed about; then it squealed as if begging for help, sinking ever deeper into the snow.

"Die!" I shouted at the dog with a mad laugh. "Perish, you beast!"

I left it in the snow and trudged on towards the barely visible entrance to a canyon. It received me with a silent darkness in which my boots slogging through a deep layer of snow sounded like a sudden storm; the sound was thrown back by the concave walls of the canyon and filled the frightening space with a deep, subdued echo.

The canyon opened up into a wide basin, closed in on all sides by furrowed rocky heights. I began to trudge across it, with the snow reaching up to my knees and occasionally higher. Halfway across I collapsed and started to cry like a baby. I could feel the strength slowly ebbing out of my body. The ice-cold dampness of the large snowflakes kept biting me in the face. I still couldn't quite believe that I was suddenly alone, abandoned in wintry wilderness.

Suddenly my strength returned, it overwhelmed me like a gust of wind. I will go back! Yes, I will trudge back to the lamasery, I will demand to be taken to the Master of the Diamond Vehicle, I will beg him to forgive me and take me back. I will humiliate myself if necessary; I will do whatever he wants me to do: if he asks me to crawl up his arse I will crawl up his arse. In the midst of the Himalayan winter, with wolves not far away, pride is the luxury no man can afford.

I struggled to my feet and started to trudge back the way I had come. Suddenly a furry shadow of the mastiff appeared before me.

"Vhhhrrrrrraaaaf." It coughed at me and bared its teeth. Its eyes were burning with hateful determination; its snout was covered in froth. It was obvious it would pounce on me the moment I took another step towards it. I reached into my pocket to feel the knife. Then I thought: even if I try to kill it, it won't give up without a fight. Its teeth are sharp, almost knife-edged. Do I really need, in addition to everything else, a face torn to pieces by a vicious dog?

I turned back and trudged on through the snowy whiteness. The mastiff followed me. Whenever I stopped to recover my breath it growled and assumed an aggressive position. It didn't come any closer, it maintained a safe distance, threatening me only if it felt that I was slowing down or that I intended to return to the lamasery. It followed me up a steep incline and into a confusion of jutting rocks, keeping close to my footsteps; when I was forced to take a brief rest, the dog rested as well. Its tongue kept shooting in and out between its teeth; its eyes were glowing at me like the eyes of a demon determined to drive me to hell.

Gradually it stopped snowing and the mountains were embraced by brilliant sunshine. I was already high on the glacier-covered slope, at the end of my strength, with my heart in my throat, overheated, sweaty, puffed-up; more than three kilometres away from the lamasery, but the dog was still there, full of strength, and in the sunshine incredibly large.

"How far are you going to drive me?" I shouted.

"Vhhhhrrraaaaf," it answered, balancing its weight on its hind legs.

We continued to climb up the slope. The moraine eventually straightened into a saddle-like pass. From the opposite side, a chilly wind began to blow into my face. I paused, closed my eyes and enjoyed the relief offered by the cold whistling air and the spray of snowflakes which the wind kept sweeping off the ground and whirling around me. The mastiff shivered a few metres behind me. With the wind pressing its ruffled fur against its body, it looked strangely emaciated, like a cat that had fallen into a pool of water. It looked extremely unhappy.

I made a threatening gesture and shouted at the top of my voice: "Get lost!"

It didn't move; it continued to stare at me mournfully, almost imploringly.

Poor dog, I thought. You, too, are no more than a dog. Both of us are no more than dogs; our bark is worse than our bite. I took off my backpack, let it fall in the snow and collapsed onto it.

Almost at the same moment I became aware of a strange movement. The mastiff rose to its feet, pushed out its neck and swivelled its head to the right. Something was moving on the slope above us, something white was inflating into a large oval balloon that kept rushing towards us. Avalanche! – I suddenly realised. By shouting at the dog I had set off an avalanche!

I was mesmerised by the seething whiteness that was rapidly growing into a huge wall, leaving behind it the black surface of granite rocks. The mastiff squealed and pulled its head between its shoulders as if expecting a violent blow. But it didn't move. It looked at me as if expecting help, but I was already half-jumping, half-flying towards the rock jutting out of the ground not far away. I managed to hide behind it the moment the white mass stormed over me.

The sound, like the patter of hundreds of horses mixed with the subdued silky slide, was swallowed by a sudden and complete silence. A heavy cold blanket pressed at me from all sides.

I was buried under the snow!

I could feel the hardness of the rock behind which I had hidden; leaning against it, I managed to push myself up on my feet. The weight of the snow slid off my shoulders and suddenly there was light. The rock had split the avalanche, forcing the snow to rush past on both sides; I was buried only by the surface layer that slid over the rock. Everything around me was white; there was no trace of the mastiff. And no trace of my backpack.

I began to dig. I pushed my hands into the snow I used them as little spades to throw the white mass up and away from me. When I reached the hard frozen ground, the hole was two metres deep, but there was no trace of my luggage. I thought that the force of the avalanche may have pushed it a few metres ahead, so I climbed out of the hole and began to dig where I thought I would be luckier. I found the mastiff, still warm, but definitely no longer alive – its snout was agape, its throat stuffed with snow.

I left it in the hole and climbed out.

The avalanche had swallowed everything: my clothes, notebooks, camera, films, medicines, documents, the lot. And not only that: also the tent and my sleeping bag. The night was going to kill me! I continued to dig as if struck by a fit of madness; I made four holes in four different spots, then I made a fifth and a sixth, but in the seventh I lost my strength and remained lying in it.

How stupid. If I hadn't shouted at the dog, I wouldn't have set off an avalanche; if I hadn't stopped, I would've been somewhere else by now. If I hadn't been born, I would not have to die.

I wouldn't have lived.

I climbed out of the snow hole and looked at the molehills of the other ones. I raised my frozen hands towards the sun. These are the hands of the child that I was and the hands of the old man I will never be. These are the hands of a young man who had gotten what he had been looking for and would on this snow-covered mountain pass finally become the Buddha, the Awakened One, sitting here until the next spring, in nirvana, a frozen tantric master who will never again expect anything. The winds will ruffle his beard and whistle past his ears, but he won't hear them, his home will be Silence.

In my heart I felt a longing for nobler feelings, for a resignation that would allow me to accept the fate awaiting me, but my subconscious was pouring out an unstoppable flow of resentment, vengefulness and fear. I could feel what was going on inside me but I couldn't help myself; the force of the outburst was too great.

So great that it lifted me up and carried me across the snow to the hole in which I had left the dead mastiff. It reached in my pocket and pressed the knife into my hand. It forced it into a swinging motion and kept stabbing at the mastiff until it was lying in a pool of blood which was seeping into the snow and into the trousers on my knees. At the same time I was stabbing at the inhuman people in the lamasery who had wilfully pushed me into the lap of death.

When the desire for vengeance was satisfied; when the child in me "showed them", I climbed out of the hole and raised my bloodied hands towards the sun.

"Laugh!" Yogananda's voice floated towards me on the sails of the wind. "The world is your home, and at home you can do what you like."

"Ha ha ha ha!" I stood on top of a mountain pass, more than four thousand metres above the sea level, challenging gods in the heavens like Lear after he had given away his kingdom. These are the hands that were most dangerous with a pen between their fingers; and happiest, really and truly happy, only when they were caressing the body of a beloved woman. And these are the hands of the man who had finally, after all his years of innocence, killed an already dead dog!

"Ha ha ha ha!" I kept laughing, no doubt already half-mad, waiting for another – this time final – avalanche to bury me. I fell on my knees and continued to scrub blood off my hands even after they were already clean; as though the soul wanted to cleanse itself of the blood spots that covered it when the knife of tantra stabbed the ego without being able to kill it.

The sun was sinking behind the white peak on my left and a dark shadow began to swallow the pass, the vanguard of the night that was creeping stealthily, like an enemy, through the canyon. Down below it won't be so cold, I thought. I may find a cave in which I can rest, and perhaps survive for another day or two.

I began to trudge through the snow which had already started to freeze into a crust on top. After five or six steps I tripped over something and fell face first into the snow. I got up and looked back.

Sticking out of the white mass was a corner of my sleeping bag.

"Haaaaaaaah!" I shouted.

I began to dig like mad and soon recovered not only the sleeping bag, but also my backpack and tent. Although the bag meant no more than I wasn't going to freeze to death the first night, but rather the second or third, I shouted with joy as if I had discovered a magic carpet to carry me across endless canyons and moraines into a warm room in a luxury hotel. Loaded with my precious possessions, I staggered towards the depths lying on the other side of the pass.

And then I suddenly saw them.

They were lying before me like an endless rough ocean, petrified during a violent storm, reaching into the depths of the universe, glistening, sparkling in the sun but interspersed with undulating shadows, a granite plain of almost grotesque configurations of sandstone and limestone, jutting white peaks, sharply pointed or carved into three or four horns, and below them a myriad of lower peaks, some black or dark brown because snow had been swept off them by the winds, others blindingly white, a petrified army of stalagmite soldiers which had, scattered about in complete disorder, frozen into an eternal armistice; and among them twisted knots of serpentine and torn stony ribs which the underground pressure had crushed and piled on top of one another, leaving among them wide depressions and narrow canyons with terraced slopes down which broken-off rocks slide year after year and keep piling up into phallic symbols of the eternal erotic game with which the mountains maintain and renew themselves.

In spite of the disorder everything was in its place. Not a single stone was where it wasn't supposed to be. Everything was immortal, free and peaceful. The mountains are free. Reflected in their eternity was my transience.

The mountains are. I am trying to be. That's why I'll have to die.

I felt tears in my eyes. A pair of wings flapped above me; a large bird was flying across the pass, followed by its shadow on the snow-covered ground.

The silence of solitude, the noise of loneliness. My life is noisy even when I'm surrounded by silence. Eternal arguments, eternal debates inside me, eternal chipping of thoughts and emotions, as if – with loud bangs and collisions and creaking sounds –mountains were being formed within me. But never the mountains like those before me, where everything is forever in its proper place.

Vague sounds of distant drumming and sonorous trumpeting of radongs floated towards me across the sea of silence. I looked back and saw, far behind the white slopes, the lamasery of the left-pointing swastika, carved into a cliff, a cluster-like jewel on the face of a mountain, golden in the setting sun, fairy-like, almost unreal, and yet, as I could feel in my blood, more real and permanent than my fragile body, than all my dreams that I call reality.

Only from a distance could I feel how ineradicable was everything I had lived through inside those walls. It was all jumbled up in my memory, all twisted into a knot of visual and aural fragments: of solemn ceremonies and secret sexual rituals, of damp underground corridors and suffocating incense; of flapping prayer flags and toothless old women; of beauty and fear, hopes and disappointments.

Of great hopes that did not materialise.

How is that possible? How is it possible that I have to live in search of myself? I am, I'm aware of the fact that I am, but there is a gap between what I think I am, and what I am in reality. Something prevents me from moving from the periphery to my centre. Something is not right. Instead of living inside myself I live in the eternal cold of alienation, circling around myself like a burglar trying to find an easy point of entry.

Have I been insufficiently violent? Or have I been asking the wrong question? How can I know myself? Should the question have been: how is it possible that I *don't* know myself? Evidently it is I, myself, who is creating and maintaining the fence separating me from myself; why am I doing that? Or, more precisely: *how* am I doing that? Why can't I see things as they are?

The problem is that I keep *explaining* reality to myself. I keep translating it into a language I can understand: the language of concepts and definitions. I believe that by doing so I can get closer to reality, but in fact I'm merely creating a dream cloud in which I can touch only my *interpretations* of reality.

Between me and reality there is the Word. I am translating things into a language I can understand, but at the same time I force upon them a context that isn't natural; it is merely a projection of my feelings at a given moment. I look across the freezing wilderness of snowdrifts and think: ghastly winter, cruel and indifferent, it's going to kill me. If my boots were strapped into a pair of skis and there was a luxury hotel below me I would think: How charming this endless whiteness is, how inviting. What a great holiday!

I moved my frozen limbs. A gust of wind swept up a spray of dry snowflakes and slapped them into my face. I felt that death was not far away.

The feeling shocked me. I had wasted my life. I had followed wrong dreams. I had constructed a fiction which I called life as a defence against true reality which I was afraid to confront because it was too rough, too cold, too indifferent. Now it had caught up with me. And I, the fool, was hoping I could cheat it again, even now, at the end.

I remembered seeing a Japanese silent movie in which the director with the orchestration of visual details succeeded in creating suspense that became almost unbearable towards the end. And I remembered how afraid I was that one of the actors would suddenly speak; that he would open his mouth and ruin everything.

It had seemed to me then that words are stones we keep throwing at the window pane of the world, turning it into a non-transparent screen. Each word, even the most honest one, is already a little lie, a translation of feeling into thought and thereby into an approximation. In all of us it is the ego that thinks, and ego is a mask, a self-image.

What I wanted to have in life were meaning and hope. The hope that tomorrow would not be without the possibility for my wishes coming true. Without hope I could not, and would not know how to live. Where would I find the strength to crawl out of the warm bed every morning and sail into the stormy weather of a new day if I could not hope that tomorrow, or the day after, or at least some time in the future, the efforts I was putting into living would bring rewards?

I was afraid to admit to myself that life is hopeless; that tomorrow is just an illusion, a mask on the face of the fear of the real (and only) life in the present. It was always easier to postpone the confrontation that ultimately I could not avoid. I could see now that I had set a big trap for myself. In my life, which is now a distant echo of unimportant noise, I had nurtured knowledge, hypotheses, philosophy, and opinions about things. Whenever I merely felt it seemed to me that that wasn't enough; that I needed an explanation, a context, a "meaning" behind my feelings. And I believed that I could discover and approach this “meaning” only through words. The words (mine, those of others, written or spoken) created the noise whose echo is now dying behind the mountains. *Yap-yap-yap, blah-blah-blah*; the echo of a life that never was.

Everything has vanished. Everything has abandoned me. No need to worry about tomorrow, what others will think of me, of my work, what I will think of myself and others, what will happen to me and to mankind.

Today I’m going to die.

32.

The noise of loneliness

As the mountains slipped under the blanket of darkness, I too began to slide into a state of isolation, surrendering to the lights inside me, to the flashing bundles that danced up and down like headlights on a bumpy road, coming towards me and blinking like the landing lights of an interstellar craft, slowly joining into a circle of light in which there was again the world – not the usual one but the world of things that did not belong in it. What was missing was the feeling that I was responsible for my actions; that I existed independently of my senses. What also wasn't there was the familiar border between me and my immediate surroundings. Instead there was an unmistakable feeling that everything was happening at the same time to me and within me: that I caused events, yet they also took place of their own free will. Because I no longer existed outside my perceptions, I lost the awareness of my usual attitude to things and events: the nouns remained without verbs, they stood alone, self-sufficient: instead of "I sit in the snow", snowsit; instead of "I'm afraid", ifear; instead of "the night is coming", nightclose.

Such is my memory of the coming night and the following day:

a succession of pure perceptions:

golden brown eyes of blue sheep, silky sparkling of their furs in the sunlight, soft noise of hooves in the snow, waving of horns, silence, pain in the legs, burning of hands in the frozen air, scratchy and crispy white surface, snow in my boots, snow in my trousers, wind a sharp dagger, falling, grabbing at a rolling backpack, falling into darkness, then shaking, flapping of something against my face, something burning inside the mouth, strong fingers on the shoulders, sharp fingers in the armpits, unsavoury breath from an alien mouth, a flash of fire or torch, a silhouette of an old Tibetan with a wide-brimmed hat, shapes of moving animals, a silhouette of the Indian hunter of blue sheep, large packs on the backs of yaks, bundles of tightly tied furs and horns, skinny statures of yak drivers, laughter, whispering conversation, moving across the snow, the moon in the sky, shining whiteness, shapes of trudging animals, one after another deeper and deeper, sticks in the snow, sticks on animals' backs, creaking of belts and loads, rest at the foot of the slope, fire, tents, sleeping bag, warmth, murmuring voices, the howling of wolves in the night, far, very far, and finally sleep

in the morning the unrest of setting off, peering Indian eyes, mysterious Tibetan eyes, the creaking of leather trousers, boots with metal heels, yaks loaded with furs of slaughtered blue sheep, staggering along a canyon, falling into the snow, spiral falling into a black hole, rocking motion, yak's back, smell of cattle, sharp mocking eyes, dance of the mountains on the horizon, dance of the mountains on the horizon, puffing mouth, stabbing Indian eyes, angry voice, "Where, where, where?", a jolt with an elbow, rage, fatigue, consultation, sideways glances, whisperings, whoknowswhere, whoknowswhy, whoknowswhat, and again rocking on a yak's back, again a broken line of yaks and their drivers climbing a slope, the hired Tibetan with the hat at the front, the Indian with the slaughtered profit at rear, and I, the Himalayan hitchhiker on a yak's back, in the middle

and the panorama of mountains, astonishing, endless, a granite teeth of the planet that is emptiness, born out of nothing and sliding back into nothing, ice under feet, again blue sheep on top of a cliff, a shot, two more shots, the rattle of running hooves, shadow of smoke at the mouth of a gun bobbing up and down behind a red turban, behind greying moustache, behind the eyes that want more and more, the reflection of the sun in these eyes – please God, let me not have such eyes, never let me have such greedy eyes another rest in a village, eyes of curious kids, alert but still innocent, drivers in a circle, chatter, laughter, a lonely prayer flag in front of an isolated chorten, stupid eyes of the resting yaks, then goodbye, sniffling kids with us to the end of the village, staying behind, a black group in white snow, a cluster of lonely melancholy, then past a line of small chortens, across a frozen surface of a mountain stream, staying behind us, below us, lower and lower, finally melting into the overall whiteness, and the grand peaks on the horizon, and the sun again sinking behind them, shadows spreading over the slopes, cold rising like mist from the canyons, exhaustion, stumbling, slipping, again on a yak's back, this mountain hero, this battered body, these frozen fingers, this ruffled unshaven bag of bones and little else, rocking across the high plain, and the dance of the mountains on the horizon, the dance of the mountains on the horizon

Who am I, what am I? A spark of light slowly fading, a frustrated lover of life, killer of a dead dog, a slave of restlessness – what am I? – blood on the sharp ends of my illusions? – why am I – oh God! Why am I not a mountain, jutting into the sky, immobile, why these thoughts, these feelings, this noise, this hell? This "I"?

Will I have to come to terms with it in the end?

dizziness, a fall in the snow, crunchy blow, ice on the cheeks, a powerful grip of a rough hand, dark Indian hand, pointing towards a pass on the left. "Ladakh," the word slipping between two lines of teeth, five of them gold, "Ladakh, Ladakh!", laughter, turning, crunchy sounds, the caravan leaving

The world without verbs. The silence of solitude, the noise of loneliness. What is the meaning of life? someone asked the Buddha. Carry on, he replied.

The verbs had returned, the border between me and the events was reinstated, I was again "I", the noise in silence. I didn't go in the direction pointed out by the Indian hunter, I didn't trust him. I decided to follow the caravan which had disappeared behind the curve of the slope. He had wanted to get rid of me. For him, the dark-eyed killer of blue sheep, I was nothing but trouble. If I had a silver fur on my body, he would have shot me; but as a man, a confused man, I was useless to him.

But that's what I am, I suddenly realised.

And I fell on my knees.

Who would miss me? Even my closest and dearest would carry on with their lives if I didn't return; they, too, in the noise of their loneliness, as always. I'm the only one who would miss me. And what would I miss? This creation, this fiction of "I", which does have an apparent existence and importance in the environment that had created him, and in which he can maintain the fiction with daily rituals of self-confirmation, but which here, in the silence of complete isolation, is fully transparent, merely the noise of loneliness, the panicky longing for his "home", for the mirror in which he could again see himself? I felt that there was no me. I was there, but I did not exist.

In silence, empty, what are you? Every organism is merely a temporary organisation of energy particles, a "personality" of opinions, reflexes and psychological mechanisms, imagining that it is a static, permanent unit, although it is no more than a brief dance of a fly. And during that dance – what is death, what is the past, what is hope? O God! Release me from the burden of this incomprehensible "I-ness", change me into an ant, a butterfly, a leaf on a tree. Into a snowflake.

I followed the trail of the caravan towards the end of the valley. Gradually it narrowed into a deep canyon with overhanging cliffs. I felt a breath of something unusual brushing past me, something darkly cold; something that was not merely the shadow of the approaching night.

After the first corner I came upon seven dead bodies. The first one was lying on its back – limbs spread out, mouth agape, eyes staring vacuously at the sky, a wound in its chest, neck half-severed, and the back of its head on a smudgy patch of blood as if resting on red cushion. Like a figure of wax, its fingers were stretched out as if fending off an attacker. The next body was crouched in the pose of an unsuccessful escape, its left leg bent sideways and the right one thrust forward, both hands pressed hard against the ground as though at the moment of death it still sought support. Its throat was cut right across, the severed trachea jutting out from a nodular mass of blood and flesh.

I recognised the third body as the Indian hunter of blue sheep. I recognised him by the red turban someone had tightened round his neck. His face had been battered into a porridge of broken jaws and teeth with the butt of his rifle which was lying nearby. The next three bodies had been placed with their heads together and legs pointing in three directions. The snow under them was dark red. The cruelty of the attack was evident from the disfigured faces of the victims: one had his eyes gouged out with a knife, another had his tongue cut off, and the third was without his nose and ears.

Who could have done a thing like that?

I staggered towards the last body. It was lying ten, perhaps fifteen metres further on – the body of a man who must have made a serious attempt to escape. A wide-brimmed hat was lying next to the grey-haired head. His leather trousers moved and creaked in the snow, the body had raised itself on an elbow and a blood-spattered Tibetan face stared straight into my eyes. A trembling hand reached towards the belt and pulled a dagger from a torn sheath (which it had no time to pull out during the attack). It lifted the dagger towards me. The man's mouth blurted out something incomprehensible, and the effort of it squeezed more blood from the wound in the belly; the dying eyes stared at me as if asking for mercy. Then the hand trembled, the dagger slipped from it into the snow, the eyes froze into an upturned gaze.

I fell on my knees. I vomited violently as never before. I grabbed around in the snow as if trying to rearrange the scene around me. If the Indian hunter hadn't gotten rid of me in the valley beyond, I would now be lying next to him without my tongue and ears. He had left me in the snow to die; he had spared me the massacre and condemned me to another few days of life. How many? Three? Two? It could be hours instead of days.

I looked along the canyon. There was no sign of the yaks and the precious furs of the blue sheep. The ambush had succeeded; the robbers had left behind only blood. They couldn't be far away, I thought; they could be no further than behind the second, third or fourth corner. They could even be coming back, maybe they forgot something, any moment they could see me …

I hurried back the way I had come, across the darkening valley which was fast filling with evening fog; a force born of fear carried me up a steep slope towards the moon hanging above the pass, it pulled me, together with the weight of the luggage, higher and higher, without my knowing where, without caring about it. All I wanted was to get away from the scene that had fixed itself in every grisly detail into my memory forever.

33.

The caveman

Through the shining brightness of the night I reached the top of the pass and began to descend down the other side. The stars kept winking at me. The moon was so close that it was almost touching my head. It was huge, as big as a mountain. The dark entrance of an underground cave appeared before me. Warm air seemed to be streaming out of it. Bear, leopard, a pack of wolves?

I went down on my knees and carefully crawled inside.

Something alive breathed into my face and touched my hand. I shouted and moved back. The next moment something cold and hard clutched at my neck. “Got something to eat?” a feverish Australian voice almost yelled into my ear.

“No!” I said, looking for a way to escape.

But then I felt the sharp point of a knife under my chin.

“I swear,” I almost shrieked, “I haven’t eaten in more than two days!”

The grip of the cold fingers relaxed, I could feel a fist punching my shoulder. “They threw you out, ha ha,” the wild creature laughed. “And now you’re free! What’s your name?”

I told him, and he laughed again. “Come on. Why don’t you admit that your name is Egon?”

I kept waiting for the opportunity to scramble past him out of the cave. I felt for my knife in the side pocket of my backpack; if I go, I thought, he goes with me.

He could see me, at least vaguely. But having come from the white moonlight, I peered in vain into darkness. I could assume where he was only by the sound of his voice.

"Don't you know Egon?" he asked me. "Of course you do. You belong to the society of Egons, held together by egonomics; you came looking for teachers to help you escape from yourself."

His voice grew louder, almost pompous; in darkness, it circled around me:

"Egon is clever; oh, how clever he is! He invents life, but then he discovers that he can't live it. He has invested too much to start using the capital. Every now and then, for a while, he lives off the interest, but because he fears that the capital isn't big enough, he finally stops living off the interest as well. And the capital grows. Egon is a speculator; he negotiates, blackmails, and cheats. Whatever he discovers, by design or by chance, becomes his property; every piece of information, however insignificant, is instantly added to his capital."

"That is not me," I said. "I know Egons like that, but I'm not one of them."

"I'm going to prove to you that you are." His face swung out of the darkness towards me, so close, so close I could feel his acid breath. Then the voice moved away and began to reverberate inside the cave which must have been larger than I thought.

"What does Egon like? Most of all he likes to dominate, and most of his goals are directly or indirectly connected with a search for situations in which he can secure a leading role for himself. Every Egon must have at least one other Egon he can dominate; and when he finds one, he would like to have one more, and when he has two or three, he would like to have many. Egon wants to be at the front and visible. He wants to be integrated into the egonomic network on his own terms. If nobody pays any attention to him, he falls ill. He starts looking for a way out: the meaning of life, mental health, liberation. That means that he wants to dominate his fate as well; he wants to be the author of his happiness. When he falls ill he visits an expert and puts his life on his desk as though he were showing him a broken watch. And it's true: Egon's egonomic machine has broken down, it doesn't run smoothly any more, something had snapped inside it."

“That’s not me,” I shouted into the darkness when he paused. “I know Egons like that but I’m not one of them.”

“That’s not me.” He laughed right in front of me. “When the broken Egon visits an egonomic expert he always says: That’s not me. Because if he says; yes, I’m Egon, the expert will have to say: that’s precisely the problem, stop being one and you’re cured! Neither of them wants to play a game like that. Egon is looking for egonomic self-assurance while the expert, who is also Egon, would never give up the role that enables him to dominate other Egons. The expert gives the impression that he is absolutely free and spontaneous. Why? Because while treating other Egons he employs non-egonomic language. That’s his camouflage. In reality, even the expert is programmed; his motives have been approved by the central egonomic committee.”

What about you, I thought, what game are you playing; what are you trying to prove to yourself?

“Here and there,” he continued, “an Egon comes along who wants to exit the egonomic game. He abandons the rules of the majority and joins a minority. Now he feels he belongs to the elite, and he likes that. *Guess What Is Reality* is the name of the new game. Egon’s reality is made up of fantasies he calls events. He rearranges and edits these fantasies into new meanings; he calls that *Problem Solving*. When an Egon starts to play with the puzzle of meanings, you can be sure he will play that until his final days. If his confusion is big enough and if he is at least mildly adventurous, he will set off to India and find himself a guru. And again he will breathe a sigh of relief. He has discovered a new game: Enlightenment!”

He fell silent and remained silent for a long time. He probably felt how desperately I wanted him to continue.

Finally he resumed, “Egon has found a guru. And he is puzzled. Very puzzled. The relationship with the guru is different from anything he had experienced. The guru sees that Egon is using his game of liberation as a camouflage for the effort to remain Egon. Don’t seek, just find it, the guru says. But Egon believes that liberation is waiting for him in the future. You don’t have to go anywhere, the guru says; you’re already where you want to be, the moment is everything. But Egon can’t accept that. The moment is just a tight space between past and future; that's not enough for him. In this little space he runs out of oxygen, he collapses and dies. That's why he puts up a fight. Surrender, the guru advises him. And Egon surrenders: to his feelings. But these feelings are merely his habits. Guru says: lie down in the grass and look at the clouds. Stop the clock; it will happen. Don't seek, don't expect. Allow it to happen. The goal is where you are. This isn't the language that Egon can understand. So he translates it into a language he *can* understand. And when the translation is finished, guru's advice has been turned upside down. Seek, doubt, analyse, measure, compare, try harder, hurry, debate. Egon the translator is Egon the traitor. That's why he is leaving no different than he was when he came."

He fell silent and didn't speak any more. After a while the sound of snoring started to reverberate inside the cave.

I didn't sleep. I stayed awake into the small hours of the morning.

When I climbed out of the cave, a freezing wind slapped me straight in the face and filled my flesh with ice all the way to the bones. In the early sun the distant ring of the mountains resembled an archipelago of ice-covered islands on the surface of a large sea. The mountain peaks were so high, so incredibly high!

And so indifferent in their immobility. They still filled me with terror, but at the same time I could already feel in my heart the stirrings of forgiveness that a condemned man comes to feel for his executioner. I didn't want to die, but with the foreboding of death a feeling of relief began to seep into me, a peculiar sort of pride that I will be killed by the mountains and won't have to expire in a sickbed.

How strange, I thought. Egon has fallen in love with his killer. Even in the face of annihilation, he would like to prove his existence. I'm dying, therefore I am.

The Australian emerged from the cave shortly after me. Out of the frizzled beard and matted hair, a pair of blue eyes looked me up and down with an expression of welcoming curiosity. He was dressed in a red-brown Zanskari coat, with multicoloured patches all over but otherwise in surprisingly good condition. His legs were protected all the way to his knees by sturdy if battered boots. Stuck behind his belt was a large Tibetan dagger. He was less emaciated than I had expected; his posture revealed a natural flexibility of a wild animal.

"I set traps," he said. "Occasionally I make my way to the nearest village and buy a sack of barley flour. Or I wait for the village women to bring me one. And a piece of meat here and there. Even some vegetables. Word got around that a holy hermit lives in a mountain cave. With blue eyes! They bring me presents. And worship my lingam."

He laughed. "They're all tantrists in these mountains. Occasionally I kill a blue sheep. Once I stabbed a large bear, but it got away. Will you stay? Plenty of room in the cave."

I looked across the furrowed surface of hills which extended, punctured by gorges and canyons, all the way to the ring of giant white peaks in the distance. Would I get used to this wilderness?

Perhaps. In my tenderness I could feel the seed of cruelty which, in the right circumstances, would come to life faster than I could imagine. I was struck by the sudden awareness of my polarity: my sincerity, inside which there nestles the seed of dishonesty; my reticence, which is merely the other side of aggressive intrusiveness; my warmth, which hides the seed of indifference; my spontaneity, which has the same source as my awkwardness. Night and day; I'm both. Posi-negative. I look for freedom, but I'm afraid of it; I reject it so that I can continue to look for it.

The wild mountain man offered me an opportunity; why didn't I grab it? There had been thousands of opportunities; why had I allowed them to slip by? I had not rejected them; whenever I sensed one, I pounced on it. And, in my eagerness, rebounded. Tantra is action without any effort, the Great Lama had taught me. Don't seek, just find, Yogananda advised me. In my love of paradox, I had for far too long seen only word games in these pieces of wisdom.

"It's all in vain," the Australian said. "Freedom is an illusion. We are incapable of reaching it. The answer is in the heart, but in our world the heart is a muscle we can transplant. Or a metaphor. We have lost the art of surrender. Attack and win is our motto. Rule, dominate, enclose inside walls. Egon continues to kill the very life he is so desperate to live."

"Look at this space." He waved a hand towards the sea of mountains. "Here I don't have to play games. I can be what I am. I can live in my centre while the periphery can do what it wants without distressing me. Here there is no room for empty hopes, for the accumulation of stupid desires, for putting up walls and facades, for creating impressions.

"But tell me: Who waits impatiently for the village women to bring him food? Who gets angry when there is too much snow and the women can't come for a while? Who had gotten attached to one of the younger ones so much that he would like to live with her, perhaps start a family? Who longs for human company, for silly chatter; who keeps asking himself where he will get a new pair of boots when these are no longer of use, and a new coat when this one falls to pieces? Egon came, Egon was driven out of the lamasery, Egon now lives in this cave. In Sydney, among the monks, in the cave, it makes no difference: always and everywhere Egon."

I felt my way into the cave to fetch my backpack, tent and sleeping bag. When I re-emerged the lonely hermit looked at me almost imploringly and repeated: "Won't you stay? The cave is big enough."

"For one Egon," I said. "For two it would quickly become too small. Soon we would start playing *Guess What Is Reality*. In fact we have already started. In a few days we would establish an egonomic system; we would start fighting for domination. Won't that be a pity?"

"The only pity is that you don't want to stay," he said.

I asked him to go with me and return to the world.

"That's what you're going to do?" He looked at me.

After a brief reflection, I said: "Only in the world that is mine and I cannot reject can I make a decisive step. Only there the question of spiritual freedom has any meaning; here it is just exotic and precious, nothing more. At the centre of my life, Egon is different than here: more violent, less predictable, in greater panic. If I want to escape his clutches I must first get to know him; and that's possible only where I live under his domination. Finally I know what I must do. Everything I have learned in these mountains; everything that Egon had translated into the language he could understand, I must translate back into the original. I must relearn the language of the soul."

"Take care," he yelled after me as I waded into the snow. He was standing at the entrance to the cave, slightly bent, with the wind ruffling his hair as if shaking the top of a lonely pine tree. Every curve of his body expressed his desire to go with me and also his awareness that he must stay.

"Look at this space." He waved a hand at the sea of mountains. "No audience. No need to act."

Except for yourself, I thought. When I was already far away he shouted at the top of his voice that I should cling to the right slope until I reached a narrow pass. On the other side of the pass there was a village, and there I could hope to get food.

I had no idea what was under the snow, so I often slipped on a particularly steep part of the slope, setting off a small avalanche that carried me downward until I was held back by an obstruction such as a jutting rock or a sturdy bush. The sun had changed the landscape into a sparkling white sea.

I closed my eyes and trudged through the snow blindly, but even so the sunny whiteness streamed through my eyelids straight into my brain. On the northern side of the curved slope the layer of snow suddenly thinned. The winds that blew through the gap on the other side of the gorge had blown the snow off the rocky ribs and exposed them to the heat of the sun. My legs, so tired that I couldn't even feel them any more, needed no guidance to drag my body towards the shadowy canyon below me. I felt great relief. My backpack slipped off my shoulders into the snow, and I fell on top of it in the shadow of a large cliff.

I felt a strangely familiar taste in my mouth. I felt that I was reliving something familiar. The feeling was so strong that I had to catch my breath.

Somewhere behind the pass there was a village, the goal of my efforts. Far on the left, I could see the glistening ring of the mountain peaks. Suddenly I realised: I know this, I have already been here. Before me an obstacle, behind it a steep incline, and on the other side a promise of safety. Always a promise of safety, and always on the other side. Village, money, knowledge, truth, love, inner peace. And far in the horizon the ring of indescribable beauty that filled me with terror.

I will walk down into the canyon, cross it and make my way up the slope, hoping to reach the top of the pass and finally the village on the other side. And then again. And again.

And again.

I have done this hundreds, thousands of times. What is the force that drives mc? Where am I trying to get to in such a hurry, why do I push myself through life? Why can't I stay put, give up whatever I think is waiting for me on the other side; why can't I surrender to the enjoyment of the indescribable beauty in the horizon: to the panorama of life?

Because I don't feel safe? Death is close behind me and on the other side of the pass I will be safe. For how long? Five minutes? And then on, and on, and on. Why am I whipping myself through life?

The night caught up with me at the top of the pass. I couldn't feel any cold, my body was giving off heat; the breath from my lungs was turning into en embrace of little white clouds around me. It was the legs that failed me; I collapsed into the freezing snow, with a huge mass of the moon again hanging directly above me.

This was the moon I used to watch from a slope under my birth house, I thought. In the evenings I used to ski across the fields down the slope and as I walked back uphill I often stopped and stared at the moon and the stars for long stretches of time, trying to figure out the mysteries of the universe in which I had found myself. This is the same moon. And I, too, am the same. I had gone round the world and had taken myself along as a piece of luggage. I cannot become someone else. Or different.

I am.

At first I felt only pain in my limbs, then paralysis began to spread rapidly through my body, then a biting cold began to flow over me, such a violent cold that I could not even shiver. Coming in the wake of the cold was dizziness. I stared at the moon and waited. There was no fear any more, only curiosity.

And then confusion, creaking, pushing, rubbing against something, a dance of flashing shadows, nothing I could identify, none of the monsters mentioned in *The Tibetan Book of the Dead*, only a tossing about that seemed neverending. The moon returned and again hovered above me, shining into my eyes. It sparkled; then it began to flicker as though it were made of flames. And so it was. Embracing me was a feeling of warmth. I was lying on a rug not far from the hearth in a room with a low ceiling, surrounded by a ring of faces. Someone was pulling off my boots and socks; someone was rubbing my feet to improve circulation. Evidently someone crossing the pass had found me and brought me to the village.

In the light of the flames one of the faces appeared to be strangely familiar. It leaned towards me.

"How is that now?" I heard the unforgettable voice of old Yogananda. "You look for me, and I find you!"

Oh God! I grabbed his hand and began to kiss it all over, wetting it with spontaneous tears. He pushed his hand under my neck, gently lifted my head and poured three glasses of sharp local spirits into my mouth.

"Have a rest," he said and lowered my head back onto the rug.

34.

The bridge within

Next morning we set off in the direction of Ladakh. I wasn't cold any more; the lady of the house had made me a pair of gloves, her husband gave me a gourd of spirits, and Yogananda lent me a pair of thick socks. Rosinante (poor old Rosinante who should have been dead but looked healthy and stronger than ever) accepted my back-pack without a single sign of objection.

One after another, with Yogananda leading, Rosinante following, and myself making up the rear, we trudged across the fields towards another canyon.

After the flashing of knives in the mountains – what relief! And in this relief – new strength. And in the strength – hope that all the dangers are now behind me and I'm on my way home.

Finally home. On the way we made frequent stops and I talked and talked; words were pouring out of me.

How strange, I thought. Never before had I talked so much, I, who prefer silence and am afraid of words because they are so often treacherous.

Do I suddenly trust them?

We spent the first night in an empty lamasery above a village of six houses. A chubby young village woman led us to the door and unlocked it with a huge metal key. A little later she returned with two blankets. Yogananda curled up in a corner. I, zipped up in my sleeping bag, leaned against the door and through a dirty window in the opposite wall stared at the starry sky.

And I talked.

Ego and soul have lost their mutual attraction, I said. Ego had become grossly inflated, pushing the soul away into its shadow. Only when ego and soul will be equally strong, once again open to mutual influences and corrections, will I be normal and healthy.

Where is the soul located? If the ego resides in my mind, is the soul hiding in my subconscious? What is the true meaning of these expressions? Disunity, polarity, synthesis of opposites, integration, becoming whole. Egon translated these words into metaphysical wool, it disarmed and hid them behind metaphorical masks; it changed them into verbiage.

I must translate them back into the original! I must try to grasp their meaning without allowing the ego to interpret them for me. I must accept them as facts. Disunity, duality, complementary polarity. Spirit and matter, spirit and body, heart and mind, soul and ego, subjective and objective. If polarity gives birth to and maintains the material world, it must be manifested on all levels: the physical, electromagnetic, chemical, biological, psychological, spiritual, linguistic, experiential, emotional; and also on all material levels, from the smallest particle to the universe.

A magnet has two poles. If I split it, I won't get two independent poles but two new magnets, each with two poles. I can continue to split them until I reach the micro level, where it becomes obvious that matter is organised on the principle of electromagnetic polarity. Everything that exists is manifested in pairs of opposites which are indestructible and cannot exist without each other. Negative and positive, darkness and light, good and evil, man and woman, left and right – are these merely words forced upon us by the dualistic nature of language, or is language itself one of the millions of variations of bipolarity?

Being is manifested by the differentiation of the basic pair of opposites into increasingly complex and sophisticated forms on increasingly complex levels. The world exists by being ceaselessly formed; it does not exist statically, it is happening, incessantly developing from lower to higher, from one to many, from simple to complicated, from invisible to visible. The basic polarity gives matter a characteristic which our senses register as "substance". Tantra claims that the substance of matter is an illusion, our projection, a dimension of the limits of our sensory faculties since we are unable to see things as they are. The same is claimed by contemporary physicists who are discovering that the smallest particles of matter are not present "absolutely" but only contingently, as micro moments of potentiality that are formed into visible, palpable matter because of the original pair of opposites. Visibility, palpability, matter – these are merely dimensions of our perception, projections of our (self)conscious minds.

The mind, too, is polarised; it does not register one reality but two: the objective and subjective. Ego and soul are the opposite poles of our mental electromagnet, a pair of opposites that creates and maintains the energetic field of our consciousness. That means that everything wrong with the world is wrong with us, and everything wrong with us is wrong with our inner energetic fields. It is there that the balance is missing; it is there where it is happening what we perceive as happening; there is the Hell, there is the Kingdom of Heaven. There, and nowhere else.

Between the two poles of our inner world, between consciousness and the subconscious, between reason and intuition, between the ego and soul there exists a field of tension. If the poles are equally strong, the field is neutralised, there are no conflicts; there is peace in the soul. The problems start when one side grows stronger at the expense of the other; when the ego annexes regions that belong to the soul. Or the other way round, in which case the result is psychosis.

If tantra is a method for outwitting the ego, if it liberates, it is more than obvious that it liberates the soul from the prison of the ego, intuition from the chains of reason, spontaneity from the grip of habit. Even so, the aim of tantric practice is not the destruction of the ego; its aim is synthesis, a bridge between the two.

Without reason, without ego, you are mad. But without soul, without intuition, you are equally mad. Health is in the balance.

I stopped talking and looked at Yogananda. He was fast asleep.

Next morning we reached the end of the valley and came face to face with another slope leading up to a glacier-covered pass. Just before we reached the top, Rosinante slipped on ice and slid back down the slope, twice overturning and finally crashing against a rock. When we reached him, I saw such terror in his stupid eyes that I was moved to tears. Yogananda ordered me to collect my backpack and other things and continue up the slope; he would catch up with me.

After climbing for five minutes I looked back. Yogananda, with a sack on his shoulder, a blanket under one arm and with his stick in the other, followed me with slow easy steps. The horse's head was resting in the snow. Dark rivulets of blood were streaming from his severed jugular vein.

I sank to my knees. Why, for God's sake? Why? My strength was the strength of believing that I was returning to the world that was familiar and predictable. I was too weak to look back along the traces of cruelty that littered my journey.

"Let's walk on," Yogananda said.

When we reached the eastern province of Ladakh the sun was sinking behind the ridge of the mountains. Yogananda pointed towards a chain of snowy peaks on the right. "There runs the border with China."

Silently we continued towards a group of square buildings on the edge of the valley. Here there was less snow on the ground. We were invited in at the first house. Hospitality in the mountains, miles from the nearest settlement, is as natural as breathing. They offered us *tsampa* and butter tea, allowed us to warm up near the fire, we drank *chang*, surrounded by a swarm of curious unwashed little kids. Then we were shown to a small room above the stables. Our host opened the trapdoor in the wooden floor and a warm air smelling of dung began to rise from below. We could hear the sounds of farm animals, mooing, mewing and bleating. We had already slept in a place like that; a long time ago, in Zanskar, behind God knows which mountain pass.

We were too tired to sleep. We sat up all night, talking.

We spent some time discussing the complementary nature of spirit and matter and finally stopped at the characteristics of human psyche. I said that I, too was a victim (and an inheritor) of the essential polarity: living within me concurrently were a scientist and a mystic. The first one keeps asking *How*, and the second *Why*. The first one measures and compares, the second one feels and anticipates. The first one employs reason, the second one relies on intuition. It seems to me, I said, that I'm talking about the two poles of my inner reality. Would I be right in calling them ego and soul?

"Certainly," Yogananda said. "As long as we understand that we're talking about the tendencies of your psycho-structure to manifest in two apparently contradictory ways."

I said that this contradiction wasn't apparent, it was real. Ego is aggressive, greedy and tight-fisted. It translates experience into information. The soul is sensual and *feels* reality; it translates information into experience. It isn't aggressive, it is libidinous; it doesn't know how to think, but it knows how to dream. The soul is telepathic, prophetic, timeless and aesthetic. Ego doesn't love; it attacks and defends; it doesn't trust, it doubts, it cannot comprehend the whole, it divides and analyses piece by piece; it doesn't indicate, it explains.

In connection to this, I keep asking myself: Why has ego overshadowed the soul in most people, especially Europeans?

"No doubt you have an answer," Yogananda said.

I don't, I replied; all I can do is guess. I think that in Europeans (and Americans, too) the ego subdued the soul because it's an aggressor and has for a long time been very successful. It conquered nature, it landed on the moon, and it penetrated the cosmos. With all these successes it grew and continued to reaffirm itself. It sparkled so convincingly that even the soul fell in love with it. Ego, feeding on its successes, inflated beyond all reason and upset the balance of the mandala; it caused a dislocation, a mutilation. Not only is every individual person mutilated; it is the whole world. Ego has reached a state of hypnosis. It is the rulers who imprison or beggar the poets, not the other way round; ego is afraid of the soul. Tantra is neutral, merely a method. But it's a method of liberation, not of suppression. Tantra is on the side of soul. That's why the ego fears it. But the aim of tantra is not to overthrow the ego; its aim is to create a balance and cooperation between the ego and the soul. That's why tantra is so successful.

“And so dangerous,” Yogananda added.

The bridge, I continued. When I arrived I saw my journey as a symbolic attempt to jump across the gap in the snow bridge in my inner landscape. I was brought here by the awareness that I was only half the man I could be and by a desire to meet the double that had accompanied me through life as a shadow of my rational deeds, never far away, but never close enough for me to be able to touch it. The double was my emotional “I”, my soul. But because I had waited too long, the bridge between us had collapsed and a gap appeared between us – a gap across which my intellect could not jump without falling into madness.

“That’s why I came. I was hoping that you would help me across the gap in my psyche. And you did. You taught me that I mustn’t think of healing as repairing the existing bridge, but building a new one. This bridge isn’t outside me, somewhere in the future. It’s within me, in my brain. Tantra is a building method.”

Yogananda laughed. “I wouldn’t employ such static similes. Tantra isn’t a structure, it’s a dance. You must create conditions for a dynamic play between the two poles of your psyche. If you are driven by thoughts, you’re a slave; if you are driven by impulse, you’re a slave no less. If you vacillate between thought and feeling, daily or over longer periods – what are you but a slave? The only freedom is in the thought that is also a feeling, and in the feeling that is also a thought. Tantra is the name of this mutuality.”

35.

Emptiness is not empty

When I opened my eyes around noon the following day and looked out of the window I saw an Indian soldier with a Kalashnikov in his hands. He was leaning against the mudguard of a grey military jeep.

"Yogananda," I called out.

The answer was silence; he wasn't there any more.

I opened the door into the main room. Two uniformed Indians were standing near the hearth. The first one, evidently an officer, stepped towards me.

"Your name," he demanded in English.

I told him.

"You're under arrest," he said drily and motioned to his colleague who pulled out his pistol. Roughly, he grabbed hold of my elbow and pushed me towards the exit.

"My luggage." I turned around.

"That's our problem," barked the officer and gestured to the soldier not to waste any time. In front of the house I encountered the unhappy face of the owner. A string of words that sounded like an apology streamed out of his mouth. Evidently he was the one who called the soldiers and was now trying to explain that he had no choice.

In less than half an hour I was in a military camp on the bank of a river. A tall bearded sikh was circling around me with his hands behind his back. He had introduced himself as Major Singh. He was polite but wary; he was looking at me with undisguised, but stern curiosity.

"What are you doing in this part of the world?" he asked me.

What indeed, I thought. To him it would sound stupid whatever I said. I shrugged.

He raised his voice. "You're in a forbidden zone. Your silence is an admission of guilt."

I laughed. My situation, so different from anything that had happened to me in the past few weeks, was exceedingly funny.

"I wouldn't laugh if I were you," Major Singh warned me with a serious look.

Which made me laugh even louder. "If I told you that I have been spying for the last eight weeks in the mountains, not for the Chinese, Russians or Americans, but for myself personally, you wouldn't believe me."

He stopped in front of me. "In your luggage we found a camera, films, a map of the border area between China and India, and notes in two languages. In English and in some unknown foreign language. You have also made sketches of a number of villages, lamaseries and mountain passes. Who are you working for?"

"I didn't know I was in a forbidden zone. I apologize and promise to be more careful in the future. May I go now?"

"No," he replied. "Tomorrow you'll be transferred to the military prison in Leh. You'll be interrogated by a member of the Indian security services. We'll check your notes word by word and prove that you're a Russian spy."

"Russian," I protested, "why not American?"

"Russian *and* American," he concluded.

I was taken to a smaller tent with a metal bed frame on which I could spread out my sleeping bag. As if afraid that freezing temperatures might kill me (and thus deprive them of potentially serious information), they brought me a very warm and very thick blanket. They were surly, but remained correct. They even brought me dinner: lamb vindaloo, pilau rice, two naans, all very tasty.

I hadn't eaten so well since coming to Ladakh.

In spite of the armed guard in front of the tent I felt strangely relaxed. The soldiers represented the world in which things meant mostly what they were expected to mean; there were no hidden meanings in their names and descriptions. Once again it was possible to talk about them. I made myself as comfortable as I could on the hard surface and returned in my thoughts to things that were more important, less temporary than my arrest.

I was relieved to discover that with a guard outside I felt incredibly free. Here there was no need to guess what Major Singh expected from me. He had told me: the truth. We both knew what sort of truth. There was nothing ambiguous about the question whether I was a spy or not. Either I was or I wasn't. A third possibility did not exist. I had returned home, to the world of *samsara*, the world of reality-by-common-agreement.

Nirvana remained far away in the mountains. Perhaps it died in the unhappy eyes of little Dolma, perhaps it was extinguished in my heart which could not accept the naked fact of winter and death.

My head was spinning. My thoughts were twisting and turning, they were sparkling, dissolving, rejoining, piling up, crumbling, evaporating, reappearing in new logical patterns. My mind seemed to have gone wild. The sorting and reshuffling and unravelling lasted well into the night, practically until early morning, when I finally fell asleep.

Not for long, for just after eight Yogananda pushed his head past the entry flap and asked me if I felt all right. I had no time to ask him where he had been, or why he hadn't explained to the soldiers that I was innocent; I grabbed hold of his robe and pulled him into the tent. I sat him down on the bed. I could see that he had news and wanted to say something, but what I had to tell him was far more important.

I said that I had finally discovered the correct meaning of the Tibetan concept of emptiness, *shunyata*. Emptiness isn't between things, as I had mistakenly thought; it is in them. What fills things with substance and gives them reality is my projection. I give objects reality by noticing them. The nature of Being is psycho-physical; mind and matter are two sides of the same coin. I think that the events of which I had first dreamt and which later really took place were arrangements of inner and outer facts: what awaited me in the material future had already been present in my subconscious. The dream yoga had enabled me to register the primary possibilities of future events as though time was an illusion and the possibility of an event was concurrent with its realisation.

God is a spider and the world is its web. Brahman had created the world by simply turning into it with a big bang. The world is Lila, a divine game; and this game is God, and God is destiny. God isn't outside the world, he hadn't made it, or started a process that would lead to it; God *is* the process.

Everything moves. In *Tao Te Ching* we read: "Man is moving by the laws of the Earth, which is moving by the laws of Heaven, which is moving by the laws of the Tao, and the Tao is moving by the laws of its nature."

36.

Hail to the jewel in the lotus

And I am moving by the laws of the Indian Army. I was led towards a military truck. The guard, clutching his Kalashnikov, followed me so closely that he would have bumped into me had I suddenly stopped. The valley was enveloped in early fog and the soldiers were emerging out of it and vanishing into it like ghosts. They were loading something on to the truck; the driver was already warming up the engine.

"Tell them," I told Yogananda who was walking beside me, "tell them, please, that they are mistaken and that I was with you."

"I never talk to soldiers." He grinned. "It would be like the deaf shouting at the deaf."

The corpulent figure of Major Singh emerged from the fog. He was followed by a soldier carrying two bags. Evidently he had decided to hand me over to the security services personally; he was still convinced he had caught a big fish; perhaps he was hoping for promotion.

Soon we were on our way. I was sitting on a hard bench between two armed soldiers. Five more soldiers sat on the opposite bench, among them Yogananda who had decided to accompany me to Leh. In the semi-darkness, with one side of the awning slapping against the frame of the vehicle, his eyes burned like those of a wild cat.

I felt a stabbing pain in my heart. Soon I won't be able to see them any more, the eyes of the only man in the world who had filled me with a desire to live in his skin for a while.

It happened sooner than I had expected. After two hours of a juddering drive along an atrocious road the truck came to a sudden halt. One of the soldiers lifted the rear flap of the awning and revealed the sharp whiteness of the snow. Not far behind, on a rocky slope, I could see the sunlit walls of the lamasery of Thikse.

Yogananda placed his hand on top of mine and gave it a squeeze. "I must visit my friends," he said with a hint of excuse. "Be ready for anything, but expect nothing."

Nimbly, like a youth of twenty, he jumped off the truck. The soldiers threw his bundle, blanket and stick after him. The last thing I saw was Yogananda bending down to collect them; then the raised awning fell back in its place and our vehicle juddered on.

Something heavy clutched at my throat. I wanted to throw myself towards the rear of the truck, lift the awning and shout, "Yogananda, thank you and good luck!" At the same time a little voice inside me whispered: he is lucky enough, he doesn't need empty words, goodbye is goodbye, you turn around, and you go. You enter the silence of solitude with the noise of your loneliness.

And yet: there were so many words we had never spoken, so many things for which I had no explanation; why must everything remain in the air, only half-answered, now, when I feel that the answers are so close? Or has he, with his last words, told me everything worth keeping in mind?

The interrogation lasted a little more than four hours. A Kashmiri with a Moslem cap on his head went through my notebooks. Every now and then he would copy a sentence or two into his dog-eared exercise book. He would follow that with a question that had little or no obvious connection with my alleged crime. Do I have any brothers or sisters? Do I like cricket or soccer? Catholic or Protestant? From time to time he placed his finger on a Slovenian text in the notebook and demanded translation.

"In fact every situation offers you only one correct step, only one move," I read. "This move determines what follows. If the step is correct and the move is crafty, the problem is solved and your opponent becomes your ally." He wanted to know why all my notes were not in English. I said that I was bilingual; when making notes I would use the language in which the thought first appears; I don't even realise that, the process is automatic.

His confusion grew; I could see that by the narrowing of his eyes. He was convinced that I was holding something back. He sank into the contents of my notes as if being swallowed by quicksand; I almost felt sorry for him. The poor chap was only doing his job. I could see that he would like to get rid of me, but was afraid he might let a real spy slip through his fingers; no doubt he had a family to support. But on the level of the problem he was trying to solve, my notes about tantra sounded like something written in a secret code.

"The problem is not where you see it, but at the point from which you observe it," I quoted to him from one of the notebooks. I couldn't resist flashing a superior smile, which worsened his distress even more. Lying on the desk between us were the same words, but instead of bringing us closer to each other, they were increasing the distance between us.

My inquisitor finally decided to throw in the towel. "And what are your plans now?"

"That depends on you," I said with a friendly smile. "To be honest, I'd like to go straight to the airport and take the first plane to New Delhi. And from there back to London."

After a long, painful silence he leaned back in his chair and said, "If you promise not to return, you're free to go."

I stood up and reached for my notebooks. He quickly pushed them aside. "These we're going to keep," he said, looking at me triumphantly; finally he had an opportunity to get even.

In vain I tried to persuade him that I needed my notes; in vain I uttered veiled threats and offered bribes; he confiscated all my notebooks and films, even my camera.

"You can lodge a complaint in Delhi," he said, holding the door open for me.

In the corridor I leaned against a wall and tried to suppress tears I could feel welling up. Without my notes I felt naked and robbed: anonymous, as if I didn't exist. I take notes, therefore I am? Must I really always write about my experiences? Is just living not enough for me?

At the airline office I reserved a seat for New Delhi the following afternoon. The official told me that I had caught one of the last flights of the season; the winter was on the doorstep, and Ladakh was getting ready for a long hibernation. Had I waited a few days longer, only the Indian Air Force would have been able to evacuate me from Leh.

I still had some time at my disposal: the whole afternoon, the night and the following morning. I stopped at the "café" Pamposh (a barrack-like building with only one wall) and drank what would have been, after a very long time (if it had managed to be that), my first real coffee. Two months before, when I had arrived in Ladakh, Pamposh was bursting with adventurous foreign tourists, mostly young. Now I was sitting alone at a rickety table, the only guest, a curiosity.

Then I walked to the restaurant Dreamland and ordered a none-too-tasteful dish called Lhasa chow-mein. My eyes were drawn towards the distant snowy peaks. There is my land of dreams, I thought, behind those mountains. Then, suddenly, it flashed through my mind: No! The land of dreams is here. Behind the mountains what I was eating would be called food. Here it is Lhasa chow-mein in the restaurant Dreamland!

I was returning into the dream cloud of everyday familiarity: into the world of categories, names, big and small lies; into the world of mutually agreed pretence. Egon was weaving himself back into the egonomic web.

Evening was not far away. The city was deathly silent, deserted; I had no desire to go anywhere.

Except…

I walked to the bus station, hired a jeep-taxi and asked the driver to take me to the lamasery of Thikse. As I was climbing past the chortens towards rectangular buildings, my heart was thumping at the thought how surprised Yogananda would be to see me.

But he wasn't. After the third corner I literally bumped into him; he was waiting for me. He must have seen me coming.

"How is that now?" He laughed. "You look for me, and again it is I who find you! Isn't it time for *you* to surprise me?"

"Maybe I will," I replied. "That's why I've come."

He led me to the main hall. Pleasant warmth was streaming from the flames in the fireplace. The monks still remembered me. I was offered butter tea, *tsampa* and plenty of friendly smiles. Yogananda and I sat down on a bench near the fire. I told him that all my notebooks and films had been confiscated. And that I don't care, I have accepted it. And maybe it's better like this. I said my flight was scheduled for the following afternoon; I had come to the lamasery because there were things I wanted to clear up with him. Would he mind?

"What things?" he asked.

I said that I had managed to get to the bottom of everything that had puzzled me; the only thing missing is the thread that would tie all the bits into a whole. For example, now I know the true meaning of words I had used merely as knots of my theoretical knitwear. The Buddhist "avidya", ignorance, I used to perceive as a lack of knowledge about things and concepts as static, independent units. Now I know that "avidya" is really the very thing I call knowledge: the tendency of the mind to register individual units and ignore the context; to isolate parts of the flow and call them events and things.

That, of course, is quite normal, without that there would be no consciousness. The problem appears when I *forget* that consciousness is the result of ignoring the whole in favour of individual parts. Then I begin to see individual parts as though they were self-existent and "real"; I begin to believe that nature is split up "naturally" and that I am merely *discovering* the multiplicity of forms.

Shunyata (emptiness) means that forms are inseparable from the context; that they do not exist by themselves, for the form of a figure is also the shape of its background, in the same way that my outer form is also the inner form of the world that surrounds me. No other thing more clearly reveals to me the meaning of tantric universal connectedness, of the world as a field of mutually irreplaceable functions.

I imagine the world as an endless number of dewdrops. If I look into one I see that it reflects all the others, and that every other also reflects all the others. And if I take these dew drops as being no more than static symbols of dynamic processes I have arrived at the concept of Lila, the divine play, and Shiva's cosmic dance. The people of the East had discovered Lila intuitively, the people of the West rationally. But there is only one Lila, and it contains all possible forms of being aware of it.

"Then there is no problem." Yogananda laughed. "You're free!" And he looked at me almost compassionately, like a father would at a child who had lost his favourite toy.

I told him that I was still far from being free. Because of my desire to become free I lack the courage to be free in reality. Because I'm unable to accept my mortality, I can't understand that being and not-being are the poles of a mutual pair of opposites, each unable to exist without the other. Because I keep pushing aside the awareness of the inevitability of my end instead of turning it into my home, I perceive existence as something that belongs to me; I don't take it seriously. In the past two months there had been no shortage of occasions when I "lived my day as though it were my last", but even that failed to give me the feeling of freedom.

That is the only problem I still have to resolve, I said. What is the "liberation" that I'm supposed to be looking for? What is awakening? From what, into what must I awake?

"Well, what do you think?" Yogananda winked at me.

"I think that you allowed yourself a nice little joke at my expense," I said. "That you cheated me. For you this was no more than a game."

"Cheated you? How?"

I said that cheating may not be the correct word. In fact it was a kind of trick of huge proportions, some kind of mental judo; a game of handball with an invisible ball.

"You never attacked," I said. "You waited for me to take a running jump, and every time I did so you gave me an additional push. I was throwing myself against a wall, and you encouraged me. I told you I was looking for truth, awakening, enlightenment, integration and God knows what else, and you said: Good! I described my distress by a succession of metaphors and every time you said that I must do what I myself thought I should do. All ideas were mine; you simply caught them, those invisible balls, often intuitively before I managed to put them into words, and you urged me to go after them. I kept scoring self-goals with your help! Every attack on the ego became a form of its own defence. Every attempt to achieve the state of non-thinking became thinking. Every attack on the map of my projections became yet another projection. With each attempt to escape I added another link to my chain. Carry on, carry on, you kept shouting, trying to hide your self-satisfaction. Forget the past, forget the future; settle in the present. I wanted to become like you, but with each effort I became even more the kind of person I didn't want to be. You knew what was happening, why didn't you tell me?"

"But I did." He laughed. "I told you: don't seek, just find. If you seek you will miss it. I told you that you can become the Buddha when you realise that you are already the Buddha. I couldn't possibly offer you a better escape from your distress. And what did you do? You grabbed my words and nailed them to the door of your prison as a list of dogmatic instructions. Do this, do that. As a decorator of your interior spaces you have no equal. Your experiences become museum pieces even before they are concluded. You measure the value of your life by the glamour of this inner museum, by your spiritual wealth, as you call it. You have come to me complaining: I feel so bad, I'm walled in, there is too much of everything, I have no space in which I could be what I am. You came convinced that you can enrich this trash through another museum exhibit – spiritual freedom, and then everything will be all right. You believed that everything will be all right when you add something to what you had too much of already. Not when you let go of everything. I don't mean that you reject everything, but merely let go, leave it where it is, such as it is."

He looked me in the eyes. "What should I do with a man like that? I allowed you to draw me into a game. I decided to play with you and pretend we were playing a serious game, and that you did have an ego you could get rid off, that you *must* get rid off. I was hoping you would grow tired in the end and realise that you can't win at this game. Just as you can't win in the game with the alienated parts of your soul. And even less in a battle you're waging against yourself."

I felt as if I had lost the ground under my feet.

"Then my feelings were right," I said. "It was a trick."

"Of course!" He laughed.

Of course! I had looked for a method which doesn't exist, I had looked for a way that isn't there, I had looked for a path the leads nowhere, I had looked for an answer to the question that is meaningless. The problem cannot be solved because I made it up!

Didn't he say to me that I was stupid because I was clever? Life isn't a problem; the problem is my belief that it is a problem. Surrender to the flow, he kept telling me. And I tried, directing all my energy into the effort to live effortlessly.

There is no flow to which I could surrender! *I* am the flow! When I resist it, I am staging a revolt against myself. I had come with the conviction that the state of enlightenment is something superior, even supernatural; something that can be of use to me. Didn't the Buddha say that he got absolutely nothing from his awakening, and that it was for that very reason the most perfect awakening?

The old master, sly as a fox, alert as a rabbit, quick as a striking cobra, how fantastically he had taken me for a ride! Be mindful, he said. And I was. I had tried to achieve the mastery of the mind. After each failed attempt, after each new realisation that I cannot achieve a state of non-thinking; that I cannot silence the monkeys inside me; that there is no master who could do that; that this supposed master is just one of the monkeys, it still wasn't clear to me that the old man was trying to push me against a wall, to make me realise that there is no thinker of thought or knower of knowledge, and that I'm destroying the true concentration by the very attempt to make my ego concentrate on *its* thoughts. He was trying to make me realise that the mind is always in a state of concentration. Whenever it thinks, it is concentrated on whatever it thinks. The mind is nothing other than a succession of thoughts.

Here and now, he had told me a hundred times. I should be aware of the moment, of each and every moment. That, too, was a trick.

Thoughts for which I claim to be memories, are not happening in the past, they are happening now. The thoughts about the future are also happening now, only here and now, this very moment. That doesn't mean that the moment doesn't exist; all it means is that there is nothing *except* the moment. I can only be conscious of *now*. The old man had tricked me in a different way I had thought. He had lured me into a trap in which I had tried with all available means to achieve what is happening by itself!

I jumped to my feet. The world was spinning. Yogananda, too, rose to his feet; his eyes were shining with expectation.

"Ego is an illusion," I said. "I am what I know, what I think, what I feel, what I sense, what I hope, what I do. I am self-happening. Ego is merely a symbol, a static symbol of the mutually dynamic union between me and my immediate surroundings."

I grabbed him by the hands and drew him into an awkward dance. The doorway quickly filled with the smiling faces of the monks.

"Let's dance!" I shouted like mad and pulled him in a circle around the hall. "I'm free because I have no choice. I'm no longer running away from myself. I'm not trying to get close to myself. I'm the one running away from myself, I'm the one getting close to myself. It is always I. I can't kiss myself on the mouth, I can only kiss others, I can only kiss you!"

I embraced him and stuck two loud kisses to his cheeks.

"Thank you," I shouted. "Thank you. I came with the desire to discover my true self. Now I know that I cannot not-be my true self. Whatever I do, whatever I don't do, whatever I feel or don't feel, think or don't think, everything is my true self. It is all me, it is all I. I don't have to reject parts of myself – I'm not split into parts. The secret is not that I should accept myself, the secret is that I can't reject myself –"

Suddenly I felt Yogananda's fist strike me painfully in the mouth. I licked my lips and tasted blood. I stepped back to get out of his way, but he followed me and slapped me hard on both cheeks.

The hall was suddenly full of grinning monks. They formed a circle and began to root for us, half for me and half for my attacker. I struck back. Yogananda ducked, my fist went past his head, with my body following, with his hand on the nape of my neck; I fell to the ground. Laughter, noise, approbation.

The old man started to kick me. I covered my head with my hands. He pulled me up to my feet and slammed his fist into my stomach; then once more into my jaw. I passed out.

I was brought back to consciousness by a bucket of cold water which one of the monks had poured on my face. I realised that they had removed my clothes and leant me, naked, against the wall. The monks had formed a group at the opposite side of the hall. Yogananda, standing in the middle, was poking fun at my nakedness, my penis, my humiliation. The monks yelled and hooted with derisive laughter.

Then they began to throw things at me: damp cleaning cloths, sandals, remains of food, rotten eggs. One of them came running towards me with a bucket of pigswill and poured it over my head. I closed my eyes and buried my face between my knees.

I remembered an event in my first year at school. The older boys had tied my hands and feet with their belts and pulled me up and down the corridor, shouting, "Flisar is a pisspot, Flisar is a pisspot!"

Poor little Flisar. What despair he had felt! And later, every time life tied his hands and feet and dragged him up and down, making fun of him, shaming him – every time his self-image suffered an insult.

But now there was no reaction. As though Flisar wasn't there any more.

I looked up and began to grin. Yogananda waved his hand and the noisy merriment came to a halt. The monks grew quiet and serious.

They looked at me, bowed and recited as one, "Om Mani Padme Hum!"

37.

Our last day

Yogananda accompanied me to Leh. Our last day was the most memorable we had spent together, most joyful but also filled with melancholy; blessed with genuine friendship although we realised that we belonged to different worlds; it was unforgettable, but also half-dreamlike, full of gentle brushing of hand against hand, eyes softly meeting eyes as if by accident, of leave-taking that started ten hours before my departure; full of superficial chatter in which we told to each other more than at any other time before.

"Maybe I'll come back," I said.

"Don't." He smiled. "I won't be here any more. And if you come anyway, it won't be you who'll be coming."

"If I ever meet someone with eyes like yours, and if that person is a woman, I'll fall in love with her, and love her forever."

He laughed. "You'll meet Lila. Everything you dreamt about will come true. You will meet her. You may have met her already and didn't know it was her. Or she may be growing up somewhere, innocently, waiting for you. She will bring you exceptional happiness. And suffering. But because you're now liberated, you'll be happy even while suffering."

"Hardly," I said. "As for liberation, I will probably have that feeling for two minutes a day. Will that be enough?"

"One moment of insight is worth ten years of ignorance," he said. "When you're home again at first it will be more difficult than when you left. Don't let that frighten you. The process you went through here will have to be repeated in your own world. For a while your ego will appear stronger than it had ever been. For a while everything that you experienced in these mountains will seem like a fairytale, useless in your everyday life. Never mind. Sooner or later a thread will appear. You will start discovering regions of exceptional light in your life. You won't know where it comes from. But sooner or later, perhaps, you will start believing that it originates somewhere among these mountains."

"As a matter of fact," I said, "it was only yesterday that I began to understand the big secret. You are free if you live naked, not dressed up in your self-image. Then there is nothing to defend, hide, lie about or build upon. Hours of planning, regrets, and psychological cosmetics are not required any more."

"As simple as that," he said, squeezing my hand. "You're free if you live exposed, not wrapped in your self-image. Everything else simply follows. There is no need to play games. Others will still want to involve you in theirs, to use you for their self-confirmation. You won't resist. Because you will no longer play games of your own, you'll be able to play others' games as though they were yours. And because you're no longer paralysed by the desire to win, or by the fear of losing, you're always going to win; even when others think that you have suffered defeat."

I said that here and now, at this moment, everything looks fine, things are clear; I feel relief which is freedom to the extent that the question of freedom no longer interests me. The only thing that worries me is what will happen when I return to the world that will immediately confront me with challenges to which I am used to respond in my old ways. Will I not instantly seek refuge in my self-image again? Defend and attack as though I am fighting for something and against something? Like always?

"That will certainly happen," he said. "The real battle is still waiting for you. How you will fare on the real battlefield, I don't know. A good apprentice doesn't always become a good master; more often he just remains a good apprentice. But even that is better than pretending to be a master while knowing that you're not. There is always a danger of that. Will you be able to avoid it?"

I don't know, I said. In my everyday life I will have to live as if my ego were real. I will have to pretend that I'm like all the others, and keep the knowledge that I'm different to myself. I don't know if I'll be able to live in a world in which I won't need my self-image but will choose one deliberately; in which I won't have to play social games but will play them anyway. It may well happen that sooner or later I will start taking my self-image and my social games seriously again.

"You will need help," Yogananda said. "The help of your lover tantra; the only one that will never betray you. Whenever you'll wake up firmly convinced that you *must* survive the day, be successful, create good impressions, insure yourself against misfortune, finish something by the deadline, be the sort of man you'd like to be, get proof that you're attractive, respected and loved, your faithful lover, tantra, will trip you up so you will fall on your nose and wake from hypnosis. And realise that you have once again been tricked by the ego. The ego is born when you start believing that you and your viewpoint are one and the same. Ego is a viewpoint attempting to prove that it really exists. Tantra will derail you. It will throw you out of your imaginary railway network along which you transport your life. But you mustn't forget the greatest paradox of tantra: it works only if you forget about it. If you never even think of it. When you talk or write about it, when you discuss it, you're not a tantrist. On a bicycle you never think about the laws of balance. You cycle. You cycle as though you were dancing."

Tantra is living life as though you were dancing, I said. I had heard that many times, and it sounded nice, but I still don't know how to dance with my life. Tantra as a dance, it seems to me, is life as rhythm, as music. The musician putting an effort into playing correctly is no longer playing; the dancer trying to be relaxed while dancing, turns awkward. There is no spontaneity without discipline, and there is no tantra without morality. But neither discipline nor morality is repressive. They become repressive with the thought that the musician is separated from his music; that the dancer and his dancing are two different things; that the "liver" (the one who lives) is something other than his life.

"Well said," he commended me. "Life is a dance. Surrender to it and you will dance beautifully and naturally. Resist it or try to guide it, and you tread on people's toes, including your own. The rhythm you won't adapt to will topple you. Tantra as a dance is a life without goals that are not life itself. When you subject the present to the future, life becomes a word. And the word isn't the same as dance. Words are empty, and if you allow your future to enslave your present, your life will be empty as well."

Yes, I said. Words are stones with which we are breaking the window of the world and turning it into an opaque shattered screen. That's why I'm most worried by what role I will ascribe to words when I return home. Will I be able to live with them and without them at the same time?

"Speaking of which," he said, reaching inside his linen bag, "I find it the right moment to complicate your dilemma even further. When you were having breakfast at Pamposh, I went to visit a friend who is connected with people who are connected with those who have connections with some of those only few people have any connections with.

With a tricky smile, he pressed all my notebooks and three of the five confiscated films into my hands.

"Yogananda!" I exclaimed, infinitely grateful.

"The story of your liberation," he said. "The chains of your imprisonment. Into what are you going to weave them; what sort of cage will you build with them?"

"I don't know," I said. "Maybe I will, maybe not. Everything will have to be chewed over, analysed, relived; I see no reason not to do that on paper. Writing about my life is not an obsession, it's me; writing and I are one."

"And then you will print and distribute it, so that others can chew it over too?"

"Yes, I probably will," I said.

"Don't mention my real name. I don't want a crowd of your doubles looking for me in these mountains. Call me Yogananda."

I promised I would.

Suddenly he embraced me and pressed me close to his chest. Then he took a step back.

"Cry," he said when he saw tears in my eyes. "Be spontaneous. The game isn't serious. That doesn't mean that you're better or happier than those who believe it is. They also play, but because they aren't aware of it, their game is more dangerous. The true point of your freedom is in your willingness to help them when they suffer a fall, and to help yourself when you slip and find yourself on the floor. And you can slip quite unexpectedly; there is no way of predicting the moment. The world is a place of deceptive appearances. A place where gangs of robbers disguised as policemen fight it out with policemen disguised as robbers. Where does illusion begin, where does reality end? The space in which you can be a tantrist is so small that it hardly exists. But it does exist, and you can live as a tantrist. As long as you don't think that you have to."

With those words he turned and walked down the road.

I followed him with my eyes, fully aware that I will never see him again, this master of wisdom who had crashed into my life like a bolt of lightning, leaving me a gift of near-magic power I could feel in my heart. There was nothing mysterious or supernatural in this power. It was merely an invitation to return to the world from which I had distanced myself; and through that world back to myself. My power is the knowledge that there is no situation that couldn't be solved, which means that each and every moment I'm a riddle that can be solved as well.

With my backpack and other gear I walked towards the small air terminal.

And now?

A Zen-Buddhist master attained enlightenment. "And then," his admirers asked him, "what did you do then?" He shrugged and said, "I ordered a cup of tea."

What else could he have done?

When the world is turned upside down, it is again standing the right way up.

"Cup of tea," I said at the bar and looked at my watch. It told me that boarding would start in ten minutes.

I released the strap and offered the watch to the astonished tea seller. Knowing well that when I reached home I, as a renewed although now only part-time Egon, would have to buy a new one.